My sister began to wail.

"Hush, hush now little one," the Reverend Mother begged. "I baptize you in the name of the Father, and of the Son and of the Holy Ghost. Amen." She made the sign of the cross on Baby Big Mouth's head. The Sister picked her up and bounced her frantically as her cries reverberated through the damp cave. She reached down and placed her hand on the motionless chest of my old self. "And I baptize you, precious child, Olivia Abigail Clancy Hersh, after your dear grandmother, your mother's mother—God, rest her soul. And I commit your spirit into God's loving hands."

Olivia Abigail. *Nice name*, I thought. The sound of it rang through me with the perfect pitch of a Gregorian chant. But the startling realization that no one would ever call me by it saddened me. No one would ever know me. Olivia Abigail was dead. I had died before ever leaving my mother's womb. I wondered why I was hanging around. Shouldn't I be going somewhere? Up, maybe? Could I stand being left here in this void indefinitely when already I longed for the physical, I ached for the intimacy these humans already shared?

The identity of my father was hidden from me for reasons only God understood, but I knew what the Reverend Mother had realized: That my father was a Negro. In 1956 Tennessee that fact alone would explain why my mother had been hidden in the convent, and why her babies would quickly be taken away.

I glanced back at my glimmering door. All I understood was a connection, a bond, tethering me by a tenuous thread of light between the physical plane of the living and the mysteries that lay beyond.

For Peter and MK.
You complete my story.

FLOWERS FOR ELVIS

Julia Schuster

Smyrna, Georgia

Bell Bridge Books
PO BOX 67
Smyrna, GA 30081

ISBN: 978-0-9821756-1-3

Bell Bridge Books is an Imprint of BelleBooks, Inc.

Copyright 2009 by Julia Schuster

Printed and bound in the United States of America.

We at BelleBooks enjoy hearing from readers. You can contact us at the address above or at BelleBooks@BelleBooks.com

Visit our websites – www.BelleBooks.com
and www.BellBridgeBooks.com.

10 9 8 7 6 5 4 3 2 1

Cover Design: Debra Dixon
Cover: Background texture: © Handy | Dreamstime.com
Cover: girl on swing: copyright Larry Inman of Inman Images
Interior design: Linda Kichline

Our birth is but a sleep and a forgetting:
The Soul that rises with us, our life's Star,
Hath had elsewhere its setting,
And cometh from afar:
Not in entire forgetfulness,
And not in utter nakedness,
But trailing clouds of glory do we come
From God, who is our home:
Heaven lies about us in our infancy!

Ode: Intimations of Immortality
William Wordsworth

Elvis Aaron Presley was born to Vernon and Gladys Presley on January 8, 1935 in a two-room house in Tupelo, Mississippi. His twin brother, Jesse Garon Presley, was still born.

Love Me Tender
Film, Twentieth Century Fox
Top 20 *Billboard* Hits Single

I came into this world and left it on the same day. I guess God knew what He was doing. Being the illegitimate daughter of a nun would have been restrictive, to say the least. Then, when you factor in that my mother was white and my father black, that they lived in the podunk town of Iuka, Mississippi, and the year was 1956—I guess I should really feel blessed to be dead. Still, it would have been nice to hang around in the flesh for a while. Instead, God put me in charge of my other half, my white twin, whose lungs were a tad bit more developed than mine at the time of our premature entry into the world. She became my responsibility—and, oh, what a time that child gives me. What a time indeed.

Heartbreak Hotel
Top 20 *Billboard* Hit Single

My sister came within an angel's breath of being dropped on her head when her body gushed from between our mother's legs. Would a good rap on the concrete have done her some good? The convent's Reverend Mother and I couldn't be sure at the time, but you know what they say about hindsight. Instead, the Reverend Mother caught her by the ankles on the fly and swooped her up into her arms like an outfielder cradling a grounder to her chest.

Midwifery hadn't been a required course of study in the nunnery, I don't suppose, but this woman could field! My sister arrived blaring like all holy fury from her first breath. But not one scream escaped our devastated mother. Not one "Jesus, Mary and Joseph," only silent tears and whispered prayers for the welfare of her twins.

Mother Superior bent down and placed my squalling sibling on the straw mat on the floor next to my lifeless shell. The stark shade of death revealed our differences. My body was blue-lipped and my skin as pale-toned as a birch crucifix, like the complexion some mixed-race babies own in their first moments on earth. It is not until breath and blood work together to energize pigment that the skin warms with the rich tones a mingled heritage affords.

My sister, however, had attained the chalky alabaster complexion of our mother, as white as the good nun's bib and coif. A barely audible "Lord, have mercy," escaped with Mother Superior's gasp. She crossed herself, staring down at my screeching sister and the inert body my spirit had briefly possessed.

Finally, she composed herself long enough to give our grieving mother's hand a quick squeeze. "I'll take care of everything Willard, dear," she whispered. "You'll have to trust me, but I promise I'll do what's best. God has a plan. We may not understand it, but in it we can trust. Of that we can be sure." She wrapped us in a tattered bath towel, rubbed her hands against the chill, and scooped us up.

"I want them to have the best home, promise me," our mother pleaded. "That's why I came here. I knew you would help me. And please don't tell anyone in my family. I couldn't bear it. Please don't tell Genevieve."

Mother Superior wiped a stray tear from my mother's cheek. "Trust, child. Trust." She turned to leave and a hush enveloped the room for the first time as she whisked us from our mother's cell. The rubber soles of her slippers slapped the concrete as she scurried down the hall, passing a long row of closed doors. Light streamed from beneath each door, but none opened with an offer of assistance. This woman was on her own.

Silence draped the metal stairwell as we descended. For the first time I recognized that my vantage point had changed. My body remained in the nun's arms with my sister, but my soul had moved away. Sometime between my death within my mother's womb and my sister's life surge, the essence of me had wriggled out of myself and squeezed into the space between my sister's heartbeat and my Heavenly Father's lap. I was stuck between the two, cocooned, but now, infused with a milky understanding and abilities I would piece together as I went along, and with no flesh to contain me, no tiny house of bones and blood and breath to keep me small, I grew in space and knowledge, all air and fog and stars, memory and thought and calm.

Over my right shoulder I saw shadows of my family's past. I grasped its meaning, comprehended its effects, but its members and their connections to each other seemed too complicated for me to decipher just then. I realized that many secrets lay in the past of my ancestors, but I did not yet have the ability to figure them all out. I turned my attention to my sister, whose present pulsed through me like the breath I never required to sustain me, urgent and still within my grasp. Ahead, though, time loomed before us, shrouded with uncertainty and a foggy translucence I knew I was destined to wade through and piece together bit by bit.

Glancing down at myself, I checked out my ethereal outfit like a skinny woman trying on bathing suits for the first time. I looked good, felt good, knew good, but sensed, too, the evil that walks hand in hand with the physical world.

A door stood partially open beside me, close enough to touch. It had six panels and a golden knob with no lock. This doorway glowed with the blue translucence of welcome. White light streamed from its crack, the triangular point of it reaching me. I shook my foot; the light shook with me, attached at my toe, my heel, my hand. This light moved with me.

I placed my hand on the door, but did not push. I knew I wasn't supposed to, not now, not yet. A parental nudge at the small of my back turned me toward my sister again, making all I needed to know for now clear.

At the bottom of the stairs, the Reverend Mother stopped suddenly and leaned into the shadows against the wall. "Go on by," she prayed aloud. Headlights illuminated the front of the building. The backward words, *Beaver's Auto Parts and Shop,* stood out in streaked red across the plate glass windows. The Sister barely breathed until the vehicle moved on.

"Curtains, we've got to make curtains," she murmured, and scuttled across the large front room, headed toward the back. I tagged along, knowing no other option. I figured God would get around to giving me details when He got a break in His schedule.

Rough wooden benches stood at odd angles on the oil-stained floor, facing a makeshift altar under a faded wall painted with signs advertising spark plugs and motor oil. A statue of the Virgin Mary stood against the far wall on an old display case. So beautiful. Votive wishes flickered at her feet. Mother Superior paused in front of the statue just long enough to whisper a prayer. Then she moved on through a crude kitchenette and into a pantry stacked with canned goods and cases of wine.

She bent low to enter a subterranean chamber through a beat-up metal door and bolted it behind us. "I just don't understand it," she told no one, as we hurried down concrete stairs to the basement. "How can one child be so light and the other so dark-skinned?" Congealed grease and heavy incense clogged the air. She stifled a cough and cleared her throat. "Help me, Mother. What should I do?"

This time she directed her pleas to a broken statue, resting on its side on the floor. This disfigured Virgin had lost her outstretched arm.

The lopped-off appendage lay next to a stack of Bibles, propped against the cinder block wall. "What will I do with these babies? How could this happen? How could I not have known?" A bare bulb cast shadows about us. She glanced down into the wide eyes of my sister. "I must protect them. I know that, Sweet Virgin. And their mother, too. Oh, their mother, the poor dear. How best can I help her? She is such a devout young woman. Help me to know what is best for them all."

As she gazed down at my vacant gray shell, struggle played across her face. Watching from aside, I knew what she was thinking; not through some extrasensory perception or mind reading benefit, but from a rumble that surged within me. She fought to stave off the thoughts pushing to the forefront of her mind: *How could You let this happen, Lord? But thank you, God, for not allowing the little dark-skinned child to live.*

The impressions sickened her, and me too, for that matter. How could it ever be good for a baby to die? Especially me. But already—by gift or curse, I couldn't be sure which just yet—I knew the inner workings of this woman, as if I possessed a sympathetic insight born of my beyond-life circumstance. This knowing was equipped with an uncertain depth, though. Resonating, as if God had added a bass bell to a deep chime, her heart's song assured me that it wasn't like her to question God. She was a kind and holy woman who would never assume that she knew what was best. In this instance, however, she was glad it had turned out this way. She cared about our welfare and how difficult it would have been for me if I had lived. Mississippi in those days—and in these days still—was not a friendly place for those born with racially mixed-up blood. God taking me out of the equation like He did relieved the Reverend Mother of the predicament of having to explain our births and the anomaly of twin girls with opposing skin hues.

The Sister knelt and laid my sister and I on the floor. Water oozed from a crack in the cinder block wall, dripping into a perpetual puddle on the floor. Despite the nuns' best efforts, this place was a cold and smelly hole. The fact that a convent even existed was nothing short of a miracle in rural Mississippi. Few people even knew of its existence.

The idiot who'd come up with the plan to turn an auto parts store

into a convent must never have visited this basement. It needed work—
starting with a furnace. Mother Superior shuddered. She had taken
vows to uphold her duties to the Church. Did that include covering up
these illegitimate births, she wondered? Making livable this inhospitable
place had seemed like a great deal to ask of one person just weeks
before, when the nuns had moved into the space. Being a cloistered
sect, these nuns faced a future alone, their days and nights spent in
silence and contemplative prayer, sheltered and hidden from the outside
world by the tall walls that encircled the property. But all of that seemed
simple in light of the situation that presented itself now, in the flesh.
The icy chill of isolation tore at her heart. Who could she ask for help?
She looked down at my sister's living face and my dead one.

Certainly not me; I had my own situation to figure out.

The good Sister bowed her head above us. A great mole stuck
out on her forehead, her public brand of imperfection for everyone to
see. Her face was pock-marked with red skin, dry and scaly around
her nose and across her cheekbones. Her thick lenses fogged. She
peeped through their haze to make sure I really was dead, that I didn't
twitch or move. Trembling, she filled a small mixing bowl with water.
Then she dipped her hand into the holy water font and dribbled the
cool liquid over our heads.

It was then that I realized the magnitude of my lacking. No greater
gift could God have taken from me than the sense of touch. I suddenly
ached to run my fingers through that water and experience its cleansing
flow. I reached out to touch the damp wall; I felt nothing. I rested my
hand on the Sister's shoulder, but no energy conveyed. My hand
indented the fabric of her sleeve, but no friction transferred. She felt
nothing; I felt nothing in return.

My sister began to wail.

"Hush, hush now little one," the Reverend Mother begged. "I
baptize you in the name of the Father, and of the Son and of the Holy
Ghost. Amen." She made the sign of the cross on Baby Big Mouth's
head. The Sister picked her up and bounced her frantically as her
cries reverberated through the damp cave. She reached down and
placed her hand on the motionless chest of my old self. "And I baptize
you, precious child, Olivia Abigail Clancy Hersh, after your dear
grandmother, your mother's mother—God, rest her soul. And I commit

your spirit into God's loving hands."

Olivia Abigail. *Nice name*, I thought. The sound of it rang through me with the perfect pitch of a Gregorian chant. But the startling realization that no one would ever call me by it saddened me. No one would ever know me. Olivia Abigail was dead. I had died before ever leaving my mother's womb. I wondered why I was hanging around. Shouldn't I be going somewhere? Up, maybe? Could I stand being left here in this void indefinitely when already I longed for the physical and ached for the intimacy these humans already shared?

The identity of my father was hidden from me for reasons only God understood, but I knew what the Reverend Mother had realized: That my father was a Negro. In 1956 Tennessee that fact alone would explain why my mother had been hidden in the convent, and why her babies would quickly be taken away.

I glanced back at my glimmering door. All I understood was a connection, a bond, tethering me by a tenuous thread of light between the physical plane of the living and the mysteries that lay beyond. I longed to be here and elsewhere. I was alone and in company at the same time. The nun couldn't see me, didn't have the slightest hint of my presence. My ethereal exile became both my blessing and my penance for sins I would never have the opportunity to commit.

Many times during that seemingly endless night of squalling, several expletive salutations came to the exhausted Sister's mind. When daylight finally glinted through the flip-out window above our heads, her back ached from hours of rocking and shushing, and my obstinate sister's wailing had grated on my last nerve. But I sensed that Sister's prayers had been answered. Providence had delivered her a solution, and for that she was truly thankful and relieved. My next questions were: Why was I shielded from the details? Why hadn't anyone informed me?

*

Mississippi mud is harder than granite, especially when it is thirty degrees outside. It took three Sisters all morning to dig my hole. Their spades picked and hacked at the earth, useless toothpicks as the sinuous roots of ancient oaks impeded their path. Gray, woolen clouds billowed above them and rained darts of sleet onto their hunched shoulders like barbs of regret. They were silent in their work, glancing up now and then, puzzled as to why their spiritual leader had requested such a task in the dead of winter and before morning prayers.

I watched from above them, around them, beside them. Moving around seemed effortless for me, the only requirement a thought, a blink, a wish, although I never felt like I could or should stray too far from my sister. She was my only real connection. At least in our mother's womb our hearts had beat in unison, our life sacks had bumped and rubbed and rolled in the happy dance of anticipated birth.

I tried to remember what it was like there. What it felt like to be close enough to touch. But nothing. I was relegated to a space apart, alone. I watched the nuns scoop each shovel full of dirt from the hole that would soon hold my body. They didn't acknowledge my presence because they didn't know of it. I was air.

Mother Superior flitted around in a state, as anxious and flustered as a canary in the sights of a prowling cat. She came out to check and recheck their progress. And finally, on her fourth or fifth trip, she dismissed her holy laborers to go on about their duties, certain of their loyalty and silent confidence. She stood at the foot of the termite-ridden wall encircling the property, her lengthy skirts billowing in the breeze, and mumbled prayers for my departed soul, making invisible crosses in the air with one hand while holding her veil to keep it from blowing off her head with the other. A stopped-up nose muffled her words. She had no more tears. Arthritic expiation settled in on her as she patted the icy earth around my crude coffin, a wooden case that had once held the finest altar wine.

A dog howled in pain from somewhere close by or some place far away. Or was it my pain escaping, a gush of sorrow released to the wind? I wanted to follow it, fly with it away, to a place that might be different, but I knew I couldn't depart. I would never really want to leave here, to leave my sweet sister. But I would always want what she had—life. Could cold be any colder than this?

Lifeless and brittle, leaves and earthy refuse blew up around the Sister's black stockings. "Sleep well, little Olivia Abigail. Fear not, for God has better plans for you, my dear."

I wondered how she knew this. Why had no one consulted me about these things? My death and birth had transformed me, yes, but into what I could still not be sure. I sensed things, knew things, but not everything. Why, I wondered?

Like an overly sensitive transistor, static often interrupted my signal. Was God still figuring out what He wanted me to do?

Sister turned, clasped her rosary beads and dried her eyes on the back of her hand. No one else witnessed my burial that day. My sister's secret birth and my secret death registered only in our mother's heart and in the heart of the kindly Reverend Mother, who did the best she could do at the time.

*

A young woman waddled into Mother Superior's office that afternoon and lowered herself into the wooden chair facing the desk. Her name was Genevieve Baxter and she was my mother's sister, my aunt, the Genevieve my mother had mentioned to the Reverend Mother. In an instant I knew this young woman, had personal knowledge about her, as if her personality suddenly pulsated through me. Her intentions rubbed coarse against my own. She revolted me instantly, as if a cloud of distrust followed her into the room. What was Reverend Mother up to? I settled myself onto the windowsill, a good vantage point for keeping an eye out.

No amount of disinfectant could remove the stench of ancient mildew and greasy rags from the convent. Genevieve's nose wrinkled. She shivered. She rubbed her swollen belly and checked herself to make sure none of the notes she had written to Elvis had escaped her jacket pockets.

Elvis, yes, Elvis. Silly details about this complete stranger came to me as if an internal movie reel played just for me in stereo hi-fi. His baritone moaned, *"Walk that lonesome valley,"* in my ear. His hips swiveled before me. His slim hand pushed a dark curl out of his face. And I knew Genevieve loved him. But Reverend Mother's plans for my sister played on stations my antennae could not locate. Was God some kind of jokester, I wondered? Was He funning with me? Was He going to keep me guessing and dole out information on a need-to-know basis? Or, rather, was I just not good enough, not smart enough for this job?

Genevieve fingered the ragged scraps of paper in her pocket. *My confession notes*, she called them. *Who needs a priest when Elvis is close at hand*, she thought. Something primitive, almost carnal oozed luxuriously from her sigh. "Well, at least they can't recruit me," she whispered to the daydream of her rock-and-roll idol. "I don't exactly fit the nun mold anymore—not that I ever did."

She fidgeted against the rough oak of her seat, wondering why the Reverend Mother had summoned her to come all the way out to the convent on such a cold and dreadful day. She wondered, too, what she had gotten caught at. She knew it was something, but with her delinquent reputation, it could have been one of any number of things. She turned, thinking someone had opened the door behind her.

This startled me. Had I done that? Had she felt my presence there? I was watching the door at the time. Had I made her look? I focused my attention on the doorway again, willed it to move, or at the very least to squeak. But no, nothing. It didn't move. Genevieve didn't look again. Tugging at her coat, she settled uncomfortably back into the chair.

A few moments later, footsteps sounded from the hallway. Genevieve brushed back her bouffant flip and stood up just as Mother Superior pushed open the door and entered the room.

"Good morning, Sister," Genevieve chimed in her best parochial-school chant. She almost choked on it, but she got it out.

She glanced down and noticed her new *Elvis Presley Fan Club* button peeking out from beneath her car-coat lapel. Tugging gently at the jacket to conceal her pride, she twisted her pearl choker around her finger to make her restlessness appear nonchalant.

"Yes, yes, good morning, Genevieve," Mother Superior replied. She crossed the room to stand between Genevieve and her desk, and motioned for the young woman to sit back down. She didn't sit down herself.

This is bad, Genevieve thought, studying how the Sister's deformed brow was furrowed more deeply than usual, and how she nervously fingered the rosary bead belt encircling her waist.

"Regardless of the outcome of this meeting," Sister said flatly, "I trust that every word spoken in this room will be kept in the strictest of confidence. I mean no one—not even your husband, Ned—can know what we discuss. Can I have your word on that, Genevieve?" She stared buckshot through Genevieve, who dabbed at perspiration that had suddenly formed on her upper lip.

"Well, uh, of course, Sister. Why? What's wrong? What did I do this time?"

The nun's lips pursed as if she'd taken a bite out of a dead rat. Something was up and Genevieve knew it—if she could only figure out what it was before Sister wielded her holy wrath.

Sister was thirty years old at the most, only a few years Genevieve's senior, but that day she looked much older, haggard and tired. With good reason, of course, considering all we'd been through the night before. Neither one of us had gotten a bit of rest.

Sister inhaled with effort. The massive crucifix around her neck rose and fell with her breath. Finally, she said, "There is a child, a baby who needs a good home. I want you to take her, Genevieve."

What? My mind screeched the question to the heavens, but no one answered. How could this be? How could I not have known? And why didn't she contact my father? Wouldn't he be a better choice? Why did I have no inkling about him?

My feeble understanding of my reality shattered under the realization that not only God, but also these people, could keep secrets from me. Until that moment I thought I could read every feeling, sense every thought of every person I had been around. *Evidently, I am not a siphon*, I thought. I wondered if I had accidentally triggered an invisible on-and-off switch somewhere, and wondered, too, what other surprises would catch me off guard.

Genevieve cocked her head, also unsure if she'd heard the woman correctly. *What's this*? she thought. *A convenient twist? Being here has nothing to do with me, or anything I've done*? She straightened up in her chair and moistened her suddenly parched lips. "A baby, Sister? Take her where?"

"Why, home with you, of course."

Genevieve's complexion grayed markedly and her muscles seemed to give way. Her eyes searched the nun's face for a hint of something other than solemnity, but found none. "But Sister, do you mean? But that's impossible. I'm pregnant myself and due any day! "

"Yes, yes, I know. Which is why, under the circumstances, you are the best choice, the perfect choice. You and your husband will care for her. No one will ever guess that she isn't your child. She deserves a good home, Geneveive."

Genevieve's legs stood her up. Her hands twitched. She needed to move and wanted to escape. Her thoughts screamed so loudly I plugged my ears, and even she feared Sister might actually hear the horror in them.

Her brain told her feet to act quickly, to take one step and then another and another until she was out the door. I urged her on. *Yes, go, go. You can't have my sister, you can't.* But holy guilt glued her to the floor.

Is this some kind of cruel joke? she wondered. Was God paying her back for all the hell she'd raised as a teen? She folded her hands in front of her, studying them. It must be God's way of forcing her onto the straight and narrow. His way of making her accept her rightful place in goodness, like my mother Willard, her saintly older sister had. She shoved her hands deep inside her pockets and once again fondled the scraps of papers hidden there. Oh, if they could only grant her reprieve.

Wavering a moment longer, she struggled to hang on to her resolve, and to avoid the cool eyes that now gripped her gaze. *Lord, that woman is ugly*, Genevieve thought. *She can't make me do this. I won't.*

But it was no use. The nun's eyes told the tale. It was easy for Genevieve to do as she pleased when no one was watching, but when God used a nun to point His finger, there was no escape. Genevieve's countenance collapsed, and she gave in like the good little Catholic girl she had never been. "But why me, Sister? I don't understand."

Mother Superior walked around her desk and eased herself into her oppressive chair. "The child was born here last night, Genevieve. Yes, that's right—here, in this convent. I'm sure you understand the consequences of such an occurrence. This child needs and deserves a loving home. You have a good heart, deep down. This is your opportunity to do something responsible with your life."

Was that a hint of mist in the Sister's eyes? I was certain of it, but she blinked it away before Genevieve could be sure.

Genevieve wondered who the mother could be, how a child could be born in a convent, what made the Reverend Mother think that she, of all people, could be the right choice for this mission of mercy. She didn't know that her sister, Willard, had come to the convent, and had no clue that Willard had been pregnant. But, being a small town and since Willard had supposedly joined a Religious Order to do mission work in Africa several months before, Genevieve had to wonder. *Could this be my sister's child? Could Willard have come here instead?* She didn't get the chance to voice any of her questions.

Sister tucked her hands inside the wide sleeves of her habit, hugging herself. I couldn't decide if I wanted to hug her or slap her silly. What could she be thinking? My *Aunt* Genevieve wasn't fit to raise a yard dog. If I knew nothing else, of that I was sure.

"I prayed for God to reveal His plan to me and He did," Sister said weakly. "I'll never understand it, but He revealed you, Genevieve. As hard as it is to believe, you are His plan. With you so close to your own due date, you can take this child and raise her with your child as your own."

"But whose child is it, Sister?"

The Reverend Mother raised her hand to silence Genevieve, a stern refusal that put an end to this line of questioning.

Genevieve squirmed. The meaning took a few minutes to seep in. While she steeped, my purpose in death rang through me with the clarity of an intelligent mind. I wasn't sure yet what, if any, effect I could have on the physical world, but if this was to be, if Genevieve Baxter was to become the adoptive mother of my sister—and I use the word "mother" loosely—she would not get off easy. She would have to contend with me.

Was I being judgmental and unfair? Maybe. Okay, yes! Jumping to conclusions? Probably. But my first concern was my sister, and I sensed that Genevieve, a self-absorbed little hussy, only thought about herself, her own desires and pleasures, and never considered charity and sacrifice for the good of someone else, even a helpless child. Sure, Christian responsibility had been drilled into her head her whole life, but the dog must have eaten her spiritual homework or, at the very least, she'd slept through class.

Suddenly, Genevieve felt hot, flushed. Glancing over her shoulder toward the doorway again, she whispered, "This place gives me the creeps." She shifted on her nervous feet, fanned herself with her open hand then rested her forehead in it. "I don't know, Sister," she told the floor. "Do you really think God wants me for this job? Me, sister?" She tried not to, but looked up into the Sister's eyes again. They grabbed her like she knew they would and pulled her in. "What about Ned? He'll have to know. Won't he?"

Reverend Mother leaned back in her chair but didn't utter a word. She leveled her gaze on Genevieve, a well-practiced terror tactic Genevieve had experienced often in parochial school. I leveled more than my gaze on her as she stood there, simmering in her misfortune.

As I suspected it might, the pause gave Genevieve's legendarily devious mind time to do the rest.

*

Three days later, another child was born at the convent.

"Oh, Good Lord, you're in labor!" Reverend Mother screeched at Genevieve, who sat sprattle-legged in the middle of the kitchen floor. She had kept Genevieve at the convent to bond with her "new daughter"—ugh, it chokes me up to think about it to this day—while the other resident nuns prayed the Liturgy of the Hours, alone. They spent their days in silence and contemplation, only speaking amongst themselves at regularly scheduled times. The Reverend Mother was the only nun allowed to interact with the outside world.

Watching Genevieve fumble, mishandle, and downright ignore my sister pained me greatly but solidified my place and duty. I'd just as soon have been damned to live with Lucifer forever as to ever leave this ingrate alone with my flesh and blood.

"Look, Sister," Genevieve said now, "my baby is coming and there's no way to stop it. Isn't this what you wanted? So, help me. Do something before I spit this baby out right here on the linoleum floor or die trying."

I could only wish.

"Yes, yes, of course. This is how God meant it to be."

At this birth, all the nuns chipped in to assist. Reverend Mother had no other choice but to trust them and enlist their help in her little cover-up scheme. All helped, except one, that is: my mother, who had been ordered to cloister herself in her upstairs cell until further notice, where she remained, painfully oblivious to the escapades taking place in the days just after she delivered my sister and me. She mourned her losses alone, not knowing that Reverend Mother had given my sister to Genevieve, not even knowing that I had died, while her convent Sisters rushed around just beneath her like a silent gaggle of over-excited geese.

The kitchen clucked with excitement. One saintly goose accepted the handoff of my twin while the others dressed the kitchen table in clean linens and boiled two Dutch ovens of water on top of the stove. Mother Superior bellowed orders like she knew what she was doing. She pushed her long sleeves up over her shoulders, flipped her veil out of her face, scrubbed down like a surgeon and sterilized a butcher knife big enough to gut a goat.

Genevieve's pains brought forth screaming obscenities. The busy flock of nuns just tucked their heads while crossing themselves obsessively to ward off any adverse effects of the curses. Finally, the tiny bundle oozed into Reverend Mother's awaiting arms.

"It's a girl. Another precious little girl," she cried out. She slapped its purple behind and cries rang out through the Motherhouse again. "I think I missed my calling," Sister said, through a flood of new tears. "Maybe a baby doctor was what He had planned for me to be all along."

She was probably correct in that assumption, but as good as she would become at keeping secrets, I knew being a nun was the right choice for her. She would need the time to spend on her knees.

*

"I think they're identical," Ned announced soon after he brought Genevieve and their new daughters home from the convent. Again, it made me queasy to say the words … *new daughters.* A sad day, such a sad, sad day. He had been suspicious at first. Genevieve had spent every spare moment at the convent, awaiting her child's delivery, since the morning Reverend Mother made her unusual request. He probably wondered why on earth his wife suddenly felt compelled to attend daily Mass with the Sisters. Why would anyone, especially his Genevieve, want to spend hours upon hours in contemplative prayer? As I saw it, and knowing Genevieve as I already did, her deception would have been evident to anyone with a lick of sense.

Guess that says a lot about our dense old Ned. But when he saw his twin daughters, all his worries were relieved. Well, almost all.

He rubbed his clean-shaven chin and pushed up his red thermal sleeves. While Genevieve gave birth at the convent that morning, Ned had been sitting alone and unarmed in a duck blind, at his morning constitutional, no matter what kind of hunting season was open. Now, with his hunting vest rumpled and empty, cigarette smoke and the light embrace of inexpensive bourbon clung to him. A new duck call hung around his neck from a leather shoelace chain. "Just look at them, Genny. They're spitting images of me."

He was seated on the foot of Genevieve's bed, bouncing as he spoke. A thick padding of newspapers, applied for warmth with duct tape at four a.m. in the duck blind, encircled his hips and thighs with news of a world he knew little about.

Genevieve moaned. She rolled away from what she called, "my unfortunate excuse for a husband," to face the tall windows that looked out over the carriage house and greenhouses of the family's once-grand Mississippi estate. The metal bed squeaked at the commotion. Icy rain pattered against the tin roof of the back porch. "You're blind, Ned. They don't look anything like you, you fool." The bed became oppressive under his weight.

"Are you sure we shouldn't get that old doc over in Iuka to drive out here and take a look at them, though? This little one's a bit pique-ed. Maybe you'd better feed the little tikes." He stood up. The bed sprang back in relief.

A yellowed wicker bassinet beside the bed held the two babies, lying elbow to elbow. One rested quietly. The new one was calm, but my sister squirmed around like a banked fish, kicking and fretting to free herself from the confines of the blanket papoose meant to keep her calm. My Little Miss Fussbudget.

Genevieve had passed the babies around so much and had then bundled them up so tightly that barely a nose peeked out. I was worried I'd lose track of my sister. Cute and as white as a lop-eared bunny, but oh, that child had opinions. She twisted her little mouth into a knot and let out a howl that scared the mice right back into the old Victorian walls. As if unwilling to be outdone, the other child tuned up and joined in. The shrill reverberated across the hardwoods and down the stairway, all the way to the parlor on the front of the house.

"Holy Mother!" Ned whooped, moving toward the door. "I'll check on things in the flower shop and let you deal with the little buggers. Thank God I'm not equipped for your job."

"Well, you sorry, good for nothing, SOB!" Genevieve screeched, flipping back over like a flapjack to face him. "I delivered our baby on the cold floor of an auto parts convent and now all you can think about is getting out of here at the first little peep."

Ah, Genevieve's true colors were showing themselves. Ned didn't catch her slip of the singular. If Genevieve wasn't careful, she would blow Mother Superior's plan out the back windows.

I could only hope and pray.

"Now, Genny . . . "

"Don't you 'Now, Genny' me." She sat up straight as a yardstick in the middle of the bed. "I won't have it, you hear? Now pick one of these squalling babies up and bounce her 'til she's quiet." Ned obeyed. "And I am not breast-feeding. Who do you think God invented that new fangled formula stuff for?"

"Now, Genny, is that stuff safe?" Ned was making tracks back and forth across the bedroom floor, bouncing and shooshing at the same time. I sat in yet another windowsill. Aren't windowsills and doorframes the place to go when earthquakes hit? I had already discovered them to be the perfect perching spots for a soul stuck between here and there.

"We're trying it," Genevieve announced, wiggling her hips back into the softness of the feather bed. "And if it doesn't work, I'll hire a wet nurse." She snatched a hand mirror from the nightstand. Staring into it, she fluffed her teased hair helmet and checked under her eyes for wrinkled luggage. "Ned, I don't even let *you* near my breasts. What makes you think I'd let the babies suckle me like a couple of hungry little pigs?"

"Okay, okay, Genny, don't get all riled. We'll try the bottle instead, but stop talking about a wet nurse. Nobody does that anymore."

Ned gently placed my sister in the bassinet next to my replacement. Then he said, "I'll get Madson to make up a bottle right now. By damn, that nigger knows how to do just about everything, but I'll bet he never thought he'd be mixing up baby formula for our twins. And I never thought I'd be glad his sorry black ass was around to do it."

"You are treading on rose petals now, Ned," Genevieve growled, pointing her manicured finger like a dagger. "Leave Madson alone. He's been my best friend since forever, a lot longer than you've been poking around."

Ned grumbled, "You hate niggers as much as I do—probably more than the Klan, and you know it. I never thought I'd see the day."

"Out Ned—get out of my sight and out of my earshot or I swear I'll . . ."

"I'm going. I'm going."

He exited the room quickly, before she had a chance to get going on some other yelling upset. The nine-foot door closed with a distinctive click. I wanted to join him but didn't dare leave. Plus, where would I go? I kept expecting my mother to walk through the door, to say it was all a mistake and that she'd come to collect her child, but I could not feel her or sense her. She was outside my realm. I assumed she was still at the convent, but I could stray from my sister only so far, directed by God's prodding to be exactly where He wanted me to be. I thought about her, though, prayed every second that she was safe and that her grief had not vaporized her into a world of despondency beyond anyone's reach.

Genevieve pushed herself up onto her elbows, wincing at the sudden jab of pain between her legs that she hadn't felt just moments ago in the heat of her frenzy. I envied her grimace, longed to feel something physical, and wondered, too, if pain felt anything like the hollowness of detachment that echoed through my bodiless soul. With some difficulty she fluffed her stack of feather pillows and leaned back into them, tucking the quilt up under her engorged breasts. For a minute all she did was stare at the wall, the babies' uneasy wiggling only a mild annoyance to her reverie. Then, from the nightstand drawer, she retrieved the small photo album she kept hidden there under her prayer book and extra Modess pads.

She thumbed through it, passing up the five-year-old wedding picture of Ned and herself under the oak trees out back, and stopped on a page with a photo of her mother on one side and my mother's First Communion on the other. I recognized Mother immediately, even as she posed as a child in her white dress and veil. They were sisters, true, but there could be no two sisters more opposite than these.

Genevieve remembered the day six months before when Willard had boarded a Greyhound bus for Atlanta, off to become a nun, to save the world, to become a missionary in Africa and teach all the little savage children about Jesus and salvation. Genevieve now suspected that something quite different had taken place. "You never left the county," she murmured to herself. "You were pregnant." *Why else would the Reverend Mother give me this child,* she thought. *And who could the father be?* "Willard, you sly bird. You had me fooled."

But Genevieve hadn't been looking through her picture album for the picture of my mother. Those suspicions would have to wait for another day. Today, her eyes longed to gaze on someone else. She pulled the snapshots partway out of the plastic sleeve and fingered their edges to free the hidden photo between them. Her cheeks warmed. A smile dimpled them as she gazed down at her prize.

This ought to be good, I thought, and eased in closer to get a good look at the sepia picture of a man standing next to several buckets of flowers. His hair and skin seemed light against the bronze background of a brick wall, his face taut. *Bland-Hersh Wholesale* was painted on the wall. His pant pockets bulged with fists shoved deep. He was not looking at the camera, but off to the side, as if he'd turned away just before the shutter flashed.

"I love you, Jack Bland," she whispered to the image. "You're the only man I'll ever truly love." She pressed the picture to her swollen bosoms and sighed. I was astonished to see tears trickle down her cheeks as she ruminated over the life she was meant to have had, but I assumed they were of the crocodile kind. This woman could not possibly be capable of real feelings, could she? With no audience present, at least not one that she was aware of, I had to wonder. Had I judged her too harshly? Okay, okay, I will admit that her life had been sad, tragic even, a life devoid of love. I guess some fast-talking lawyer could make the case that, since no one had ever shown her love, how would she know it if it bit her in the backside? No one had ever loved her for herself. Who would want to, I wanted to know?

She thought it wasn't fair. She thought she deserved better, that she was worthy of more. How would she ever get that life now? The lace curtains on the window next to the bed billowed up suddenly like a puff of summer breeze had caught them and tossed them into the air. The window was shut tight to keep winter's fury at bay. Again I asked myself, *Was that me?* Had I ruffled the curtains? Genevieve pulled the down coverlet up to her chin, shivering. "Who is it?" she whispered, hoarsely. "Who's there?" The lace relaxed.

After several minutes, she shook off the mood and reached over the edge of the mattress. From there she pulled out a magazine that she'd tucked under her side of the bed. Before opening it, she glanced over at the window to make sure the curtains remained calm. I gave them a wave, but to no avail. Both babies started fretting, but Genevieve couldn't acknowledge their cries. The magazine's front cover caption read: *Tupelo native Elvis Presley hits the charts with Heartbreak Hotel*. She flipped through the pages and creased their corners each time her dreamy-eyed idol appeared.

"I can't love who I want to," she told Elvis, "but I can love you. Oh, yes, baby cakes, you'll do just fine." She propped the open magazine against the lamp on the bedside table. "I don't care what Ned says. I'm your number-one fan. And you know all of my secrets. I may have to hide my real love, but I won't hide you away. Ned can just go suck a snake egg."

A passing thought darted though my mind, but didn't stop long enough for serious consideration. I had to wonder, though: Was her relationship with Elvis real, or just some fantasy she had dreamt up for herself as an escape from her pitiful life? I was privy to much of her past, but some things seemed evasive, shrouded in deep folds of her psyche that I hadn't learned how to unfold yet. Like I said, the idea was too ludicrous. It exited as quickly as it had arrived.

A soft rap on the door roused her from her daydreams. "Cover yourself," a voice said. "I'm coming in." The door squeaked open, and a lightly bronzed man slipped into the room. He was wearing crisply ironed jeans, rolled up twice and precisely at the hem, revealing their lighter underside. A crease down the front of each leg was so sharp it could cut you if you got too close. He wore a starched white shirt, buttoned up tight to a pole-thin neck, and black shoes so shiny one could mistake them for onyx rocks. He wasn't any bigger around than a cedar fence post, but his hands were large and strong. He crossed in front of the bed with the easy gait of belonging, stopping to place a vase of Sonya roses on the dresser and to straighten the tatted doily beneath it before approaching the bed.

"Oh, thank God," she said, holding out her arms to him for a hug.

He considered her distance from the edge of the bed, hands on his hips, brows raised in jest. He moved in once. Then rethought his position and came at her again. Leaning forward at the waist, he readjusted his trajectory several times. Then with his knee supporting his weight, he leaned in and placed his hands on top of the bed covers on finger tripods, one on either side of Genevieve, as if touching any part of her body might harm her somehow. When their cheeks met, her arms flung around his neck with such force he almost toppled. His eyes bulged.

Shaking his head, he pulled away and retreated. He scooped both babies up in his wiry arms and laid a child into her lap with a tenderness no one I had met thus far possessed. Then, like magic, he retrieved two baby bottles from the wide pocket of his flower-shop apron and handed one to Genevieve with fingers like the petals of a bony flower.

Livvie's Heavenly Bouquet was embroidered in fine script across his chest in light green with *Madson* written beneath it in simple block letters.

"I heard you hollering all the way downstairs," he said, poking the rubber nipple into my sibling's mouth. I watched her suck, mesmerized by the action. *What must it be like to taste?* I wondered. I imagined the warmth of the white liquid traveling from lips to mouth to throat to soul.

But my images held no flavor. I was distracted by my own longing, and I had to force myself to concentrate. "It ain't good that you've been giving that husband of yours such a hard time," he was saying to Genevieve. "He's a new daddy. He's got no clue what to do with twins, and he never knew what to do with a crazy wife like you."

"No clue is right. The flowers from you?"

Madson shook his head. "Jack Bland told me to take some out of our last order and make you up a bouquet. Sends his congratulations."

"Humph. Make sure he makes up for them on the next shipment. It'd be just like him to forget."

Madson sat down on the edge of the bed and picked up the conversation where he had detoured. "You might as well make up your mind to settle down and forget about that Mr. Bland. You're a momma now. These young'uns need somebody to bring them up right and take up for them when times get rough, not someone living in the past, pining over a man she can never have. "

I liked this man already. Words of wisdom, how refreshing. Where had he been all this time?

"Like you took up for me, Madson?" Madson looked away. She went on, "You did, you know. Time and time again. Especially when I . . . when I killed Grandpa Clancy . . . Oh, I'll never forget it, Madson. I'll never forget what you did for me."

I almost fell out of the windowsill. *Killed Grandpa Clancy!* How could I not have sensed that in my first impression of her?

"Hush, now," Madson warned. "I've told you about that. You never killed anyone; stop saying that. He died of natural causes. You had nothing to do with it. You've got to get those crazy ideas out of your head."

She smiled up at Madson and drew her legs under her to support the feeding infant in her arms. "What would I have done, what would I do now without you to help me survive my life? Tell me that, Madson."

"Don't know, but chances are you'd be locked up in some nut-house somewheres. Someone needs to help you recognize reality. You ain't perfect, but you're no murderer. Now hush with that kind of talk."

In the span of a few minutes Genevieve's revelations had terrified me and Madson's had relieved me. Somewhat. I wondered what other surprises this woman might reveal. For the first time in days, though, my fears for the well-being of my baby sister eased a bit. I had just met my first ally and could not have been more thrilled, knowing that Madson would be around. He finished feeding my sibling in silence. Then he laid her on the bed and left Genevieve to mull over her new life.

Staring down at the infants, she seemed engrossed for the first time by their presence. She had expected them to be whiter than a freshly burst cotton boll, but they weren't. Her child resembled a new bruise, still puckered and swollen from its struggle to exit the womb. But my sister's complexion had cleared to reveal a buttery softness the color and consistency of whipping cream. Genevieve stroked the cheek of her child as it suckled the rubber nipple. Guess who squirmed within the confines of her blanket, almost satisfied for a time at least? Genevieve smiled, happy and overwhelmed at the same time. *Maybe I am a good choice for this job,* she thought. *Maybe I will be a good mother to both my girls.*

So often she let life's goings-on consume her, a convenient way to disengage herself from anything that might hurt. But how could she detach herself from this, she wondered? She had never held a baby until the last few days. She had always felt leery around younger kids. And Grandpa Clancy had never allowed her any friends of any age. Now, what would she do with two arms-full? How would she raise these babies with no foundation in the art? Maybe osmosis would prevail. She could only hope.

We could only hope.

Tears brimmed again. She blinked, letting them roll as motherhood—or more likely, raging hormones—engulfed her. Her chest tightened with a warmth she'd never known, a warmth that both calmed her and scared the bejeezes out of her.

"We'll have fun," she whispered in an effort to shift her mind gears. She could almost hear them grinding hard to thwart emotions she could never let herself feel. It was too risky, letting them in, letting anyone in. "If nothing else, we'll have fun." She swallowed hard. "And I won't let anyone hurt you, babies." Memories washed over her like dirty rain. "Nope, no one will hurt my babies. I won't let them. I won't let myself."

Even coming from Genevieve, those were the best words I had heard since my death.

Hard Headed Woman
Top 20 *Billboard* Hit Single

While Ned steered his flower shop van with his knees along Mississippi Highway 72 East, he picked at the skin on his cracked fingers. They had been sliced one-too-many times by the shop's pick machine and had stripped a thousand-too-many leaves from prickly stems. As he turned off the main road headed north toward Iuka and Pickwick Lake, he vowed aloud not to accept any more excuses from Genevieve. "It's time my family lived together in Memphis—not way out here in the boonies of Mississippi on my in-law's God-forsaken old place." It was a Saturday evening in late April of 1966.

The twins, as they were called, were almost ten years old now. And an interesting ten years it had been. I had learned to accept my place in limbo, although reluctantly and not without the constant yearning to be human and to experience the senses my spiritual existence lacked. Either God had given up on me, or He had never intended to invite me into Paradise from the get-go. The strong, silent type, He remained aloof and incognito, languishing behind my doorway in a realm I dreamed about often, but doubted I'd ever encounter. He never spoke—but made certain that I caught His drift—never conversed with me other than with an occasional ethereal nudge to keep me in line, which didn't leave me much opportunity to ad lib.

I hung around, mostly, keeping watch, but managed to get my two cents' worth across in a variety of small ways now and then. It had taken me a few years to figure out the scope of my unearthly abilities, what I could and couldn't do, but once I got the hang of it, sending chills up Genevieve's spine became one of the highlights of my days, especially when we were gallivanting around to Elvis concerts with the girls.

And my girls, oh, my girls. What precocious little marvels they had become. I loved them both dearly, with a devotion that blurred the edges of simple sibling ownership and taught me the unconditional virtue of hearts joined, fingers intertwined.

As gravel crunched under the tires of Ned's old Chevy van, he noticed the girls daredevil-jumping off the porch and vaulting the old World War Two torpedo that lay on the front lawn. No one knew how the relic happened to find its way to the yard, but we didn't mind it being there. It was a conversation piece, the girls said.

They had painted it bright pink in an effort to make it stand out "in a feminine way," and to look pretty when the azaleas were in bloom. Genevieve worried that "relatives" had deposited it there and might decide to blow them all to Kingdom Come with it, but the girls remained fearless, and were determined for torpedo-vaulting to become a new sport in the Olympics one day.

Genevieve suspected me in her warnings, I suppose. Or more probably the ghosts who roamed the property like disgruntled centenarians, aimless and ornery, wrinkled and weary. I steered clear of them most of the time, and they had no use for me, either. Watching them, however, had taught me a thing or ten about the celestial food chain. I ranked high above them, I was certain. I had purpose and light; they had only shadow and destitution.

The van's motor knocked a few times before it finally coughed and relieved itself with a great sigh. Ned climbed out and patted the hood as he passed. He was forever working on that vehicle, even though he knew little about mechanical things. If God hadn't invented duct tape, Ned's favorite fix-all, that old jalopy would have fallen apart years ago. He walked up the front steps to the porch, and the girls flew into his arms, screaming, "Daddy, Daddy." They almost knocked him back down the stairs. He scooped them up, tickling them as he swung them around. His comb-over flew up in the breeze and remained there, standing at attention. Not even the thick Brylcreem he used could keep that flag from waving without the help of a hat.

Anna Beth was a stocky little thing, short for her age, all muscle and mischief, with a rough and tumble attitude that would spit in the eye of authority given the chance. She'd stick out her chin like a target, asking for a fight. And just try to get that child into a dress. Ha! But she was an artistic little one. From the time her stumpy fingers could grip a paintbrush she recreated with shadow and light and striking detail whatever she happened to rest her eyes upon.

Louisa, on the other hand, was tall and lean, decidedly prissy. She had a thin nose and a flirtatious glance that could unnerve even the most liberal adult. She had the habit of talking to herself in the bathroom mirror for hours on end with puckered lips, hands raised in model poses and fingers worrying her hair. The only thing she wanted to paint was her face. Her fondest wish was to be old enough to wear makeup, which, if Ned had his way, wouldn't be until she was twenty-five.

Not long after Genevieve had brought them home as babies from the convent their physical differences mellowed. Their baby bodies had developed similarly into cherubic rolls of skin, all cheeks and chubby fingers and toes. With being dressed alike until their fifth birthday, and being passed around between family members and flower shop employees, I had trouble keeping up with which one was which. Even their infant dispositions became similar. I worried often that I might have lost track of which one was my sister. I loved them both, of course. There was no distinction in my affection, no special affinity to one child or the other. Had God intended it that way? Then, as they'd aged, new differences became clear. Most of the time I was fairly certain I knew which one was my sister, but there were times when I questioned my choice. Did it really matter, I wondered? Was my job here not as protector for both?

It was panty-sticking hot that day, even though spring had barely caught hold. Stretched out on the porch swing, Genevieve snoozed like a lioness with her eyes closed and one leg dangling off the swing. An Elvis tea pitcher and matching set of glasses sat on a wicker table beside her, its ice melting slowly in the late spring warmth. A sign that read *Elvis Slept Here* hung above the front door.

Ned put the girls down. He patted their rumps. "You're getting too big for me to do that," he said. "I'll fool around and throw my back out, if I'm not careful. Then I'd be in one heck of a mess."

They ran down to the opposite end of the wrap-around porch, squealing and laughing like monkeys in a zoo. And me? Well, this Windowsill Princess had graduated to the Queen of Doorjambs, Porch Railings, and even Laps. Always as watchful as a screech owl, as silent as a hummingbird's wings.

"These girls are going to kill each other one day," Ned yelled at his wife, stomping dust off his work shoes on the top step. "A little supervision might help." He had reason to worry. The girls were fearless in their antics, often jumping from tree branches into Genevieve's persuasive arms. Or crossing the highway without looking so they could torment the neighbors' chickens. Or throwing eggs at cows' backsides to see if they could make a *butt*-bull's eye. I had a Dickens of a time keeping up with them. And when Genevieve wasn't pretending to work in the flower shop, she was right in there with them, planning the next escapade and plotting how to keep from getting caught.

She yawned and stretched, sitting up. "They're fine, Ned. They're having fun. We always have fun. So, stop griping and leave them alone." Then she grumbled under her breath, "Leave us all alone," unconcerned if he overheard her or not. A minute later she asked, "How was your trip?"

"Too long. I've had it, Genny. Ya'll are moving to Memphis with me this weekend. Do you hear?" He didn't know that they made regular trips into the city to camp out in front of Graceland, Genevieve always hoping for a glimpse of her King, or better yet, an invitation to enter those musical gates so she could get a taste of the good life.

"I hear. I hear." She slid her feet into her pink-satin pom-pom house slippers and hoisted her chiffon-muu-muued self off the swing. She hollered toward the yard. "Now girls, you can jump on that instrument of death all you want, but don't beat on it with that stick, Louisa. It's a bomb, not bongos. You'll blow us all to where Grandpa Clancy is, and believe you me, you don't want to go there."

I wondered how she knew where he'd gone, or if she'd seen him roaming about. I certainly had. My Great-Grandfather Clancy spent his eternity tortured and removed from anything good, wandering the property in the hell he'd created for himself. He was a scary reminder of what sin can do. I was glad he couldn't come near me, and wished I hadn't been burdened with the ability to know of his place. I feared for Genevieve, too. Much as I disliked her, I wouldn't wish first-hand knowledge of his place on anyone. Her guilt over *killing* him eat at her soul, in spite of Madson's assurances that she had nothing to do with Grandpa's death.

She stretched her arms up over her head to knock the kinks out, rotating her hips this way and that. Ned's trousers suddenly poked out in front, his serpent coming to life and sticking straight out like a divining rod. The evening sun backlit Genevieve's slinky duster, one fashionably similar to Doris Day's in *Pillow Talk*. She gave him a free shot of the curvaceous figure he hadn't seen naked in almost a year.

Good Lord, I thought. *Here he goes again, poor fool*. I hated being privy to this kind of stuff, but sadly, I had gotten used to it after all these years. That's not to say that I didn't want to know what it felt like to be sexually aroused, but I won't tarry on the details of my lusting. This story is supposed to be about the girls.

"And please Ned, for the love of Jesus, Mary and Joseph, don't call me Genny," she said for the millionth time. "You know it crawls all over me. Now, go on inside and get cleaned up. You smell like sweaty vinyl and road kill."

Ned shook his head but obeyed. He tried so hard to fit the good ol' boy mold of manliness and prowess, but she only mocked him. His pocket protector and comb-over gave him away every time. Slumping at the familiar rejection, his destiny for another cold shower rang crystal-clear.

After the screen door slammed, Genevieve whooped, "Come on, girls. Stop hogging all the fun. Give me a turn." She hiked her duster up over the lace of her long-line girdle, threw her leg over the porch rail, perched on her tiptoes on the porch's lip, and leaned forward, arching her back and holding on to the rail behind her. "This is the arched butterfly position," she informed them. "Pretty good, huh? Now, fly girls. Let's fly!" She threw herself into the air like a Hawaiian butterfly and sailed, muu-muu flapping. Slippers took flight. Azaleas took cover. Children clapped and squealed as Genevieve landed, feet perfectly together, arms spread like an Olympic gymnast for a perfect ten not two inches past the nose of the pink lawn torpedo.

Even I applauded. No one could deny that Genevieve knew how to have a good time.

*

Chairs scraped across the hardwood floors as the Baxter family gathered to eat their only sit-down meal together all week. I plopped myself down on the sideboard above which hung two gold framed posters of Elvis. This position offered me a clear view of everyone present. The sideboard was also located next to the kitchen door, a convenient escape hatch when their bickering or Genevieve's whining made me wish I owned the capacity to puke.

Ned's brow furrowed as he watched disaster in the making. The girls' manners needed polish. Louisa's slender fingers cocked her hundred-year-old sterling silver spoon and shot a field pea across the table at Anna Beth. It missed its target, bounced a couple of times and rolled in my direction. I focused my attention on it and smirked, pleased, when its buttered shell burst open and splayed its innards into a squash spot on the floor. As usual, no one noticed. But I would not give up hope. It seems juvenile, I know. But field pea exploding might come in handy for me someday.

"Now, Louisa, that's enough," Ned barked. "I'll not have any child of mine acting like trailer trash at the table. Uh uh, Anna Beth, don't you dare toss that roll!"

Ignoring him, Anna Beth reared back with the arm of a quarterback and fired the yeast roll with precision. Louisa ducked, but not in time. The roll caught her square in the left brow, and its puff of self-rising flour left a white bull's eye from her hairline to her chin. Giggles erupted and quickly bloomed into full-grown howls.

While Ned sat there with his mouth gaping in a kind of shocked pause, Genevieve struggled to keep her last bite of meatloaf in-house. Anna Beth tried to squelch her laughter by taking a sip of milk when she noticed Ned's face reddening to a dangerous shade, but that mistake became clear when she couldn't swallow, almost choked, and a thick white shower drenched them all.

At that, Louisa was overcome. She gave up and fell out of her chair. She heaved with laughter as though she had invented comedy.

Ned bellowed, "Genny, you should have taught them some kind of manners by now. Settle down, girls—I'm telling you—or you'll be excused from this table without so much as another bite." Louisa clambered back to sit upright, and hands rose to cover snickering mouths.

Genevieve exhaled with great dramatic effect. Her husband's ill-fated attempts at discipline were laughable—but at least he tried. He hadn't a clue what wild-spirited high-jinks she put up with—and encouraged—day in and day out, while he piddled his time away at his dismal excuse for a family business in Memphis.

It was common everyday fare for Anna Beth, the tomboy and most imaginative of the bunch including Genevieve, to plan out detailed covert maneuvers for the three of them to play. Although it usually took some coaxing to get Louisa involved.

Everything from water-balloon bombings of greenhouse workers—justified as being refreshing on hot summer days—to pebbled raids with slingshots upon unsuspecting highway motorists. Ned didn't know the first thing about playtime at the Baxter house. Staring across the table at him, Genevieve lifted her fork to her mouth with all the delight and expectation of a truckload of manure headed down her throat. She wondered why she had let her grandfather talk her into marrying such a depressingly boring man.

Ned wasn't really Grandpa Clancy's fault, though, and she knew it. Every other heartbreaking thing in her life had been, but not Ned. No, Genevieve had picked Ned because he happened to be conveniently unattached and in the wrong place at the right time. Poor fool. At that moment almost fifteen years ago, Ned was her way out of the abusive hands of her grandfather and into the loving arms of her true love.

Or at least, that had been her plan. Jealousy was her motive. She'd hoped that seeing her with Ned would make her secret lover, Jack Bland, jealous enough to leave his wife. Unfortunately, Ned was only the first of Genevieve's schemes to backfire with an ass-kicking punch. Now, her only hope was to endure the dreary torture of Ned and pray that he'd die an early death.

With dinner over, Genevieve retreated to the parlor with her latest romance novel. Ned poured himself a tottie, and then went to check up on Madson, to make sure he'd locked up the flower shop and battened down the greenhouses. The girls, ever plucky and full of mischief, evaporated into the spring darkness with flashlights and Mason jars to catch spiders or torment any other nocturnal creatures they could scare up. I delighted in shooing bunnies into their path. There is nothing quite as soothing as squealing, giggling kids.

Two geological ages later, or at the very least sometime long past any child's decent bedtime, Louisa and Anna Beth sneaked out of the hall with Louisa and me close in tow.

"But why doesn't Moody want to go to Memphis?" Louisa asked. "Elvis is there. Seems like she'd want to be on the first bus. We could have tons of fun there, don't cha think?"

"I don't get it either."

"What do ya suppose'll happen?"

Anna Beth considered it all as Louisa crawled back into bed. They had always lived right there across the driveway from Grandma's flower shop, on land that still undulated with perennial waves of flora planted by Olivia, the grandmother whose name I shared, thanks to the Sister's benediction at my funeral. Olivia had given them purple, yellow and white iris, delicate baby's breath, hardy chrysanthemum, fern varieties numbering in the hundreds.

But the possibility of moving, of living an exotic city life in Memphis with Genevieve leading the way, sounded great to the girls on the surface. And seeing Ned more often than once a week might give them a life resembling normal. Wouldn't that be a twist? They were open to the idea, so young, too young to know better. The essence of the place, of home, hadn't yet solidified in their bones. They hadn't matured enough to realize what they'd lose, what they would forget.

But for me the prospect was rattling. I had followed them around the property, even across town and out to Pickwick Lake, but would my tether span far enough? Would my hold on them be that strong? Or would they disappear from my reality and leave me wasting away with the other lonesome souls who meandered through death without a cause? The thought left me winter-chilled.

"Naw, Weesa, we're going nowhere," Anna Beth proclaimed. "We'll live out here 'til we've got false teeth, blue hair and support hose. I don't ever want to leave here."

*

What's that old saying, *When you least expect it*? Or maybe a better choice is: *Beware of Murphy's Law*. The next morning destiny rang the doorbell, and Anna Beth and Louisa raced to answer its call.

Usually, people came to call over at Grandma Olivia's flower shop, *Livvie's Heavenly Bouquet*, across the driveway. No one ever bothered to stop at the house first. Everyone knew that, if the sun was up, all living creatures at the Clancy/Hersh/Baxter house spent their days over in the shop or in a greenhouse. Even Genevieve stayed over there all day. She rarely lifted a finger to help out, but she gave orders and bitched and moaned about the weather and the price of roses well enough to appear involved.

The frosted oval glass in the front door framed the stranger like the old pictures sitting on the tone-deaf piano in the parlor. Sassy little Louisa won the race and swung open the door. Anna Beth's sock feet slid her into home plate next to Louisa, and the two girls gazed up into the kind eyes of a tiny woman wearing a flowery skirt, sensible shoes and a peasant blouse.

"Well, hello there," the woman said. "And who might you two be?"

Louisa bounced on her toes, her mossy eyes sparkling. "I'm Louisa Marie Clancy Baxter and this is my twin sister, Anna Elizabeth." She always used their full names when showing off, which was most of the time.

The girls were hard-pressed to keep from staring, as was I. The woman couldn't have been a breath more than five feet tall, and her delicate features and wild hair gave her the look of one of those beatnik types that Genevieve always talked about running away to become. I was doubly surprised because she looked quite different than the last time I saw her. But mine was a happy surprise, joyous indeed.

"Well, I'm pleased to meet 'cha," the woman said with a smile. She presented her miniature hand.

She was my mother. I was so thrilled to see her I didn't have time to wonder why she wasn't wearing a habit.

Anna Beth grabbed her hand and shook it vigorously. Finally, Louisa snatched it away and warned, "Good golly, Sis, don't shake the poor lady's hand off her arm."

Anna Beth blushed, tucking wild corkscrews of amber hair behind her ear with one hand and pinching Louisa's butt as hard as she could with the other. They had both developed rather demonstrative personalities.

The woman smiled. "It's okay, really. I'm your Aunt Willard. Is your mother around?"

The girls looked at each other, then back at Willard and back at each other again. They'd heard of an Aunt Willard once or twice, Genevieve only divulging the sketchiest of details about the sister that had "abandoned her," but they never thought they'd ever meet the woman. Louisa backed away from the threshold, mouth ajar. Anna Beth followed suit with a similar expression on her face. I fought to keep my aura from beaming like a lighthouse. I had never been so happy to see a person. I punched my sister in the arm when I realized that she didn't have a clue. Look, look who's here! Praise the Lord! Mother has come for us at last. But my urgings didn't get through and I wondered again if I had the right girl.

"Well sure, well, uh, come on in," Anna Beth said. "Moody's out in the kitchen. Madson's cooking up pancakes, fried eggs and sausage gravy for breakfast. He always makes enough to feed the dead troops at Shiloh. I'm sure you could join us, I guess, if you like. But Daddy's getting ready to leave for Memphis and ... "

"Moody? If you don't mind my asking, who is Moody?" Willard followed the girls down the long entry hall.

"Oh, Moody's our mother," Anna Beth explained. "Are you sure you're our aunt? We've called her Moody since we were knee-high to a spider, Daddy says. 'You girls figured her out before you ever uttered your first word,' he says. 'You knew right away that Moody describes her perfectly cuz she's all over the place.' I'm not sure what that means, but I'm sure he's right."

Louisa looked crossways at Anna Beth. Willard shook her head, covering her smile with her hand like most people did when they met the girls. *Precocious* was usually the first word that came to people's minds. Other, less flattering adjectives usually followed. *Devilish* was Genevieve's favorite. Typical. She would think of them in unflattering shades. Mine had always been *precious*—with a mischievous edge that could be softened if their "mother" had any sense in her head.

They led their newly-discovered relative past the parlor, under the staircase and down the back hallway to the sloping kitchen on the back of the house. When the girls pushed through the swinging door with my mother sandwiched between them, splattering sausage was the only audible sound in the room. The girls stood there on the buckling linoleum, grinning so big their molars showed.

Genevieve looked up, her mouth full of pancakes, her fork paused in midair, Aunt Jemima syrup dripping from her gaping mouth and down her no-longer-perfectly-made-up-chin. Ned shot out of his seat like a private whose general had just barked an order. And Madson dropped a skillet full of sausage grease into the porcelain sink. The hazelnut color of his face vanished to a shade just this side of Caucasian. It took him several seconds to recover and for his face to meld shock into a grin of delight, one he covered quickly by tucking his head and turning away. I wondered what it was about my mother that affected him so.

"Well, good morning all," Willard said with an awkward hesitation. "Looks like I got here just in time."

The rest of the day held more chafing than starched underdrawers. Louisa and Anna Beth couldn't figure it out. Due to their relatively sheltered existence on the home place, they hadn't become masters yet at recognizing the manipulative aspects of Genevieve's personality, except those she wielded daily on Ned. After Genevieve's initial shock of seeing Willard wore off, she acted as if her sister came by to visit every other day. She laughed and cut up like she usually did when church ladies came to order flowers, all proper and sweet. She wore that pasted-on kind of smile. The kind that looked like it might crack and fall off if she moved the wrong way.

Ned was supposed to leave right after breakfast to go back to Memphis. He had a business there to run. But I knew right off that a hatchet loomed overhead and threatened to fall hard when he picked up the phone and called *long distance* to make arrangements for someone else to open his shop. He had never done that before. Then he settled himself in. His grumpy disposition— from losing another moving-to-Memphis battle—vanished, replaced by a smug assurance I had never seen before.

The girls mooned over their newfound aunt like adoring fans, lathering on their sweet little girl acts, taking every opportunity to make points with Willard, just in case she might be rich. And their special Moody Radar picked up the signal: *Getting chummy with Aunt Willard steamed Moody's oats.* They laid it on thick while Genevieve threw dagger eyes at them from across the room. One thing those girls thrived on was making Genevieve stew. They were good—I mean really good. I couldn't have done it better if I'd been there in the flesh.

After a day of stiffly pleasant chitchat, long walks over the entire two-hundred acres, wandering through eight greenhouses to marvel at how Madson had increased the planting productivity, and finally, strolling out to the family burial plots so Willard could pray over—and Genevieve could spit upon—the graves of relatives best forgotten, Louisa and Anna Beth had had it. They couldn't figure out to which planet they'd been taken. And they were certain that Martians now inhabited their Moody's body. She had never been so restrained.

This new relative, Aunt Willard, puzzled them, also. She was too nice; too pretty; too sincere; *too calm*—much too normal to have Clancy blood pulsing through her too-tiny veins. Little did they know that it was Genevieve who had received the mutated genes in the family tree, not *my mother*, God bless her heart.

*

Nine o'clock in the evening meant lights out, but that night the girls just switched on their sonar to navigate in the dark. Anna Beth spent most evenings drawing or painting at her desk. She couldn't seem to sit still without doing something creative with her hands. Soon she put away her sketchpad, eased their bedroom window open and leaned out. The warm spring breeze filled the room with the smell of honeysuckle and freshly cut grass. Her complexion now resembled the color of a Sonja rose, a peachy pink so delicate you wanted to wash your dreams in it.

It shone as luminous and soft as the moonlight reflected off the tin roof. In daylight or when challenged, however, a red-orange fire deep within the folds of Anna Beth's petals took breath away from the most composed of souls and caused havoc so upsetting Madson threatened to lock her in the tool shed more than once to calm her down.

She owned a resilient little body and temperament, quick to bristle, reluctant, but willing to forgive. Calling her a spirited child was an understatement, but she was caring, almost to a fault. Of course, filling up the empty spaces in the turbulent relationships of the Baxter family's life demanded an attitude that could put a positive spin on their extraordinary reality. Being tough was mandatory at the Baxter house, and Anna Beth handled the challenge well. I was glad she had her artwork, though. It kept her focused on the beauty in life. Now, leaning out over her dominion, she breathed in deeply, savoring the night air.

Meanwhile, Louisa had brought over feather pillows to cushion their elbows from the rough windowsill. The window seat was just big enough for both of them. Kneeling, their baby-dolled rumps wriggled this way and that as if keeping time with the cicada's call. Anna Beth scratched at her backside. She hated anything with ruffles and was not happy that Genevieve had made her "dress up" for bed.

I squeezed in between them and draped my arms around their shoulders, hoping they would sense the electrical connection linking us through space and time. My essence expanded to envelope them, like a bubble-gum bubble growing with the hot breath of hope and love. Anna Beth unwittingly nudged over a bit to allow me room. Louisa shivered, then reluctantly acquiesced to giving me more space.

Louisa's personality bore traits more reminiscent of a deep-throated tulip than a rose. Red, yes, definitely red, as they both shared the inherited curse of turbulence that ran rampant through the Clancy bloodline. It manifested itself in different ways, but it was there, oh, yes, it was there in both girls. As long as Louisa's petals were meshed closely and kept cool, she was radiant and at ease with the world, but give her a little freedom or let her get warmed up and she'd burst into a full bloom that proved impossible to explain or contain.

Even more troubling was the dark center captured within the softness of her folds. She was a lonely child, even though she was rarely alone, and quite stuck on herself, self-centered, much like Genevieve. She longed for someone to love her in a way she didn't have the intellect or capacity to describe. Figuring out her "whys" and "what fors" was a challenge for everyone who cared for that girl.

"Think we'll ever get out of here?" Louisa asked. She peered outside of the window to make sure no ghosts lurked about. Silly girl. For some reason, she sensed the more unfriendly presences that prowled the property, leaving me unnoticed most of the time. However, Anna Beth, God love her, chose to ignore anything dark. She had her world under control. ("She's got it by the balls," as Ned or a more indelicate spirit might say.) Her determination toward the affirmative made me proud.

"I want to go somewhere," Louisa was saying. "And I want to be in love." She tossed her brown braid over her shoulder. It slapped an unfazed Anna Beth in the back of the head.

"What? I never want to leave, and I don't know why you do. And what in God's universe? Love? We aren't even eleven yet."

Louisa didn't respond. She just gazed out the window, all wistful-like, as if wishing on every star she happened to see.

Anna Beth nudged her. "I've been thinking, Weesa. Like I keep telling you, I can't imagine living anywhere but here." With the crudeness expected more of a son than a daughter, she hocked a wad of spit into her mouth like Ned did so often and let it fly, just to see how far it would go. The majority of it exited her lips weakly and dribbled down her chin and onto her hands, but she seemed satisfied with the effort just the same.

"Ugh," Louisa moaned, her face sliding into disgust.

Anna Beth dabbed up her saliva mess.

After a minute, Louisa said, "Only thing I'd miss is Madson's cooking. I want that more than anything in the world."

"Madson's cooking?"

"Noooo, a man to cook it for me, wait on me hand and foot, treat me like a princess. That's what Moody says every lady wants."

Anna Beth and I groaned in unison, like we did so often at Louisa and Genevieve's outlooks on life. This latest remark was the perfect example of Genevieve's bad influence on these children. Lord, what a job I had on my hands, what a job indeed.

Louisa said, "Moody would cook up pig slop. She's good at a lot of stuff, but cooking isn't one of them."

Anna Beth shook her head. "You've been watching too many soap operas. But you are right about one thing—Moody's cooking. Heck, we could die from that stuff."

"Maybe Daddy'd let us take Madson along," Louisa said, hopeful. "Or Elvis could lend us one of his cooks when we get to Memphis. Bet he's got lots of 'em, don't you think?"

Anna Beth didn't answer. Why bother? We were not moving. Period. End of discussion. And she refused to ever discuss Elvis. Neither one of us could understand why Genevieve was so devoted to the man.

plan, the way it is meant to be."

"My eye," Genevieve moaned under her breath, as the shadow of Madson left the doorway.

Up on the roof Anna Beth and Louisa sat as breathless as if they had run a race and lost. They squeezed each other's hand so tightly their knuckles turned white. Eavesdropping was one thing, but tonight, the moments it took Genevieve and Willard to regurgitate a lifetime of bitterness and heartache had altered their world.

Even at their tender ages they recognized a family history marred by painful memories of which I hoped they would never know the full extent. But their immediate concern was moving. Louisa's excitement blossomed while Anna Beth shored herself up against loss.

And I, well, I prayed for elasticity; I needed my love to stretch almost eighty miles. As I worried about the logistics of highway travel, the girls eased back through the window to begin their first of many sleepless nights.

*

The next morning my family arrived earlier than usual for seven-thirty mass. Genevieve had made a habit of skirting in well after the processional, sometimes as late as the Gospel reading, and grabbing a seat in the back row. On high holy days when every Catholic in the county showed up, she preferred sneaking in barely in time for the Eucharistic Prayer, pacing the narthex without ever sitting down, and then exiting by the side door immediately after receiving Communion. This morning, however, my mother's cheery, "Anna Beth and Louisa, wake up, wake up! Time to prepare ourselves to receive Our Blessed Lord in the Divine Mystery of the Eucharist," roused the girls at five-thirty a.m. The girls were a bit shocked, but they did as they were told. I'd never heard such moaning and grumbling from Genevieve and Ned.

At the church, Ned held open the front door for Queen Genevieve, the girls flanking her like pages. The narthex was crowded as people filed into the nave to take their seats. When Willard appeared at the door of the church, a voice from the crowd rang out, "Oh, my Goodness, look who's here," and all eyes turned to focus on my mother, who wore a simple black skirt and white blouse, her hair pulled back in a simple bun.

Genevieve also turned to look. The prayerful Sunday expressions of the parishioners were replaced by broad smiles, as if a local hero had returned home from the war. The stream turned as old family friends surrounded my mother, smothering her with hugs and cheek kisses and pats. "How are you, child? It is so good to have you home," and, "Oh, my, you haven't changed a bit. What a blessing, a blessing indeed."

I realized that these people all thought my mother had been away for the past ten years, off doing mission work somewhere. They all knew *about* the little cloistered convent on the outskirts of Iuka, but the nuns there lived such a secluded and solitary life that the townspeople had no personal interaction with them, other than occasionally seeing the Reverend Mother picking up their grocery order or other supplies, and no reason to believe that Willard had been one of them.

When the priest entered the space, the crowd pulled him toward Willard. "Look Father. Look who's here." His eyes met my mother's and he smiled reassuringly. His hand in hers transmitted a visible warmth. I realized that her presence was not a surprise to him, but he didn't let on to that fact. Instead, he said, "Welcome home, Willard. Welcome home," loud enough for all to hear. As he hugged her, he whispered, "I told you everything would be alright," but only I overheard.

Genevieve, Ned and the girls had watched in awe as Willard's joyous reception unfolded. They had always been greeted at church with polite nods or questions about floral deliveries or upcoming weddings. Social niceties of an impersonal nature. Genevieve had always longed for more and courted the parishioners, anxious for their acceptance. Her need carried a palpable desperation to fit in and her tactics were flawed by her own feelings of unworthiness. Now, witnessing the affection these people had for Willard, Genevieve realized the extent of her own delusions. She would never gain that level of honor. She would never measure up.

The first booming chords of the processional hymn put an end to the celebration. Parishioners quickly filed into the nave to take their seats, Willard caught amongst them and carried along by the flow to a pew right up front. Genevieve, Ned and the girls were left stunned and alone in the foyer with the priest who gestured for them to enter ahead of him. The only pew left was the back row, their usual spot, a place that now held great symbolism for Genevieve. She would always be last, always be left out, always be an outsider, always be alone.

*

As Ned navigated the narrow driveway of the small three-bedroom house in Memphis he had lived in but never called home, Genevieve strangled the armrest. The van's tires slipped off the concrete strips and dropped into the deep grooves of adjoining dirt. She climbed out and winced at the sight of the place, while she gingerly placed her feet, one in front of the other, moving toward the steep front steps. She waded through waves of full-grown goldenrod, dandelion and crabgrass that grabbed at her legs on her descent into her version of suburban hell. She had been to Memphis many times to visit Graceland, but never to visit her own husband and to see where he spent his weeknights, and realized now that life as she wanted to live it would have no chance of blooming here.

We had listened to Ned yammer all the way from Iuka: how great our life would be here, how wonderful for the girls to attend the Cathedral of the Immaculate Conception School for Girls, how splendid for Genevieve to work with him at the shop. How unremarkable, how mundane, how drab! As I suspected, even before she dumped her make-up bag in the dog-trot entry hall floor, plans for drastic action bounced like ping-pong balls of future regret off the walls of Genevieve's designing mind.

The catawhompus angles from which she viewed her world puzzled me still. It had taken me years to learn not to hate her. And even longer for me to give her a break once in a while. She didn't deserve pity. No, not even she wanted that. She thought of herself as a Venus Fly Trap, divinely carnivorous in her attitude toward anything threatening that came within reach. But a fragile side hid beneath her bravado. Like the too-sweet fragrance of a gardenia whose scent seems delightful at first—for one whiff or two—but stand beside a bush full and don't be surprised when you're knocked down by the stench. Even she had to back away from herself to appreciate her will. But gardenias bruise at the slightest touch. Genevieve's abrasions remained fresh. Now, standing stoically in the foyer of her misfortune, a noncommittal expression of mild annoyance shadowing her face, she cradled her favorite picture of Elvis and devised her strategy.

"You girls go on up to your rooms," Ned said, lugging in the first of their bags. The girls had been standing motionless in the almost empty living room, staring at their meager surroundings in a kind of dazed suspension. I zipped hither and there, impressed with myself for still being *attached*. I had passed between the two places like a weaver's shutter. And my doorway to Paradise stood brilliant and ever-inviting just over my left shoulder. My beam of elasticity still seeped from its tiny opening, a connective tissue of hope. Maybe someday I would know what lay beyond. I prayed that every thread I discovered in my web of existence would someday lead me beyond my place to a life elsewhere.

"Just up the stairs," Ned said, "the two rooms on the left with the bathroom in between. Moody and I will share the big room on the back of the house." He looked over at Genevieve and grinned.

She swallowed a gag.

Anna Beth led the way up the hardwood steps. Louisa followed, wearing the face of someone who had just stepped into dog poop. On the claustrophobic staircase, Anna Beth turned and whispered, "Not exactly what you had in mind?"

Louisa glowered. "Not just me. Did you see Moody? She looks like she might fall out in the floor any minute—or kill somebody."

Standing in their side-by-side bedroom doorways, the girls glanced in, unsure if they dared enter. Identical twin beds without headboards posed like overdone beauty queens in the center of the rooms, dressed in enough pink ruffles to deck out Scarlet O'Hara's hoop skirts. The beds were flanked by similarly dressed windows facing the street. A Pepto-Bismol sea of shag carpet covered the hardwoods. Loosely stretched and lumpy, the carpet undulated under their gaze. Louisa leaned against the doorjamb to steady herself. Single four-drawer dressers, painted white with pink knobs, stood against bare walls, and matching wooden chairs sat in naughty corners, naked and alone. The girls looked at each other with squenched-up noses. They had outgrown these rooms before they were born.

"A far cry from home," Anna Beth said, not realizing that Ned was coming up the stairs. Louisa's expression alerted her. She turned to face him. "But it's real nice here," she lied. "Yep, this is just fine, just fine. Don't you think it's fine, Weesa? This will do us just fine. I think we're gonna like it here." Louisa rolled her eyes and stepped into the first room.

"You girls'll get used to it. City life is different, but that don't mean it ain't just as good," Ned said. He squeezed past Anna Beth's back.

I hoped he was right. I wondered when I would see my mother again. Would I be able to visit? I was already feeling a little homesick for her, and peeved at God for giving her to me and then taking her away again. The cocoon of my reality didn't leave much room for gadding about. God made sure of that. It was comfortable, though, a bubble roomy enough that I could pace when Genevieve drove me crazy, or dance a jig when the girls did something cute. I often wondered what lying in a bed felt like, or tiptoeing through tall grass. Not to mention the whisper of someone else's skin against my hand. Oh, how tortured I sometimes felt. Even the girls' pink carpet looked fascinating to me, in a kinky sort of way. I knew so much and knew so little at the same time.

Downstairs, Genevieve eased herself into a kitchen chair, Elvis resting in her lap. She had no desire to see her new bedroom. Out of habit she scanned the kitchen looking for good places to stash things. She had plenty of "confession notes" to Elvis to hide, a suitcase full, in fact. Written ramblings that detailed everything she had done that would certainly send her south for eternity some day, and lots of things she hadn't done, but felt guilty about anyway. The house in Iuka had been well-suited for hiding secrets. This place would have to be carefully scoped out. As the olive green Frigidaire whirred behind her, she stared into the black womb of the ancient electric stove, scheming wheels still buzzing in her head. "This will not do," she told the Formica tabletop. "Nope, this won't do at all."

Ned shuffled into the kitchen, huffing and puffing from the exertion of carrying in the luggage. "I could have used a little help, Your Highness." He scratched his nether regions with staggering confidence. Then he swung open the refrigerator door, its only occupants a carton of lonesome eggs and enough bottled Blue Ribbon to open a bar.

"Gimme one of those," she said, flatly.

"What? You don't drink beer."

"I do now." She slumped against the table. It leaned with her weight.

"I've got to work on those dad-blame brakes," Ned griped. "They're squealing to beat sixty. Like to have drove me nuts all the way home."

Genevieve chugged half of the frothy excrement, then rolled the cool bottle across her forehead. "You do that, Ned. But remember, you've got to make another trip to Iuka tomorrow to get the rest of our stuff."

"I don't know how I'm supposed to do that and run a business at the same time."

Genevieve leaned back in the chrome-and-vinyl dinette chair. "Oh, don't worry, hon." She chugged long on her beer. "I'll take care of things here. We're a team now, remember? Me and the girls will open the shop all by our little lonesomes. Consider things under control."

Ned smiled, as if his fondest dreams had come true and things had fallen into place like he had planned. But he couldn't see the Fourth of July sparklers and Roman candles firing in his wife's conniving head. Did his crotch rule his life, I wondered? I could have knocked him in the head with the sugar bowl and he still wouldn't have had a clue. I had to wonder: should a person be punished for just being butt-dumb?

*

Ned left early the next morning. Genevieve had told him that, if he hurried, he could get to Iuka and back before late afternoon. She and the girls arrived at *Flowers by Ned* at nine o'clock, early for Queen Genevieve, who liked to sleep in past ten. Mildred Minniver, Ned's lead designer and part-time manager whenever he wasn't around, must have tired of standing on the curb waiting for him. She had opened the shop herself. When the bell over the front door rang above our heads announcing our arrival, the high-pitched bellow of a housefrau calling pigs greeted us, hollered from the back room. I recognized trouble in the making before we had advanced two feet inside the shop.

"Well, it's about time, Ned," the woman yelled. "Good Lord, do you know what time it is? We've only got ten dollars in the cash drawer and the Wilson's dinner party is this evening. We've got to get a move on. But if you didn't go to the bank on your way in, turn right back around and get us some cash." This tirade was followed by indiscernible grumbling. *Oh, my Good Lord,* I thought. I could hardly wait to meet this woman, who I was certain had already become a rose thorn in Genevieve's eye.

Genevieve stopped midway across the showroom floor. "This is gonna be interesting," she said under her breath. She patted the girls on their shoulders. Louisa and Anna Beth looked big-eyed at each other and snickered. Genevieve led them past the cash-wrap stand, their eyes darting around the cramped and cluttered space. Then she held her hand up like a crossing guard, a signal that she intended to handle the woman alone.

The shop was not nearly as pretty as Grandma Olivia's shop. Here, cheap knickknacks littered makeshift shelves that threatened to fall off the wall at the slightest breeze. Unadorned plastic containers held enough green plants to fill the Peabody Hotel's lobby. No one had bothered to dress up the pots with colorful cellophane or a bow. Strewn around the showroom without rhyme or reason, the foliage jungle tickled the girls' legs, quite similarly to the lawn at the house that was in desperate need of a wide-mouthed John Deere.

Louisa punched Anna Beth to get her attention and pointed to the glass-enclosed refrigerator against the wall to their left. "I can make arrangements prettier than those," she whispered. "Kinda looks like football helmets lined up on the shelf."

Anna Beth nodded. "I'm glad Madson's not here. He'd have a conniption fit. Why, he'd gut this place and start from scratch."

Genevieve had paused in the doorway of the workroom; the girls wriggled in beside her, flanking her on both sides and peeking through the parentheses her elbows made as her fists rested on her perfectly rounded hips. "Well, hello, folks," Genevieve said, coolly. "Allow me to introduce myself. I'm the boss's wife." Her mouth drew up into a sour pucker. "Ned won't be coming in today, and it's a good thing. This place looks like a chicken coop. And you can consider me the fox."

Mildred Minniver's mouth gaped open as she wheeled around. A stout woman with no waist, broad elastic held up her pink polyester pants. Hawaiian flowers, stretched tightly across her over-blouse and mid-section, did a poor job of concealing the rolls that lay beneath. She had folded down the top of her apron and tied it low around her abundant hips. It hung almost to the floor. She glanced sideways at the other two designers whose hands had frozen in mid-air with flowers poised, ready to be shoved into wet Oasis. One of the men placed his stem knife on the table and wiped his palms on his apron. The other sat heavily onto a metal stool. Then he hung onto his table for support.

"Why? Where's Ned?" Mrs. Minniver asked in a huff. Unlike the others, she hadn't stopped working. She sliced flower stems so fast the knife blurred, then she crammed them into the arrangement perched on a Lazy Susan before her. "He asked me to open up for him yesterday, but he didn't say nothing about you coming or about him not being here today. I'll swear; ya'll can't treat me this way. I've worked here forever and a day. I've put up with some kind of mess since Ned bought this place. But I am a professional floral designer. Operating on a shoestring is one thing, but I've got to know what's happening and what all's expected of me."

Sensing trouble, Louisa and Anna Beth took two steps backward, wanting to get as far away from Genevieve as possible, whose buttocks had tightened under her A-line. She patted her high-heeled foot a couple of times and crossed her arms. "Well, Miss Mildred Minniver, professional floral designer," she hissed sweetly, "I hate that you've had such a hard time around here and I mean to change that for you, honey." She took a few steps toward the woman, her eyes dilated, fixed. One finger caressed the edge of Mildred's worktable as the other hand delicately removed the curved knife from the woman's hand. "I want your life to be easy, sugar, a peaceful Garden of Eden. That's right. You shouldn't have to put up with anybody's crap, love, least of all mine." Genevieve leaned over and pulled the woman's purse from its hiding place under her table. Her jaw clenched as she said, "So take your tacky, ten-cent-store pocketbook and get your sorry self out of my shop . . . now!"

"Well, I never," should have been Mildred Minniver's last words as an employee of *Flowers by Ned*. But I knew she'd be back. As usual Genevieve hadn't thought ahead far enough to realize that she'd need this woman, that she could use this woman. And Mildred Minniver wasn't smart enough to go far, far away and to stay gone.

After Mildred's exit, a tense calm settled over the other two employees until Genevieve approached the elder of the two men, who recoiled visibly. Her pointed finger not two inches from his nose, she said, "Your only job is to please me and it is my pleasure for a dozen white roses to be arranged and delivered to Elvis at Graceland every day at precisely three p.m. I will hand-write the card. Do that to my satisfaction and you might have a prayer of staying around here for a while. Understand?"

The man almost choked on his own spit, but he managed to get out an audible, "Yes, ma'am," before scurrying into the refrigerator. When he came back with a bucket of white roses, his fate as a lackey was sealed.

*

"I thought Mrs. Minniver was gonna pop she was so mad," Anna Beth said. She and Louisa had hunkered down near the back door and busied themselves watering down a new shipment of carnations and daisy mums. The Bland-Hersh Wholesale delivery truck had just left and they figured keeping busy was the best way to keep Genevieve's sights off them. Louisa lifted the blunt side of the meat cleaver high in the air and brought it down hard ten or fifteen times on two-dozen freshly cut carnation stems.

"Don't beat them," Anna Beth warned. Water splashed out of a bucket. Her tennis shoes got dowsed. She shook her foot.

"I know what I'm doing, Miss Bossy Britches. Just hand me that bucket. You're falling down on your job."

"I can't wait to see Daddy when he finds out that Mrs. Minniver is gone." Anna Beth reached down and grabbed up a bunch of roses. A thorn bit her. She shook her finger several times, then stuck it in her mouth and went about chopping off the stems of some yellow roses.

"Oh, Moody will smooth things over," Louisa said.

When they finished the watering, they moved up front to man the cash-wrap stand so Genevieve could take a potty break. A mere ten-years-old and they could already run a business better than most adults. I wondered if they would ever get the opportunity to just be kids. Oh, sure, they were mischievous and *played* with Genevieve, but they had no friends their age, had never been on a sleepover or to a birthday party, had never dressed in ruffles and patent leather shoes, or experienced the magic of playing dress up—not that Anna Beth would, if given the chance—or the wonder of being mother to a doll. No, their job was the same as the employees'—to please Genevieve. The minor rebellions they tossed her way never really amounted to much and only proved their dedication to turn out just like her. I could not fathom how she did it, but Genevieve had convinced them she was someone to be admired.

As they stood there making bows the size of pumpkins for the naked pots we'd noticed when we arrived, the front doorbell rang. They looked up at the same time with welcoming smiles.

"May we help you, sir?" Louisa stood on her tiptoes to appear older.

The thin man approached the desk. Perspiration ringed his short-sleeved shirt. His collar curled like heated paper. He yanked off his clip-on tie and stuffed it into his pants pocket. "I'm looking for a Missrus Baxter," he said. He wiped his face with his handkerchief. "Might she be somewhere hereabouts?"

"Oh, yes, sir, she is, but I'm sorry, she is indisposed at the moment," Anna Beth offered, cutting her eyes toward Louisa who was making fun. *Indisposed*, Genevieve's favorite excuse. She'd taught the girls well. Anna Beth threw her shoulders back, standing at attention. Her moon-shaped face glowed with a toothy smile that could light the world. "We can help you, though. Are you looking for some pretty flowers for your wife, an anniversary gift maybe? We have some beautiful arrangements already made up, or one of our talented floral designers could whip up something special in a jiffy, if you have time to wait." That flowery language was Madson's contribution. Always trying to teach them the proper way to serve the public.

Louisa interrupted in a low growl, "Jeeze, can't you see he's not here for flowers? That's a badge on his pocket, you ninny."

The man shifted back and forth on his feet. "Is she 'indisposed' here? Mind if I look?" He leaned so hard against the counter the girls took an involuntary step backward and stood frozen in place, somber as funeral sprays. They looked at each other, then back at the gentleman with eyes wide and mouths clamped shut.

When Genevieve reappeared in the doorway to the back room, she said, "Girls, why aren't you assisting this fine gentleman? Looks like he might need to stand in the refrigerator for a few minutes to cool off. Is it that hot out there, sir?" She smiled one of her church lady smiles, wrinkling up her eyes more than she usually liked to do.

"Missrus Baxter? I'm Officer Percy Markham of the Mississippi Highway Patrol. May I speak to you in private, please?" He glanced down at the girls. Anna Beth had begun gnawing on the side of her thumb, while Louisa twirled her hair compulsively around her index finger. Their eyes bounced from his face to Genevieve's.

"Why certainly, Mister, uh, Officer Markham, is it? Right this way, sir. I hope there's nothing wrong." Her smile faded only slightly as she walked in front of the girls and opened the door to Ned's office. "Girls, go on back to the workroom, now. Help the boys for a while." Louisa and Anna Beth didn't budge. "Go on now, git. I'll be along directly. I'm sure this man only needs some flowers."

The girls couldn't figure out why he'd need to speak with Genevieve alone for something as simple as that, but they obeyed reluctantly and took their bow-making with them to the back room. I settled myself on the corner of Ned's desk, since the room had no windows and I didn't want to miss out, with my feet propped on the armrest of his vinyl swivel chair, close enough to kick Genevieve if the opportunity presented itself.

Officer Markham didn't sit down when offered a seat. He reintroduced himself and reconfirmed her identity as the wife of "a Mr. Nevens Poindexter Baxter of 842 Palisades Avenue, Memphis, Tennessee." For a few seconds he just stood there playing with the tie hanging from his pocket. Finally, he inhaled deeply and dove right in. "Ma'am, I hate to just drop this on you, but the Mississippi Highway Patrol is investigating a fatal traffic accident that occurred this morning on Highway 72 East, just this side of Slayden."

Genevieve gasped, bringing her hands to her face, as her imaginings of the night before replayed themselves in her head. Had she heard him correctly? Fatal? Ned *really* dead? But, but, how is that possible, she wondered. She hadn't really *done* anything to the van, had she?

"Ma'am, from the license plate number and the ID we found on the victim, we have verified that your husband's vehicle left the road and landed upside-down in a culvert about twenty miles south of the Tennessee line. No other vehicles were involved, ma'am. It seems your husband's brake line was secured with some ill-applied duct tape that came loose and allowed all his brake fluid to leak out. I'm sorry, ma'am, but your husband is dead. We think he expired instantaneously. He couldn't have survived that crash, no, ma'am."

Tears welled up in Genevieve's eyes faster than her favorite soap-opera star could invent them. The sudden reality and repercussions of innumerable possibilities washed over her like sewage backwash. But in true Genevieve-style she mentally justified to herself that there was really no way to know for sure, for proof-positive, that her mental scheming the night before had had any real effect on Ned's brakes. *A person can't wish someone dead,* she told herself. She had visualized the possibilities, imagined how she would lift the hood and find the brake line, but she knew she wouldn't have been able to determine its exact location. She had just thought about it. The same way she had imagined Grandpa Clancy's death so many times. *Oh, my God,* she thought. *I did it. My wishing made this happen, just like back then.* This certainty left her with one more sad consequence to live with, but she couldn't think about that now. She sobbed into her hands.

"I suppose you'll want the body transferred up here to Memphis," Markham said, staring at his hands. "Don't worry about a thing. The coroner's office takes care of all that. They'll just need to know which funeral parlor you'd like to use and there's some other paperwork, of course. I'm sure you understand."

Oops, that turned off her water faucet fast. Her ears perked up. She hadn't considered this—Ned's body and a burial. Last night was just a fantasy after all. She hadn't thought over anything past wishing he would never come home. That is all she had done—wished for deliverance from Ned. She hadn't actually tampered with the vehicle, but she *believed* that she had willed the accident to happen. Just as she had blamed herself for somehow deserving Grandpa Clancy's abuse, and blamed herself for his death, she was now convinced that her ill will had caused Ned to die. That mind of hers was a scary place, yes, scary indeed.

She took a few extra minutes to wipe at her tears and allowed herself time to think of a retort. Finally, she cleared her throat, and said, "No, Ned wouldn't want to come back here, Officer Markham. He'd want to be buried next to his parents down in Jackson. He was a Mississippi boy at heart, born and raised. Never considered Memphis home. Burying him here just wouldn't be right. Can we have him sent there?"

"Um, I see. Well, I'm sure they can take care of that for you, ma'am. Just call this number." Markham presented her with the Marshall County Coroner's business card.

Reaching for the card, Genevieve's body started trembling suddenly as if God himself had grabbed hold of her by the shoulders and planned to shake some sense into her at long last. It was me, of course. A little trick I'd picked up after years of practice. Lord knows, somebody had to rattle her cage. She inhaled loudly, clutching her chest like her lungs failed to provide her with enough air to live.

"Ma'am, you all right? Ma'am?"

She slumped back into Ned's desk chair, startled by her sudden bout of the shudders and fanned away the vapors Southern women have always been known for. "Damn him," she whispered. "Lord, forgive me, but damn him. How could he do this to me and our girls?"

Now I was the one considering murder.

Officer Markham dug deep into his pocket and pulled out the handkerchief he had used earlier on his sweaty face. "Ma'am?" he asked, a little confused. He walked around the desk and started to place his hand on her shoulder. She grabbed it, supposedly reaching for his handkerchief, and didn't let go.

"I said, damn him!" She squeezed hard, crushing the man's fingers in her grip. "I always told him he was gonna kill himself if he didn't hold on to that steering wheel and quit driving with his knees."

"His knees, ma'am?" Markham stuttered.

"And the duct tape, well, that's just like him! Too cheap to pay somebody who knows what they're doing to fix the van." Little whimpers overcame her. "But, dad-burn-it, that's part of what I loved about him. Ned, my dear sweet, Ned. Oh, how will I ever tell my girls that their dear father is dead?"

I guess a life devoid of love and riddled with guilt can callous the heart so it no longer feels. Or maybe it feels so deeply that the emotions contort into a hideous mass that no longer makes any sense. Hers certainly exemplified that tragedy. She was known to pray, however, daily and fervently, that her luck would hold out and that she'd somehow be forgiven for the sins she committed and those she merely thought into existence. And that the plethora of ghosts that tormented her—including me, even though I didn't fit into that category—wouldn't reach down and thump Detective Markham on the head. Hey you, don't you see what she's like? Are you so blinded by her polite hysterics that you can't see guilt when it weeps crocodile tears in your face? How I wished for a voice.

Even though I knew she had not really done anything to sabotage the van, even though I knew that Ned's brakes had failed because of his own sloppy application of duct tape, I also knew that Genevieve had *thought* about causing him harm. She had wished for it and was not devastated that his life was now gone. To Genevieve, survival was the root of all action and imaginings. Keeping her head above water simply meant holding her breath and taking a dive into the muck.

*

The girls appeared at the doorway of Ned's office only seconds after they heard the doorbell signaling the officer's departure and found Genevieve sitting at the desk. The adding machine cha-chinged several times, then Genevieve jotted numbers on a piece of paper.

"Moody?" Anna Beth asked softly from the doorway.

"You okay?" Louisa echoed, when Genevieve failed to look up. "What's the matter? Did something happen? What did that policeman want?"

Genevieve raised her head slowly and sat back in the chair with her forearms still resting on the desk. In slow motion, her blank expression remolded itself into the semblance of a smile. "What? Huh, oh, him? No, no, he was just here about some flowers for an officer who died in the line of duty. A sad story, really. Very tragic. He had me in tears." Her words sounded heavier than usual, labored, while her mind struggled to file away the reality, cramming every hint of encumbrance into files marked *Necessary Survival Tactics*. She shuffled the papers in front of her, a tactile exercise of what her mind attempted to do. Then she stacked them up and plopped them down on the opposite side of the desk. "Now, what time is it? Has your Daddy showed up yet?" She looked down at her wrist without realizing she didn't have on a watch. "He should have been here by now. Maybe he went on to the house to unload."

"Moody, are you sure?" Anna Beth asked, moving from the doorway to stand in front of the desk, her face pleading.

Louisa followed. "You don't look so good. You sure everything's okay?"

Genevieve placed her hands on the edge of the desk as if striking the final chord of a piano concerto. Her eyes focused on the impression her fingers made in the leather desk pad. "Sure I am, honeys. What makes you think anything's wrong?" She stood up abruptly. "Now, let's close up this place and head home. I'm sure Daddy will be waiting there with dinner cooked." She lumbered from behind the desk, a sack of regret weighing down her movement toward the door.

With that, I left. I couldn't stomach any more for one day. I traveled with all the fury and frustration that Ned must have felt daily, hourly, every second he'd suffered with Genevieve, to the sight where he took his final exhale. I was glad God let me go. It was the least I could do, even though his spirit had long since taken flight. I guess I wanted to make sure he had gone, somewhere, anywhere, and wasn't hanging around like I'd been doing all these years. I knew I wouldn't find him, of course. He had no good reason to stay. Only love or purpose have that hanging-on power, I had finally figured out. Ned had neither. But as I gazed down on the tangled mass of metal that was left of the old van, I couldn't help but wonder why she had fallen to this desperate level, why her heart had so little room for love, and so much space for guilt.

Ned was the only normal, constant thing in her life. And why hadn't she told the girls he was dead? None of it made sense. Would I ever figure her out? Would I ever understand and complete the divine objective that kept me around? I also had another struggle to deal with—I had to convince myself, yet again, that nobody needs love more than someone who does not deserve it.

Jail House Rock
Top 20 *Billboard* Single
Film, Metro-Goldwyn Mayer Released

Two months later, Anna Beth and Louisa grumbled under their breath as they folded clothes straight from the dryer and tucked them into the two suitcases Genevieve had set out on the kitchen floor. She was at the kitchen table drinking coffee and chain-smoking, her auburn hair tightly teased into a tangled mound on top of her head, comma-shaped curls stuck to her cheeks, secured with Scotch tape. Her hair looked like a family of rats had moved in to stay, and I wondered how bouffant had ever become the latest style. Red lipstick ringed the filter of her cigarette. The only sound in the room was her matching red fingernails clicking on the Formica when she flicked inch-long ashes into the plate-sized ashtray that lived in the middle of the table.

"Moody, we don't want to go off to another church camp," Louisa whined in a voice so similar to Genevieve's it made me want to plug my ears. It broke the silence with a shrill jolt. She flipped her bangs out of her face and her braid over her shoulder, perturbed. "Can't we just stay home? The Methodists were nice enough, but . . . "

"But they were boring," Anna Beth interjected with a huff. A navy blue baseball cap hugged her head, her gray eyes shaded by its bill and her honeyed curls exploding from beneath it in a mass around her neck. She wadded up a T-shirt and tossed it in the direction of her bag. "The Presbyterians seemed okay, too, but yawn, yawn, yawn," she continued. "Besides, heck fire, we're Catholic! So, why do you send us off to other churches' summer camps?" She had been cussing fluently for several weeks now, ever since Ned 'disappeared.'

"Because Catholics don't have summer camp," Genevieve replied, glumly, staring idly at the glow of her cigarette, and ignoring Anna Beth's language. She sucked her teeth. I focused on the hot tip of the butt between her fingers and blew on it. Little flames ignited and jumped in the air. She sprang out of her seat, dropped the fireball, then picked it up gently after it burned itself out. She stamped it in the ashtray to make sure it was out before sitting back down.

"But what if Daddy comes home while we're gone?" Louisa pleaded. Her tone had developed a grating pitch that could raise hair on your arms and make your teeth ache at the nerve. Neediness now possessed her—with good reason, I guess—but the attention she sought was out of Genevieve's realm to give. "I miss him. I want to be here when he gets home."

Genevieve lifted her legs, one at a time, to get them unstuck from the vinyl seat. It had somehow turned into sandpaper under her, a common reaction these days whenever Ned's absence came up. She wanted to blurt out, "He's dead. Let it go," but for her own twisted reasons, she remained silent. It was easier this way, she thought. Yes, easier to let the girls think Ned had abandoned them without a word than for them to know the truth.

"He's not coming home," Anna Beth snapped, her anger boiling into reddened cheeks. "Haven't you figured that out yet? And speak for yourself. I'm more than happy to sing *Kumbayah* for a week. At least the Baptists want us around." She looked crossways at Genevieve, who ignored the stare. She didn't even snap "wipe that look off your face, young lady," like she usually did. Guilt had shrouded her in complacency that didn't allow anything to faze her anymore.

The girls finished packing. Then Genevieve stood on the stoop and watched them load up the new van for the flower shop. This would become our third weeklong summer camp away in two months. Needless to say, traveling far distances no longer worried me. The Methodists had taken us to the Tennessee mountains, the Presbyterians to the Ozarks of Arkansas. But the Baptists were high-style campers; they sent their kids to the pristine beaches of Destin, Florida, on the Gulf Coast. Bring on the fun, I said. I was happy for the reprieve from Genevieve, who couldn't muster up an ounce of enthusiasm for anything lately. Even I might have thought that guilt and mourning had caused her doldrums, but no, not when I remembered that Elvis was out of town.

Louisa took her place in the only passenger seat of the van. Anna Beth always either rode facing backward on the hump or she sat on the floor in the "back forty," hanging on to the sketchpad she never drew in anymore and the rickety wooden shelves built to hold flower arrangements. Me, well, naturally, I was all over the place. Genevieve tucked her new skirt under her, just so-so, and climbed into the driver's seat. She wished she could have bought a regular car with Ned's insurance money—a new Chevrolet Corvette or something jazzy like that—but since she now owned the flower shop, she figured she'd need a van, if for no other reason than to make sure her special arrangements to Graceland arrived on time. Plus, anything snazzier might have seemed flamboyant and, under the circumstances, suspicion was the last thing she wanted to rouse.

"Okay, sit down and hang on," she yelled, revving the engine. She threw it into reverse and pulled out of the driveway, headed for Second Baptist Church's parking lot on Walnut Grove Road. She hardly spoke as she drove. Putting more than a few words together at a time seemed overwhelming. Liability has a way of clogging brain pores, I suppose. For one, I was enjoying the peace and quiet. I had heard just about all I could stand from that woman. I didn't give a flip if she ever uttered another word.

Hordes of squealing children and aloof preteens hugged the necks of their parents in the parking lot before boarding the two buses waiting to transport them to their destination of sand, sun and fun. Genevieve patted her face with pressed powder from her compact. The July heat and humidity rendered havoc on her makeup and frizzed her hair. She just wanted to see the girls off quickly so she could find air-conditioning in a shopping center somewhere.

The girls formed a miniature assembly line to unload their bags from the van and transfer them to the compartments under their assigned bus.

"Well, I guess we're off again, whether we want to be or not," Anna Beth griped, tears not daring to brim on her eyelashes.

Genevieve opened her pocketbook and dug out two twenty-dollar bills. "Here's some spending money, love bugs. Have some fun, but not too much. Those counselors had better not be calling me again with horror stories about the trouble you two cause."

"Why Moody, I thought epoxy on the music director's shoes was a brilliant idea. Didn't you, Weesa?" Anna Beth boasted.

"You're right, honey. That one made me proud," Genevieve admitted. "But the Ex-Lax in the chocolate sauce was a bit over the top, doodle-bug. I had to pay two-hundred bucks for an extra night's stay in the mountains for the whole bunch of you. I should have taken it out of your hides." She fanned herself with her white-gloved hand. "A couple more boxes of that stuff and those Presbyterians would have been sending me emergency room bills."

"Why don't you come along as a counselor, Moody? You'd be the coolest one ever. We miss all the fun we used to have," Louisa said.

"Not this time, hon." Genevieve ruffled Louisa's hair. "My King will be back in town next week. He needs me at his side. Ya'll just don't get caught this time."

"Humph," Anna Beth said, refusing to hug Genevieve's neck. "I'm gonna be sick when it's my turn for KP duty."

"That's my girl," Genevieve said, reaching long to pat her on the rump.

They both waved good-bye over their shoulders to Genevieve and boarded a bus filled with strangers for another week in exile.

*

These weeks and weeks of summer camps had kept me hopping. Spending time with my girls was my main priority, but I could never leave Genevieve alone for too long. The trouble that woman masterminded should have kept a jailhouse warden busy, not me. On one of my check-up trips back to the house, I found Genevieve flopped down on a brand-spanking new overstuffed sofa admiring her new living-room suite. Large, framed posters of Elvis hung on every wall. Many were signed, *With Love to my Genevieve,* followed by Elvis' unique signature. When the girls weren't along, God didn't allow me to accompany her to Elvis concerts, not that I really wanted to tag along, but her obsession for him was infamous. I often wondered if she really had gotten to *know* the man, or if all her talk was just another dream she had thought into reality.

"The girls won't believe it when they get home," she told her photographs. She talked to her Elvis relics as if his velvety voice might actually answer back. I often wished I could figure out a way to make that happen. *Ooooooo.* Throwing ghostly moans across the room and seeing her oxidize with fear would have been the highlight of my death. I asked some of the professional ghosts to teach me a few tricks, but they looked at me kind of like white folks look at Negroes and told me to stay out of their realm. So much for wishing.

She propped her feet on the new coffee table. "I couldn't fin-niggle a new house out of this deal, but I guess new furniture will do," she said.

The girls had been gone only a few days, but Memphis' finest interior decorators handled the transformation of the house with almost effortless ease. New furniture, sleek and contemporary, now filled every room. Wall to wall carpet—plush stuff, not that tacky looped pile everyone seemed so fond of—cushioned the hardwoods. Light wood and marble-topped tables gave the elderly place a new attitude. "Elvis, hon? Did you see that snooty decorator woman's face? When she arrived here, she thought she'd been sent out to reupholster the slums." Genevieve swizzeled a glass of sweet tea. "Well, I deserve every lick I can get, yes, siree. No matter how I have to get it. Using what I know to better our lives only makes good sense, ain't that right?"

In the kitchen, pale green cabinets with shiny brass hardware and vanilla Formica replaced the aged knotty pine and dark wrought iron. When the Sears and Roebuck delivery truck had pulled into the driveway two days before, every nosy neighbor on the block gathered in the yard across the street to watch them unload the latest model of every appliance the department store sold.

I had been with the girls at camp—wishing I could feel the sun beat down on my face—when Genevieve worked "her deal," but it didn't take much imagination to deduce that either foul play or blackmail had played a role in striking this goldmine. I suspected that it had more to do with Jack Bland than Elvis, but I couldn't be sure of it … yet. The high side of it all was that for the first time my girls would have bedroom suites—complete with headboards, bureaus and nightstands—as unique and individual as their tastes. Even considering the way she got it all, Genevieve felt proud of her accomplishments in the few weeks since Ned died. She smiled to herself. "Make 'em pay, yes sirree. Make men pay for hurting ya, the living and the dead."

After a while the doorbell rang, disturbing her afternoon of luxuriating, and I was glad I had not jetted off to be back with the girls. "Damn neighbors," she grumbled and hoisted herself out of the couch. "They never darkened the door when Ned lived here," she bitched. "Why won't those busy-bodies leave me alone?" For the past several days people had come out of the street cracks to bring neighborly offerings of freshly baked confections so they could catch a glimpse of the inside of the newly-remodeled Baxter house. Genevieve swung open the door, ready to blast the latest brownnoser with "Get the hell off my porch," but her words choked in mid-sentence. "Get the . . . well, I'll be."

"Why, hello, Genevieve." My mother's hand had already pulled open the screen. She eased her way over the threshold as Genevieve backed up without realizing it. "I came to town to do some shopping."

She threw kiss-kisses to her sister's cheeks, but I caught them instead, one and all. Oh, to kiss her back and breathe in the sweet nectar I imagined wafted off her skin. I almost swooned with the joy of seeing her again. Genevieve didn't kiss-kiss back, of course. "I had some business down at the Bland-Hersh wholesale house and thought I'd drop in to see ya'll." She turned and headed toward the living room. "How are the girls? And Ned? I'd love to see them before I head back down the road toward home . . . " Her words trailed off and her forward motion screeched to a stop in the entrance to the living room. The new crystal chandelier hanging in the adjoining dining room sparkled in the gilded mirror over the sofa. One of Elvis' mellower tunes drifted softly through the room from the new Hi-Fi.

Genevieve pushed past her dumbfounded sibling and strode across the room like a stork in tweeds. She resumed her position in the middle of the couch. "Well, Willard, come on in and stop your gawking. Don't just stand there with old-lady dribble running down your chin."

Willard took a few more steps into the room, looking about. "Well, Genevieve, I see you've been hard at work. Have you spent every living dime of Ned's money?" By appearance only, anyone could tell these two were sisters. My mother's hands were perched on her hips the same way Genevieve's usually did when she was making a point. "You've taken a simple, God-fearing man and ruined him, turned him into a money-hungry maniac to satisfy your own extravagant needs, I see." She dropped her practical leather pocketbook onto the new carpet and collapsed very ladylike into the closest chair. Her delicate frame sank only slightly into its soft embrace. She tucked wisps of wayward hair back into place, and then folded her hands neatly in her lap.

"You don't know a thing you're talking about . . . Sister," Genevieve said. She lifted a freshly lit Lucky Strike to her lips. "Ned's gone. You know, vamoose. He took off. He left me high and happy to take care of the girls alone and fend for myself, the sorry SOB."

Genevieve's mind had somehow edited her reality. She actually believed her own lies. She thought that, if she repeated them often enough, they would gain the power to mutate into truth. After all, she had been left before. First by her parents, who dropped her and Willard off indefinitely at the Clancy place in Iuka while they went to Memphis to start up the wholesale business alone, then again when their car and a tree met angrily and ended their lives prematurely. And again by *him*, Jack Bland, the man she pined her life away for, the man she felt had left her repeatedly, yearly, monthly, daily for years on end. The man who had inherited her parents' wholesale business. The man she could never have. She spun the scene over and over in her head, like a scratched record that plays to a point, then jumps back and plays the same song again and again. Admitting her faults had never come easy, but in this case blaming someone else spread her problems as smooth as cream cheese. It baffled me still as to why she put the girls through the torment of thinking that Ned had just up and walked out of their lives.

It took Willard a few seconds to process the information of Ned leaving, since such an act went against everything good and decent anyone knew about the man and the way he lived his life. He had been flabbergasted and honored when the high and mighty Genevieve Clancy Hersh had demanded that *he* become her husband. Everyone knew that Ned would never *leave* Genevieve on purpose, that is unless he was obeying some hare-brained order she'd concocted that his dim mind couldn't maneuver around.

"Well, it sure looks like he left you in fine style," Willard said. "What? Did he just hand you a treasure chest and say, 'Have fun,

Genny, but I'm outta here?' Or did all this stuff magically appear at your door?"

Genevieve dragged hard on her cigarette, sucked it deep into her lungs and held it there. "I guess magic did have a little to do with it, but no, all of this I did on my own." She still hadn't let out her last drag. Finally, a thin veil of smoke escaped her tight lips, spiraling around both sides of her highly teased head like a funeral wreath.

"I can only imagine. I'll swanee, Genevieve, you always manage to get every blessed thing you want outta life."

"Humph, that's a joke."

"And nothing you need," Willard added under her breath. "I don't even want to know how you managed this." She physically shook off the urge to ask. "I came here to make peace, not to start another rile. So, tell me—where are my nieces? This whole adventure into Disneyland would be a waste of my good time if I didn't get the chance to see the girls."

"They're at church camp. Won't be back till the end of the week."

"Where?"

"You heard me. So, you'd might as well fluff up your angel wings, start flapping and fly on out of here. You won't be spending any time with *my* girls anytime soon." Genevieve stood up, ready to usher Willard to the door. Willard didn't budge.

Just then the screen door squeaked open and the mailman dropped a short stack of mail through the slot in the door. Genevieve's eyes shot to where the letters fell, nervous and cagey all the sudden. In an ill attempt to act casual, she bolted for the entry hall, moving with such precision that Willard didn't have a hope of getting up out of her chair, much less beating her sister to intercept. When Genevieve scooped the letters up and turned back around, her face beamed with the satisfaction that she had averted a catastrophe.

Willard sat forward in the chair and studied her sister with raised eyebrows. "Important mail?"

"No, just bills. Er, uh, junk mostly." Genevieve thumbed, oh so slowly, through the stack. Her eyes landed on the letter she'd been expecting and a sigh of relief escaped her for being able to grab it before Willard could.

"Well, from the way you flew across this room, I thought maybe you were trying to save my life from a cherry bomb attack or, at the very least, hide something crucial to your clandestine way of life." She picked up her purse and fished out a stick of Juicy Fruit.

"Now, whatever gave you that idea, Sister?" Genevieve sauntered back to her perch on the couch with the letters cradled to her bosom like a secret FBI file. She leveled her most piercing gaze on Willard and decided it was time to do a little information fishing. "If anyone in this family has something to hide, dear sister, it is you. That's right. You! And the most amusing and satisfying thing about that is: I know all your secrets."

Have you ever had one of those off-guard moments that catch you by the throat and squeeze? That's what happened to my dear sweet mother that morning. It was as if all the air in the room suddenly sucked itself into her lungs as Genevieve's evilness vaporized and moved in to attack her very core. I watched the old ache in my mother's soul open fresh, as if God played the movie reel just for me. She was taken back to the day of her most devastating pain—the day she lost her children, the day I died in her womb in an auto parts convent, the day my sweet little sister was whisked away and given to Genevieve.

But Willard didn't know any of that. Mother Superior had assured her that her children, yes, children, "were fine," had been given to "a good home," and would be raised by a "sweet, loving family." With descriptions like that, no one could have guessed Genevieve. Knowing how devastated my mother was about having to give us up, Reverend Mother hadn't had the heart to tell her that I had died. She let her think we had been adopted together, to believe that the two of us were living a nice life and had each other to love. No, Willard hadn't a clue that her own sister had taken one of her children, or that the other child, me, Olivia Abigail, had died.

Oh, if I could have told her, I would have, even though I knew it would hurt her so. I had a difficult time accepting that God might actually know what He was doing, especially when His plans went against what I thought was best. All these years, no one had been able to comfort my mother, not even me. I knew that the Reverend Mother had done the best she could do at the time, that she had been *directed* in her decision, but I wondered how she could remain silent now, in light of my mother leaving the convent and being reunited, such as it was, with Genevieve.

Now, God allowed me to stumble back in time with my mother, tripping over the events that had sent her to the convent in the first place, the secret pregnancy, the unspeakable fear. Many of the details hadn't been revealed to me before. And the identity of my father was still hidden from me. I could not fathom why.

Willard wondered how Genevieve had found out? More precisely, *what* Genevieve had found out? Certainly she couldn't know. Could she? No, she was working on supposition, speculating on what she assumed happened to see if Willard would cough up the truth.

Not even a fresh stick of Juicy Fruit restored moisture to Willard's parched mouth. She strangled her purse straps, and with great effort, worked up enough spit to ask, "Wha . . . whatever do you mean? What do you think you know?" Silence buzzed in her ears. I tried to comfort her, tried to hold her close to relieve some of her fear. But Genevieve wouldn't poke a dead horse. No, Willard was a live one and she had never been good at hiding anything, especially pain. "Go on," she almost shouted. "Go on, spit it out. You're itching to say it. You can't wait to rub my face in the secrets you *think* you've dug up."

Genevieve reclined sideways on the sofa, propping herself on the armrest. Drawing her tanned legs up under her, she caressed her calf. "I'm not stupid, Willard. I figured it out," she purred.

"Figured what out?"

"I'm not blind. I saw the way you and Madson eyed each other the day you came home. It did surprise me a little, I must confess, but *you* in love with *him?* Saint Willard in love with a black man, 'the hired help,' as Grandpa would have said. I thought I was the only one who even liked Madson. I'll swear, I almost didn't believe it myself, but then I know you better than most."

Madson? Madson. Madson! Why had I not considered him before? But I would have sensed something familiar about him, a bond. And my mother's reaction to him would have given their feelings for each other away, I figured. Wouldn't they? Still I was not sure about my own parentage. Why did God do this to me?

But other revelations became clear.

Willard stood up without speaking, still gripping her pocketbook to her chest like a shield. A white girl loving a black man was almost as bad as her having children out of wedlock. But not as bad as the other truth, the truth of what Grandpa Clancy had done to her. I winced as the images came to me. Blow after blow, fist after fist. Now, I prayed that my mother could just bluff her way out of there so Genevieve wouldn't probe more. And I prayed Genevieve would never put my mother through the heartache of regurgitating the source of her shame. Sometimes all you can do is pray, after all. And trust. Yes, trusting God's wisdom is a must, but learning that lesson is a difficult task to achieve.

My mother moved toward the door.

"How long have you two been lovers?" Genevieve prodded. "Is that why you ran off to the convent? Grandpa Clancy found out and shipped you off to the nuns to keep you two apart and to save face?"

Willard stopped and turned back to face her sister. She held onto the doorframe for support as her body regained the ability to breathe. She allowed herself one long, slow inhale. Genevieve only knew part of the story—or thought she knew—and was now filling in details. My mother would have to choose her words carefully and lie to keep the rest of it from coming out. Anything to protect her babies, she was thinking. She leaned forward and whispered. "Don't you dare, Genevieve. Don't make fun of what you know nothing about. Yeah, I left home to save Madson. Accept that if you need something to believe."

"Yep, Madson would have been dead all right. Grandpa would have staked him out in the front yard and gone for the kerosene."

"Oh, hush, just hush. You have no idea what you're talking about and know nothing about what I've sacrificed . . . what I've done for this family, for you. You piece things together to suit yourself, so just shut up, Genevieve. Shut your spiteful, trashy mouth. It's my life and you have no right, no right."

Trembling, she jerked open the door. Humidity thick enough to stir with a spoon slapped her, but instead of popping out in a sweat, chilly bumps trailed across her skin like ants on the march. The *thwack* of the screen door punctuated her grief.

It killed me all over again to see her leave in such a state, and to know I couldn't follow her, God's tether keeping me in place. I had to go back inside to Genevieve. How tortured I was, knowing so much and so little at the same time. I wondered if Madson really was my father, or if my mother was protecting someone else against Genevieve's spite. It seemed that Genevieve's thoughts pulsed through me with viral intensity, but seeing my own mother's history was often like looking through pond water. Mud and algae kept blurring my view.

Certainly, from day one, my understanding of the whys and what-fors of life had soared to a realm no human could ever imagine, but that knowing wasn't the sum of me. Not really, anyway. I always thought of myself as being like the girls, a friend, the same age. I even dreamed myself a physical body, hair like my sister's, eyes wide with wisdom and white shining teeth. It was an illusion, sure; my ethereal form was much more obscure, but it was my illusion just the same. When the girls were six, so was I. When they reached ten, ten I longed to be. But on this startling day, my spirit creaked with old age. While knowing too much buoyed me into youthfulness, today, knowing too little wormed holes into my resolve. How could I be bound to this monster and be unable to comfort the dear woman who bore me? Why was I limited and limitless at the same time?

I trudged into the house, bereft, and found my burden smiling, another cigarette lit and dangling from her hand. "Oh, don't worry, honey." She was talking to her Elvises again. "Willard'll go home to her lover and be fine. She could've done worse, ya know. Madson's a good man. I just wish she had given me a hint about a pregnancy, if there was one. Then I would know for sure." She explained to a photograph that she couldn't have Willard guessing about the girls, but she had had to let her know who had the upper hand, just in case. Willard and Madson could have their little life in Iuka, but if they had had a child together, they would never have their little girl. "Nope, she's mine, and I'm keeping her. My girls are all I've got left."

The fault line across my heart created by her the first day I met her widened. She pressed her lips to the pouty face of a framed Elvis and kissed the photo softly. Then she rested her face against its cool glass and closed her eyes. Tears trickled from her lashes, smearing mascara across the glass and blurring Elvis' face. I fought the urge to curse her and reluctantly won. I wanted to leave her, to vanish in a puff of disgust to be with my girls, but hard as I tried, I could not pull myself away.

*

Icy air spilled from the open freezer of the Frigidaire as Genevieve unloaded its contents into the kitchen sink. Six layers of plastic wrap waterproofed the envelope to assure no moisture could penetrate it and ruin the papers concealed within, double-wrapped in Reynolds aluminum foil, folded, overlapped and creased just so to protect it from any adverse effects freezing might cause, placed gently on the freezer floor, stacked with pork chops, bags of creamed corn, breaded okra, field peas and TV dinners to make it blend in. She stared at eyelevel at her handiwork and smiled. Couldn't take the chance of anyone, especially the girls or Willard, finding the Court of Records envelope and the death certificate it contained. A satisfied master of concealment, Genevieve filled a glass with ice cubes and treated herself to another glass of sweetened iced tea.

*

Summer oozed slowly into fall and our life in Memphis settled into as normal a rhythm as could be expected with Elvis's greatest fan at the helm. Anna Beth and Louisa attended The Cathedral of the Immaculate Conception Academy for Girls while Genevieve pretended to run the flower shop. Ned's whereabouts were never discussed, at least not by Genevieve.

No one ever proved brave enough to inquire about the identity of the Furniture Fairy who supplied a seemingly unending stream of ready cash. We could never relax fully, though. If word-one got out that Elvis was in town or visiting in Tupelo at his momma's place, Genevieve snatched the girls out of school and here we went to swoon at his every wink or wiggle. We trekked the South, juvenile vagabonds looking for the excitement Genevieve preached was "essential to a full and frenzied life on the edge." She should know.

In the presence of anyone who might matter, Genevieve played pitiful, abandoned wife and single mother to the hilt. Privately, she tortured herself with guilt and got writer's cramp writing confession notes to Elvis, outlining her multitude of sins.

As I had suspected, she'd coaxed Mildred Minniver into coming

back to manage the flower shop. "You're such a dear, dear woman,"
she told Mrs. Gullible. "I was out of my head the morning I fired you.
It's *so* out of character for me to act that way. A premonition, it was.
I knew Ned was in trouble and that he was leaving us high and dry. I
knew something awful was happening, and it made me a little crazy."
She needed this woman and nabbed her. Mrs. Minniver never saw it
coming, but with her holding down the shop, Genevieve indulged in
some of her other non-traditional forms of fun.

One afternoon, I waited with them in a place I could have never
guessed we'd ever be. The Union Avenue precinct of the Memphis
Police Department reeked of stale coffee and human sweat. The ride
in the police cruiser had been harrowing for the girls—it being their
first time to be arrested with Genevieve when she got caught
shoplifting—but Genevieve seemed to glow with the fuss of her Rights
being read and the sirens blaring.

The officer had called her by name as he led her to the squad car.
Now, she said to Louisa, who sat next to her on the wooden bench in
the precinct hallway, "Cover my hands up with your sweater. Will
you, honey?" Louisa unfastened the gold-colored clasp that kept her
navy blue sweater from falling off her shoulders and did as she was
told. She carefully tucked the garment around Genevieve's wrists,
making sure to conceal the handcuffs that bound them together in her
lap. Then, without speaking, Louisa settled herself back against the
concrete block wall. She yanked up the regulation Argyle knee socks
of her uniform, set her jaw and stared straight ahead.

We had been waiting for over an hour, made more torturous by
the minute by Genevieve's rambling dialogue to no one in particular.
"It's a fact," she was saying, "Clancy women have needs, and I don't
just mean the sexual kind. It's inherited, so you might as well accept it.
You girls have got it in your blood—just like me." She squirmed a little
and tugged at the hem of her pencil skirt with the tips of her fingers.
Typewriter tapping drummed from desks all around us.

Anna Beth nudged in closer when a loud commotion startled her;
two policemen wrestled a convict through a doorway just down the
hall. Even tomboys show fear. She sat up straighter, smoothing her
plaid pleats, grooming constantly, twittling strands of hair, adjusting a
collar or sleeve, and trying to act like sitting in a police station with her

shackled mother didn't bother her in the least. At times like this I was certain that Anna Beth was my sister; such a tough little soldier she had become. But other times Louisa's rebellious nature caused me to rethink my certainty. I wondered if knowing really mattered. I was so proud of them both.

Witnessing Genevieve's mental decline was painful for all of us. Lately it seemed she got weirder and weirder by the day. Sometimes she would gaze into space, her cigarette burning to a nub in her hand, never puffed. She mumbled undecipherable stories about "the bad old days" or how she loved the girls more than life but knew she would lose them one day. She'd hurry the girls off to school on a Saturday and get rattled and furious when they proved her mistake. Or she'd take them to Mass when none was scheduled, and stand outside on the steps, waiting for them to come back out so they could go back home. On these occasions the girls and I would sit quietly for a while in a pew praying the rosary—thank goodness for the faithful foundation they received at Catholic school—before rejoining her for a confusing ride home.

Now, the pungent smell of polyester sweat hung thick around us, trapped and rank, that nervous kind of sweat no deodorant can cover up. Louisa whispered over Genevieve to Anna Beth, "Have any of these people ever taken a bath?" A wino sitting across from us belched. Invisible fumes rose from his chapped lips. Louisa turned up her nose and looked away. I tried to lighten the mood a little and goosed one of the officers as he walked by. Big mistake. I thought he was going to shoot the girls. He wheeled around, glaring, with his hand on his pistol.

"It's simple really," Genevieve continued, unaffected. "Once we've had a taste of something good, anything good, we're like those doped-up hippie freaks out in California. We've just got to have more. Whiskey—that was your great-grandmother Olivia's favorite vice. I just barely lived through her drinking spells." She waved her sweater-covered hands in the air in front of her as she spoke. "Consider yourselves lucky to have me, girls. At least I've got a little class."

The girls were almost twelve years old now and were finally catching on to Genevieve's ways of twisting the truth to suit herself. But Genevieve was too preoccupied with her justifications to notice anyone's annoyance.

"Money—now there's one that'll get you in trouble every time. What is it about money that drives us to do such crazy, hare-brained things?" She didn't wait for a response. "And what about love? Everyone's got problems with that one. Ask your Aunt Willard. She knows about forbidden love better than most. Yep, sometimes our needs overtake us. They become compulsions that make us do butt-dumb things. Nothing we can do about it, really. It's just part of our lives." She shook her head in resignation, and nodded to herself, satisfied.

"Moody?" Anna Beth whispered, leaning in still closer. "Are we going to jail?"

A fat police officer walked by. His belly protruded over his waistband, buttons straining against the confines of his coffee-stained shirt. He wobbled like a top, wide at the middle with a point on each end, tipping one way and back again as he waddled down the hall. Louisa watched him teeter by, his heavy breaths struggling to keep up with the overexertion walking put on his fat-clogged system.

"Well, of course not, darlin'. I'm no *crim-in-al*." Genevieve straightened up. She started to lift her arm to put it around the girls' shoulders, then remembered the handcuffs and readjusted herself politely on the bench instead. "Besides, this little misunderstanding will be fixed up in a jiffy. Don't worry your pretty little head. They can't hold a person for something as minor as this. Plus, I can't help myself. It's a sickness. They know that. This wrinkle in our day will be ironed out, and we'll be on our way—just like that—just like always." Her fingers snapped beneath their cable knit shroud.

Anna Beth relaxed a little, but her saddle oxfords swung under the bench like pendulums of distress. As complacent as she appeared on the outside, molten anger simmered within her and I feared the day it would boil over and scorch us all.

Louisa stared, wordless and wide-eyed, into the toothless face of the derelict sitting across from us. She was well on her way to figuring Genevieve out, but sadly, dealt with her knowledge much like Genevieve would have—with spite.

The fat policeman stepped out of an office down the hall. "Baxter!" His yell rang hollow through the crowded hallway. Genevieve stood up proudly. "You got one phone call. You can make it in here." His chubby finger pointed the way.

"Wait here, girls. Sit up straight and put your knees together, Louisa. And don't talk to strangers. I'll be right back." Clutching her handbag with shackled hands, she prissed down the hall with the uppity trot of a governor's wife headed to a debutante ball. Her nylons whistled underneath her skirt; the black lace of her slip peeped out from under her hem. The tapping of her high heels blended with the typewriter chorus as she disappeared into the office of Burglary, Robbery and Fraud.

Three-and-a-half hours later, a stick-skinny officer, as opposite from the other man as a person could be, shouted down the hall. "Baxter, you're free to go."

Genevieve walked over to him, holding up her wrists. "You might be needing these, sir," she said. "If you would be so kind?" He fished around in his pockets for his key and unshackled her. She turned on her spiked heels and, marching past us, said, "Come along, girls. We've got better things to do than hang around here all day."

The officer waved at our backsides as we pushed through the double doors at the end of the hall. "Nice seeing you, Mrs. Baxter. See you again in a week or so, I suppose."

Part Two

Wild in The Country
Film, Twentieth Century Fox, including
the song, *I Slipped, I Stumbled, I Fell*

Pickwick Lake is a reservoir on the Tennessee River not far from
Iuka and the old home place. Every summer weekend that Elvis wasn't
in town, we rode out to the lake and slept in a tent. That's right, as
foreign to Genevieve's nature as it seems—a tent. Jack Bland, the
mysterious man who tiptoed through Genevieve's dreams and had
inherited our grandparents' wholesale house in Memphis, owned a
nice place on the water. I'm sure he rued the day he told Genevieve to
"bring the girls up to the lake for a visit when you're in the
neighborhood." And he certainly didn't mean it as an open invitation
or an offer of squatter's rights.

As we drove along Highway 57 South, Genevieve didn't even
flinch when we passed the culvert that had claimed Ned's life. Soon
the stench of the Counce paper mill welcomed us to the crooked
shores of the finger lake. I should have taken that sulfuric smell as a
signal that trouble was close at hand. I wondered what was brewing
in the recesses of that devious mind of Genevieve's—it had to be
something really big for her to lower herself and sleep in a tent—but
she had the darnedest way of locking me out of certain historic rooms
in her psyche. Probably not such a bad thing. There's no telling what
horrors were hidden away in there.

I will always think of the summer of 1970 as "that summer." That
summer down at the lake—that summer of Anna Beth's maturation at
the old age of fourteen—that summer when Louisa lost her virginity
for the hundredth time—that summer when I almost gave up on the
whole lot of them. Louisa had had four whole years of monthly periods
to forget to mark her calendar. She'd had four years to ignore

Genevieve's pitiful reminders that "punctual periods prepare our systems for the excruciating pain of pregnancy and birth." I could only hope that Genevieve meant post-marriage pregnancy in her warnings, not the kind Louisa was oblivious to as she paraded down the bank of Pickwick Lake in her blue dotted-Swiss bikini, daisy lace rimming her concave belly and unassisted breasts.

As Louisa's honeyed complexion browned and Anna Beth's perpetually pink skin broiled under the mid-July scorch, Anna Beth and I wondered what next summer would be like with Louisa's baby along. Of course, I knew Louisa was pregnant before anyone suspected it. And, oh, our poor, dense Louisa didn't have a clue as she sauntered to the edge of the boat dock, tossed a truck tire inner-tube about twenty feet out, took three steps back, two skips and a hop, and arced into an effortless swan dive that barely rippled the water's calm. When she came up a full thirty seconds later in the black bull's eye of her drifting inner-tube, she wasn't even out of breath. She pulled herself up through its middle, brown water slicking back her waist-length hair. She swung her legs up and over, so the rubber donut cradled her around the middle and only her rump remained dowsed. She floated like a bronzed lily pad in water the color of mud.

As Anna Beth watched Louisa, she wasn't even considering— and had no point of reference to speculate upon—how Louisa's pregnancy and a baby might irrevocably change their lives. She just lay there in the water, hoping the little bugger wouldn't eradicate the weekends at the lake altogether. She, unlike me, enjoyed being "away from it all." She was so new at the menstruation blessing it had taken her a while to figure out what was up with Louisa. But she knew how to count and realized that Louisa hadn't marked her calendar in a while. Genevieve had given them only the sketchiest explanations about the facts of life, referring to "it" as "the monthly torture of dribbling red goop." Could she not see the miraculous in a woman's menses? It seemed so obvious to me.

For the longest time I had worried that Anna Beth would never start her period, never bloom into womanhood and enjoy the mystery that sets women atop the throne of near-godliness where the creation of life reveals itself so intimately, the mystical experience bestowed by a God with a sense of humor and fairness. Louisa, on the other hand, had started her monthly flow when she was only ten, too early to know how to deal with all those pulsing hormones.

And now this!

"Come on, paddle over to me," Louisa yelled in Anna Beth's direction. With her feet barely breaking water, she kicked and flailed about like an upended turtle until she finally hooked ankles with Anna Beth.

"Why didn't you ever teach me to dive like that?" Anna Beth asked, knowing full-well Louisa had tried unsuccessfully for summers on end. Anna Beth squinted through water-speckled sunglasses against the mid-afternoon sun, the war paint of zinc oxide smeared across her nose and bony cheekbones to protect her fair skin.

"Grace and practice, Bethy," Louisa reminded her. "That's all it takes." She had started calling Anna Beth "Bethy." The junior-high school giggles had attacked her early on, and now everyone needed a nickname ending in "ie" or "y." I suppose she would have called me Ollie, or Livvie like our great-grandmother, given the chance. But mostly she just ignored me, her head too consumed with teenage flirting and romance to give this guiding spirit a second thought. She grabbed hold of a thick hank of her hair and yanked it out from behind her. A stream of water pelted Anna Beth in the face as she flung it about.

"Hey," Anna Beth yelled, dodging the spray. She was covered head to foot in Coppertone. Protecting her dead-of-winter complexion from sunburn had become her most agonizing duty during our summer weekends at the lake.

Louisa relaxed her head back and stretched her firm torso out of the water, her hair fanned out in the murkiness like the train of a stained wedding dress, and her skin glistened with baby oil and iodine. She was a young woman who had come into her own.

"I've had plenty of practice," Anna Beth barked, sinking lower into her own black hole. Being such an athletic little ruffian made it difficult for her to handle Louisa outdoing her in any sporting effort. "But you must've gotten all the grace in the family, if grace is the right word for what you flaunt."

In an angel's wink Louisa had bloomed into a sexpot, while Anna Beth only molted in pubescent limbo. It wasn't that Louisa was gorgeous and Anna Beth ugly. No, Anna Beth just hadn't figured out how to use her physical assets yet. She relied more on her brain to see her through, smart girl. Of course, she had her good points physically.

Tall and lean now, her legs stretched three-quarters of the way to her armpits, shortening her waistline and giving her the statuesque posture of a marathon runner. Genevieve often told her that long shapely legs were one of the first things men looked for in a woman. Anna Beth didn't have to wonder what the other things were. She only had to take a gander at Louisa, who possessed them all. She may not have rounded quite as stylishly as Louisa had, but her time would come soon enough.

The current drifted the girls at will as they played footsie to hang on and not lose touch. I hung out on the breeze nearby, floating a few inches above the water's surface. Our weekends at the lake are some of my most cherished memories. This day was especially glorious. Wispy clouds grazed across blue skies that made me think heaven couldn't be any better than this. Louisa dozed off, as usual, and I delighted when her eyelids fluttered, and her hands twitched as if brushing aside my invisible hand.

In contrast, Anna Beth rarely rested. She fidgeted constantly, studied our surroundings and took on the familiar responsibility of making sure we didn't drift out too far. Smiling big, she winked in my direction and the thrill of it lifted me off the waves, a loving tide to ebb away any worries having to do with Genevieve. Yes, Anna Beth felt my presence, sensed me there; she always had. (Louisa did too, but wouldn't admit it.) I had whispered my name in their ears for eons it seemed. I hoped that someday they would know me as Olivia, not just recognize me as someone supportive who urged them on. I would, however, take whatever acceptance I could get. Sometimes Anna Beth stared right into my eyes, thoughtful-like, and tried to convince herself to believe. But those moments were usually fleeting—like today. I took them as they came and was thankful.

Louisa crinkled up her perky nose and, peeping out through a squint, said, "You're sure gloomy today." Rubber crunched under her, sticking as she tried to sit up straighter in its hole. "You mooning over that gawky boy pumping gas at the marina?"

Anna Beth's toes released Louisa. She buckled and allowed her donut to swallow her up. "No," she moaned, when she came up for air, "Just thinking. That's all. Is it a crime to just sit and think every once in a while?"

"Well, don't overwork that brain of yours. It's still summer and besides, eighth grade classes will demand more than any you've known so far."

You should know, Anna Beth thought as she pulled her legs back up and got situated again. Louisa had jumped ahead of her in school just after we moved to Memphis and Ned "disappeared." But now they were back in the same grade because Louisa flunked the eighth grade and had to take it a second time.

Twirling her fingers through chocolate water, Anna Beth wondered what Louisa would look like with a big baby belly poking out in front. She'd envied Louisa's concave one for so long. Might be a nice change, she thought. But would her breasts grow even bigger? Neither one of us could imagine that. Louisa's perfectly shaped orbs had drawn the embarrassing attention of every boat-full of schoolboys, fathers and granddaddies for as many summers as we could recall. Anna Beth looked down at her own pitiful excuses, and inhaled deeply, sticking them out to compare. Finally, dejected, she sank back into her flotilla's concealing embrace to daydream of coming into her own—whatever that meant.

After a few minutes, she glanced up at the bank. Genevieve's massive brimmed hat marked her spot. She sat with her left side to the lake, never giving the girls her full attention, with her other side positioned facing the cabin of her dearest delusion, Jack Bland. Everyone called Genevieve *Moody* now, except me. Anna Beth wasn't sure why, but wasn't surprised that the whole world had "figured her out."

The screen door of the cabin opened and Jack Bland stepped out onto his porch. Genevieve waved up at him, grinning as if one approving glance from him would reconcile her life and make her complete.

There is just something about that man, Anna Beth thought, twirling her fingers through the water.

Spector "Jack" Bland owned not only the cabin, but also the boat dock and acres upon wooded acres around the site. Anna Beth always thought he must be a millionaire to have enough money for a fancy home in Memphis and one nicely equipped at the lake. Jack's father had been in the wholesale flower business with Grandpa Hersh,

Genevieve and Willard's dad. The Blands had run the Bland-Hersh wholesale houses in Birmingham, while Grandpa Hersh managed the one in Memphis until his and Grandma Beatrice's unfortunate and untimely death-by-tree. Genevieve and Willard were just teenagers at the time. Soon the oldest Bland son, Jack, moved to Memphis to take over the operation, and somehow became our family's financial adviser, consoling supporter, and blessed supplier of indoor plumbing when we made our frequent camping trips to the lake.

Everyone called Jack Bland, Jack Bland—never Spector or just plain old Jack. And certainly not Mister Bland. Even the kids got away with it, which was the only example of a sanctioned, total disregard of manners that I can recall. And his wife, Mabel? Well, she never showed her powdered nose at the lake. Genevieve always talked ill of her, cutting her down to the quick for not being a better wife to Jack Bland or a better mother to their three sons. Good ol' Genevieve—hypocrisy epitomized.

Now, watching Jack Bland as he stood on the porch, and at the way Anna Beth zoned in on him, I began to worry. He was a handsome man; even I could see that. I had often longed to feel the sensations of lust, the quickening pulse of attraction, but one look at Anna Beth's flushed face reminded me of my place in the girls' lives.

Stop that, I yelled at her. *He's too old for you, by many long, gray and wrinkled years.* The stubborn little cuss never listened when I needed her attention. Just when I feared the worst, hope joined him on the porch, Little Spec, Jack Bland's oldest son, who got his good looks from his father. I realized that Little Spec was who had caught Anna Beth's attention, not Jack Bland. (Fantasies were often hard for me to delineate.)

She heaved a sigh. It was Little Spec who had supplied Anna Beth with her first pubescent daydreams of what it would be like to fall head over painted toenails in love. She fanned herself, splashed water on her face to ward off heat stroke at the sight of him.

What an inventive little imagination she's got, I thought, but then worried that she might follow in Louisa's footsteps. Of course, taking notes from Genevieve's behavior around men—and Louisa's too, for that matter—were Anna Beth's chief sources of research. Their take on womanly manners gave a slightly distorted picture of what flirting should look like. It was a wealth of information, just the same.

The lazy hum of a motor roused her from her mooning and she looked up just as the two younger Bland boys pulled into the cove. They gunned their outboard, chopping the water into undulating ribbons of rough wake. They always showed off, acting as if they owned the world and everyone in it. I wondered how they could have possibly come from Jack Bland's near-perfect genes. Anna Beth held on tightly to her float as the waves hit.

Dutch, short for Derrick, the cocky middle son, kept a wad of tobacco in his cheek and enjoyed spitting its black juice at unsuspecting feet just to see them jump. And Bart—short for Andrew and just the girls' age in years, but not even close in intellectual or emotional IQ— laughed with the whinny of a pack mule, even when nothing the slightest bit funny had been said. I never understood how they came up with Bart out of Andrew or Dutch out of Derrick. Humans do the strangest things with their names.

Even with all the commotion, Anna Beth's attention had not wavered from the porch. Hormone-charged from using Genevieve's romance novels and naughty magazines for inspiration, Little Spec seemed almost attainable to her in his Bass Weejuns, khaki shorts and white button-down.

It horrified me, but she actually had dreams of him clutching her in his arms, breathing words of endearment in her ear and making love with her in those same murky waters just off his father's dock. Lord, help me, but I braced myself daily for strength to handle what lay ahead.

She held tight to her rubber raft for another swelled ride as his brother's outboard came back around. Louisa hadn't heard the boat coming, and the swells tipped over her raft. She came up spitting muddy water and puffing smoke.

The boys circled a few times to keep the girls off balance. They cut the engine back to idle when their father let out a holler from the porch. Jack Bland motioned an angry cutthroat and his boys eased the boat into the dock to tie up. Then, like a caring Bobby Kennedy, Jack Bland swaggered down the tree-root steps toward the lake, staring out at where we drifted near the mouth of the cove. Little Spec waited on the porch, his hand shielding his sensitive eyes from the afternoon sun.

Anna Beth paddled over to Louisa, and said, "Jack Bland is waving us in. He thinks we're out too far. Maybe we ought to go in closer to the bank."

Louisa shaded her eyes to check him out. Her freckles swarmed in the sunshine. Then she shrugged, laid her head back again and closed her eyes. "Nah, he's just an old worry wart. Relax. We're fine."

Anna Beth dog-paddled toward shore anyway, slowly pulling Louisa along behind her so she wouldn't feel the tug. She secretly hoped Little Spec would still be out on the porch, hanging around to visit awhile or to invite her inside to dry off. But as soon as Jack Bland saw that we were headed back to shore, he turned, climbed the steps, patted Little Spec on the shoulder and led his son back into the cabin to be their usual aloof and alone selves.

Anna Beth's imagination took pleasure in building her up to hopeful splendor, then releasing her to plummet headlong into the depths of adolescent despair. She let go of Louisa about ten yards out—left her to fend for herself—and climbed the bank to where Genevieve ignored them. Before she even made it up the hill, the afternoon sun squelched her. Her potato-white skin shrank, tightened around her bones like cellophane, and she realized she'd done it again.

"Where's the aloe plant?" she asked Genevieve as she shuffled past her on the way to the tent.

"Check the floorboard of the van, honey," Genevieve mumbled without looking up from her *Woman's Day.* "I hope I remembered to bring it this week."

Yeah, Anna Beth thought. *Me, too*.

                              *

Later that afternoon, when everyone else was preoccupied with swimming, skiing or napping, Genevieve sauntered up the tree root steps and onto the porch. She checked to make sure no one was watching as she opened the door to Jack Bland's cabin and slipped inside. She found him where she knew he would be, at his desk in the knotty pine paneled library. The room was finely appointed with a rich-hued leather sofa and matching chairs, Oriental rugs softening the hardwood floors and English hunting lithographs framed on the walls.

"What do you want?" he asked without looking up and before she had the chance to cross the threshold. "I've told you to contact my lawyer when you get into a bind." His hand fondled a piece of Stuben crystal from a collection of figurines on his desk. Genevieve noticed that he'd chosen the ram from the group, his favorite, leaving the horse and the lion untouched.

"But I'd rather deal with you personally, Jack Bland. Ah, come on. For old time's sake. Don't you miss me? Even a little bit?"

He leaned back in his chair and stared at her for a moment. She moved closer to him, placing one foot strategically in front of the other in a choreographed dance directed by lust and flirtation. He showed no visible reaction to her movements, but let her make it all the way across the room, until she got right up beside him, before he raised his hand dismissively and said, "This isn't going to work, Genevieve. Not now. Not ever. Get that through your head."

Her confidence deflated, as if his words had held the power to fill her or release her to sputter out, her esteem escaping in little gusts through a fresh hole torn by his harshness. It took a few beats for her to recover her composure, the moments suspended between them in silence as if neither of them dared disturb the effort for fear that all hope of recovery would be lost. Then, finally, her hand drifted to his face. Her fingers traced the line of his jaw, gently at first, then harder. The sound of her nails raking over his razor stubble made her quiver. "Forever, Jack Bland. Our love is forever," she whispered, her fingers now reminding themselves of the softness of his lips.

He didn't move or respond to the display, but he also didn't rebel. She turned then, and left the room more quickly than she had entered, not even pausing at the doorway to glance over her shoulder at him again.

*

By Beanie Weenie time, Genevieve had had her limit. Yes, she had graduated from sweet tea to more mind-numbing libations. Since her orange juice and vodka took up most of the room in the ice chest, she made a point of finishing them off the first night so the cold cuts could enjoy some of the ice. It also gave her an excuse to go to the "store" the next day to restock. She only drank when we were at the lake and, when we were at the lake, she only drank.

The sun had dipped below the ridge, but refused to give up without a fight. It threw daggers of red, orange and violet up and over the treetops, a warning that it would be back tomorrow with a vengeance and to be ready for temperatures over ninety degrees. I accompanied Anna Beth as she walked their aluminum dishes and plastic forks to the trashcan behind the cabin, then headed for the tent. There we caught Louisa in the middle of wiggling into her favorite halter-top. She tied the strings around her neck and slipped into her skirt.

"Come on Bethy, gimme a hand. Zip me up." Louisa leaned forward at the waist to shake her bosoms into place. Anna Beth grabbed the skirt zipper, and Louisa sucked it in. "I'll swear, too much sun swells me up," Louisa griped. "Or maybe it was that beer I stole out of the back of Spec's car."

Anna Beth bristled, irritated at how Louisa magically maneuvered herself into opportunities to be near Little Spec. And since when did anyone call him just plain *Spec?* It seemed awfully familiar coming from Louisa. Too familiar as far as Anna Beth was concerned. "Somehow I doubt it's the sun or the freakin' beer that bloats you," she grumbled as the zipper caught hold and whizzed up Louisa's side. She hadn't figured out *if* or *how* she was going to warn Louisa that pregnancy was the major cause of *swelling* for a girl with her expertise.

Louisa slicked down her skin-tight mini and slid her bare feet into platform sandals while rummaging through her macramé handbag for lip-gloss and a hair pick.

Anna Beth peeped out through the tent's slit to where the adults hunkered around near-empty coolers for their usual riverbank chat. Mrs. Crump and Mrs. Brazelton, other flower business friends, clutched their husband's arms, warding off Genevieve's singleness. They needn't worry. Men only mattered to Genevieve when Jack Bland or Elvis were involved.

"Moody's not gonna like you going out again," Anna Beth warned, while standing shotgun. "And you'd better hurry up. Her screwdriver's running on empty and . . . uh oh. It's too late now. She's getting up and headed this way." She rushed to the opposite side of the tent, grabbed her sketchpad and pretended to be engrossed with her artwork. It meant a lot of pretending since she hadn't drawn, painted or even doodled since Ned disappeared from their lives almost four years ago. She merely carried a pad around with her all the time, clutching it to her chest.

"Oh, dad-burn it all," Louisa hissed. Both girls had developed mouths as trashy as Genevieve's. Louisa scurried to gather up her necessities for the evening. "With her out there, I had a chance of being polite to the adults and excusing myself when she couldn't object. In here, we'll have to listen to her whining all over again. Didn't she used to be fun to have around?"

A sloshing Genevieve fell through the tent flap and landed catawampus on her cot. Her head lolled to one side. When her vision didn't clear, she blinked and whispered hoarsely, "And where is our pretty little street-walker headed tonight?" She tried to push up onto her elbows, but the struggle was too much for her so she let her torso collapse back onto the cot.

Anna Beth erased furiously, almost rubbing a hole through her paper, as if the action could erase the pain and anger that was spreading its blackness throughout her. Louisa fussed with her hair, looking here, there and everywhere, except at Genevieve. And I did my best to calm the airflow through the tent. I wished I could do more. At times like this I cursed my limitations. Had I remained in this disjointed void as punishment for sins of a past life? I had to wonder, even though that reasoning never felt quite right to me. But the torture of standing by and doing nothing while Genevieve ruined the girls' lives drove me to the brink. Every time she got drunk, the canvas walls cornered her murmurs, cloistered her moans in a flimsy privacy.

"Off to cat around with the Brazelton boys again? Or is it that little dockhand this time?" Her words had no bite. They slipped off her thick tongue with despondent ease. "But no, he's just a boy, and much too low-class for you, Louisa dear." Anna Beth's eyes rolled as Genevieve's hand groped the open space between them, searching, but only grasping stagnant air. "You just better remember what I told you, missy. Keep those pretty legs of yours *shut*. Boys want only one thing."

The slurred whispers danced around us like voodoo dolls, painfully stuck. The girls pretended to ignore her like she'd ignored them all day, all summer, everyday since Ned "left." But I couldn't. I sucked in her words, hoping to purify them somehow, all the while hoping they didn't stain my soul beyond recognition, or to the point where God would never allow me entrance through my door.

"Which one tonight, Louisa? Little Spec, I'd s'spect." Genevieve chuckled to herself. "No, that Dutch boy is more your type, ain't he?" Her giggle warbled and she rolled over, wrapping her blanket around her like a granny shawl. "Ya know, if my momma and daddy hadn't died as young as they did, those Bland boys out there just might see you as a proper pick." She wiped her mouth with the back of her hand, then laid her hand over her eyes.

I had taken about all I could stand. We deserved so much better than this. My girls deserved a mother, a real mother, *my mother*. Louisa crossed and re-crossed both legs and both arms, tapping her toes in midair to fast music no one could hear. Anna Beth rocked back and forth on her cot, gripping her pad so tightly the spiral wire cut into her fingers and hand. We couldn't wait for this weekly torment to be over. There was nothing they could do to make Genevieve stop, and sadly, nothing I could do either.

When she was drunk not even my most practiced goosebump whizzing had any effect. Louisa checked her watch and huffed a few times, but it didn't change their plight. They were captives. Getting hot and bothered couldn't change that.

Cradled in loose-weave cotton arms, Genevieve stared blankly into space, her mouth slack, hair untypically lank. Her eyes misted over, but she didn't notice the salty dread trickle across her temples and pool in her ears. "You might as well face it, honey. We're nothing but squatters to them. There was a time, though, a time when Jack Bland looked at me with different eyes. But I've ruined all that, I guess. And since your daddy left me with only that dinky little flower shop to support us, we'll never rise to their level, no matter how nice or generous they seem." Her eyes shut like shades.

Louisa almost popped her zipper. She jumped up, stood over Genevieve and spat, "Oh, get off it, Moody. Daddy didn't just leave you. He left all of us, but at least he's gone and he doesn't have to put up with all the bitching and whining you've dished out for the past four years. He didn't have to see you dragging us from here to Kingdom Come to get your precious Elvis fixes, your King." Genevieve rolled away. "Oh, what's the point? Anna Beth, I'm outta here."

Cricket chirps and bullfrog croaks replaced the hostility. Anna Beth stood up and moved over to Genevieve. She lifted her legs onto the cot and tucked her in. Then she turned, smoothed down her own T-shirt, and shook her curls out of her face. I had no way to prepare them for what was to come, no way to show them how drastically their lives would be changed by Louisa's desperate longing to be loved by someone, anyone—and by her total disregard of Genevieve's warnings to keep her legs shut. And no way to defuse Anna Beth's powder keg.

The fuse had already been lit. Anna Beth snatched back the tent's flap, drew in a fierce breath and pasted on the smile of a prizefighter. Then she stalked proudly down the bank to join the other kids out by the lake who were too young and obedient to escape.

*

Anna Beth rejoined a slumbering Genevieve in the tent at about ten p.m. After a couple of hours of fighting with her sheet and failing to block out Genevieve's chainsaw snoring that rattled around the enclosed space, she gave up. She dowsed herself in Off and wandered back out to the tree-root steps. "There is nothing more peaceful than a bug-proof evening at the lake, huh?" she mused aloud, trying to lighten her mood. She chattered on for a few minutes about nothing in particular, and I was certain she was talking to me. I answered, of course. After a few minutes, she looked up at the cabin. It was dark, so she sneaked up onto the porch to peep in the windows. *Wishful thinking*, she thought. She couldn't see past the front hall.

The porch light lit our way down to the dock and, even knowing the rules about not swimming alone or at night, she dropped her shorts and shirt into a rowboat and herself into the hot black murk. She thought about practicing her swan dive—no one could have heard her that far from the campsite—but instead she just floated, seeing how still and low she could lie in the water without going under. I relished our time alone, so peaceful, so intimate. We'd been out there long enough for her skin to prune when voices from near the cabin startled her, and we moved in closer to the dock. Water lapping against boat hulls made it hard to make out who was coming but, within seconds, footsteps clomped onto the dock above us. We cozied up to a piling to get a juicy earful.

"We can't keep doing this," a masculine voice said in a loud whisper. "It's crazy. We're gonna get caught."

Anna Beth covered her mouth to keep her giggles to a dull roar, and I snuggled in around her like a teddy bear's hug. My presence didn't startle her, or make her uneasy. Instead, she embraced the feeling of me and pretended she was sharing this naughty adventure with the good friend she'd never had. Our connection was solid and being with her like this was so much fun. Eavesdropping with me was certainly better than perusing Genevieve's tacky magazines. Real-life drama had a different kind of spark.

"Awh, come on. Don't you want me?" Louisa whined.

Anna Beth almost choked on her own spit. Her ears perked up.

"I know you love me. You can't say you don't," Louisa said, burrowing in closer to him.

Anna Beth moved silently through the water until we were directly underneath them and she peered up through the wood slats of the dock. Their shadowy bodies came into view, but she still couldn't make him out. One of the Bland boys, she was certain. Or it could have been that Brazelton brat. But which one? It didn't sound like Little Spec—thank God—but she had to know for sure. She figured it had to be Dutch. He had flirted with Louisa ever since she bloomed—at about age ten. Anna Beth thought, *you little Dickens. You've been fooling around all this time and haven't breathed a word of it to me.* Her arm hairs stood on end, and it wasn't me giving them.

Louisa flipped off her shoes, and her zipper hissed.

Guess he'll have to zip her up this time, Anna Beth and I thought in unison.

"Come on," Louisa purred, "let's go for a swim."

Holy Mother of God, Anna Beth thought, *I'm a goner now.*

There was no way for us to get outta there and nowhere to hide. She cuddled up to a ski boat to wait it out, hoping they were too busy to look around. Just then, something cold slid past us in the water, brushing up against her arm like a wet finger. She almost yelped as the woolies quaked her body and chattered her teeth. It dawned on her that there were other deadly reasons—besides drowning—not to swim in those waters at night and alone. She stayed as still as she could until the snake passed.

Then it got real quiet. She didn't hear a splash and finally figured out why. Moans escaped Louisa, fabric rustled, and soft smacking sounds made Anna Beth want to gag. They were kissing and she knew it. Suddenly her childish voyeurism lost its appeal. She jumped when their bodies crumpled onto the rough wood above us. *You dummies*, she thought. *On the dock? Put the seats down in the boat, for Christ's sake. But right out in the open? How will you ever survive all those splinters in your bare butts?*

We endured what seemed like hours of heavy breathing, clutching, pawing and unison moans, but finally her question was answered. At the pentacle of their puffing, Louisa howled, "Oh Spec . . . Spec . . . Spector, you are soooooo good."

Poor Anna Beth almost died right there. *Just as I thought*, she thought. *You picked the one I like. How could you? My sister, the slut.* She slapped the water, but the splash didn't even draw their attention. *Of course, you picked the one who'll inherit.* She thought Louisa was growing more like Genevieve everyday and wondered why she couldn't have picked "one of the other boys, anyone but Little Spec." One of the boys Anna Beth couldn't care a flip about.

Ah, our first experience with sibling rivalry, I thought, and wondered how bad it would get. They had always been so close. I hated that something so silly could come between them, especially since her assumption about the identity of the man was all wrong. But my immediate concern was getting Anna Beth out of there. In her eyes, all her dreams had just been pissed on by Louisa; those fantasies of first love bite hard when they die. Her lungs tightened around her heart like a bridesmaid's grip on a wedding bouquet.

She sank lower into the shallows and skimmed along the surface like the snake that almost got her. Louisa and her *Spector* never even looked up. Anna Beth reasoned that Little Spec had chosen the easy one, the pretty one, the one who would hand her virginity over to him time after time on a silver platter and yell, "Come and get it. Dessert is served." Anna Beth and I both wanted to puke, but for different reasons. Only I knew the true identity of Louisa's lover. It was Jack Bland himself. Anna Beth didn't realize this yet, though I was certain she would figure it out soon enough. I also worried about my ill-advised Louisa and what would happen when Genevieve found out.

When she'd made it out of earshot around the bend, Anna Beth broke into a full breaststroke, and then swam to the bank on the far side of our camp. She inched through prickly underbrush that scraped her bare legs and pulled at her panties, not caring if copperheads sleep soundly or not, and trying to force herself to concentrate on something else. She failed at that.

"My life is over," she said aloud, hoping I could answer. "No one will *ever* grope me in public, rip off my clothes in the moonlight or make love to me under clandestine stars. I hate myself. I hate my life." She wheeled around, searching for me. "Why don't you answer me? I know you're there. Say something, please. Help me!"

I did. I did. I talked and talked. Comforted and consoled. I caught myself saying the things a loving mother might say. *No, this will pass. He's not who you think. Just wait, you'll see.* But she did not hear. She mourned her fantasies with Little Spec in anger, the way she handled most of the disappointments in her life. She turned that fury inward and let it join the pool of darkness locked away in her sad and aching heart.

And she vented it outward, not at Louisa, but instead, at Little Spec. He became the bad guy. He should know better, after all. She plodded, dripping wet and half naked, through the un-pathed thicket back toward the tent and realized that being fourteen would have been only mild adolescent torture without witnessing her fantasy love god make love to her sister on a rough wooden dock.

*

One morning three weeks later, Genevieve joined Anna Beth in the bathroom with a new box of Kotex and six rolls of toilet paper to store under the sink. Anna Beth was brushing her teeth. Her eyes widened when she realized what Genevieve wanted to do. "Here, I'll put them away for you," she mumbled in a panic through a mouthful of foam. Even in her pain she'd still do anything to save Louisa. She reached for the Kotex, but it was too late.

Genevieve squatted at Anna Beth's ankles and opened the cabinet. Her expression slid quickly from bewilderment to shock when two unopened boxes of Kotex stared her in the face. She counted soundlessly on her fingers for a minute, and when her mathematics came up with an overage, she sprang to her feet, and yelled, "Holy Mother!" still clutching the new box to her breasts.

"Are you marking your calendar, young lady?" she asked Anna Beth's reflection. "Have your periods been regular and on time every month?"

Anna Beth nodded, her mouth gaping with the toothbrush frozen to her tongue and toothpaste dribbling down her chin.

"Louisa. Where's Louisa?" Genevieve growled. Her pupils constricted to a pinprick.

She didn't hang around long enough for Anna Beth to spit and respond.

*

Anna Beth had learned early on that if you wanted to keep up with the going secret in the family, you had to listen carefully, listen often, and listen covertly so that no one knew you were around. Must be in the genes. She never thought of this as spying, just as a way to avoid surprises. And our family was well endowed with surprises— the life-altering kind.

Three days after Genevieve informed Louisa that "not having a period for two months in a row means you're pregnant," the long distance bill went up. Iuka, Mississippi, and Willard were only ninety miles from the front porch, give or take a few. Iuka rested just south of Pickwick Lake. Close enough, yet far enough away. Anna Beth knew Genevieve's telephone conversations with Willard must be important enough to eavesdrop upon, because Genevieve made them daily and before the rates went down.

"You've got to do this, Willard," Genevieve whispered angrily to the floor as she leaned over at her shapely waist to rest her forehead on the kitchen countertop. "Memphis may be a big city, but in the flower business, it's a Pony Express stop. What about the Junior League? And the Circle women? They're my best customers. They'll eat this up with a silver fork and swallow me whole right along with it. And I've got the shop to think about. It has a reputation, you know. I could lose a lot of business if this gets around."

I perched myself right there next to her. This was going to be good. Anna Beth hunkered down beside the contemporary china cabinet in the dining room, and drew her knees up to her chest so she could peek around the doorjamb from below eye-level as Genevieve paced the length of the phone cord and back across the kitchen floor.

Genevieve was losing the battle. She stopped every so often, held the receiver out from her ear and mouthed silent screams at it. She could over-dramatize afternoon tea at the park. "Okay, okay," she bitched, "I know you don't agree with my mothering methods, but Elvis Presley and my love for him have nothing to do with this. I wish it did. He's the only man who could save me from this life."

She listened for a minute, then held the receiver out from her ear again and hollered toward it, "No, I don't happen to know who the father is, but I can make a few good guesses." She listened again. "Who cares, Willard? She's not keeping this baby. She's a child herself. Give the baby away. I'm certainly not gonna raise it, and she's not capable. That's that. That's it. Case closed." She clapped a hand to her forehead like an actor playing torment.

Willard must have really gone off the deep end on that comment, because Genevieve dropped the receiver from her hand, barely catching it by the cord before it hit the floor. She then swung ol' Ma Bell around in a huge circle so she wouldn't have to listen to Willard's speech. When she brought it back to her ear, she got a word in edgewise. I knew this was it, and so did Anna Beth, who brought her hands together in silent prayer and closed her eyes.

Genevieve straightened her bony shoulders, craned her neck a few times, and fisted her perfect, thirty-six inch hip. "Okay, Miss Know-It-All, you're gonna listen to me now. I didn't want to do this, but you leave me no choice."

Anna Beth strained her ears. I thought, *No, Genevieve, don't. Don't let your mouth get overloaded and blow this. Don't hurt my mother again.*

Genevieve shielded the receiver with her manicured hand as if that could contain the power of her words. "I've been keeping a big ol' secret for you, Miss Big Britches, for umpteen years. You know what I'm talking about, Willard. And now it's your turn. It's payback. You owe me big time, and I'm collecting. You will help me with these girls until the baby comes, or I'll spill everything I know to whomever will listen."

The air compressed around us. I wanted to fly off to Iuka to check on my mother, but couldn't. God had a way of keeping me put when my desires deemed otherwise. Plus, one look at Anna Beth and I realized that she, too, needed me here. Genevieve spilling whatever she knew didn't concern Anna Beth, yet. But Genevieve's use of the term "these girls" buzzed around in her ears like she'd been knocked out in a fight.

Genevieve wasn't just sending Louisa away. Anna Beth was going too.

Return to Sender
Top 20 *Billboard* Hit Single

We piled into the flower shop van and headed out early the next morning. Anna Beth took her place in the back forty, hanging on to the rickety two-by-four shelves that were usually loaded down with boxed roses, tussie-mussies and potted mums. She balanced her denim butt on her suitcase with her legs wrapped around the lamp from her bedside table, and clutched the only stuffed animal that had survived her early childhood.

Louisa smoldered in the passenger seat. She sniffed into a Kleenex like she'd just heard Paul McCartney had died. She hadn't taken a bath, changed clothes or washed her hair since Genevieve told her, "You're gonna end up just like me, young lady. Alone, all alone, with younguns' to raise and no one to love you. Having fun is one thing, but this . . . this . . . You mark my word, little girl. You are well on your way."

Genevieve downshifted into second to make the turn onto the highway. She'd applied lipstick so many times that morning that little red-devil lines bled spider veins up to her nose and half-way down her chin. She cleared her throat and bared her teeth in what was supposed to be an encouraging smile.

"Aunt Willard is so excited that you girls are gonna be so close to her now. It's better for you both to go, you know. That way no one will suspect the real reason I sent you away." She cut her eyes toward Louisa, then back to the road. "I'll say that Great Aunt Edna left us some money in her will, so you girls could go away to school. That makes perfectly good sense. She was always as dizzy as a whirly bird. It'd be just like her to stipulate how her benefactors spent her wad. Besides, children get sent away to school all the time. Now, doesn't that make sense? Sure it does."

She had repeated this litany at least twenty times since she'd made her pronouncement about them leaving—not five minutes after she hung up the phone the day before. Anna Beth had almost broken her neck to keep from getting caught spying. She'd bolted over the sofa, scrambled up the stairs and threw herself onto her bed only seconds before Genevieve stopped outside the girls' doorways and yelled, "Get packed, girls. Ya'll are going on a field trip." Louisa hadn't stopped crying since.

The van hit a pothole. Louisa's head hit the roof, leaving a handful of hair twisted around a metal screw. Anna Beth bounced off her suitcase and skidded along the floorboard, slamming into the back doors of the van.

Genevieve was unaffected and in mid-sentence. "You'll live at the Catholic Home for Unwed Mothers. You'll like it fine, just fine. It's out a-ways from town—not too close to Iuka and Willard—but she can come out and visit once in a polka-dot moon, if she likes. I'm sure she will, in fact. I just hope not too much." She paused to light a cigarette and shoved an Elvis 8-track into the tape player. "You'll both do just fine. Willard has it all planned. You'll school with the Sisters of Mercy and meet other girls in just your same spot. Now, Anna Beth," she said, craning her neck to make eye contact in the rear view mirror, "you're not supposed to take notes, ya here? Just mind your business and keep your ears shut. Yep, it'll be just like the old days when we all lived out there in the country. The only difference— you won't have me along."

The van's right tire dropped off onto the gravel shoulder and Genevieve fought the steering wheel to keep on track. "Willard'll meet us at the Dairy Queen in Corinth. We'll have a nice lunch, and then ya'll can ride the rest of the way with her." She patted her teased finger waves and pulled at the strained buttons of her blouse. Then she rested her smoking hand back on the wheel to tap her clean, shorn fingernails some more.

She had come to the end of her hope. She had made a bed for herself that was so lumpy, so impossible to sleep in, to live in, that now she could see no other escape than to just roll over and fall out. She'd also backed herself into a corner of one-sided love and loneliness, but she'd given up looking for a way to escape that. And now, something unexpected, something out of her control, threatened to derail her misguided life. No one really knew about her convoluted lifestyle, except me. No one knew what all she had done, what all she thought she had sacrificed to carve out the life she had made for herself and the girls. Now, she was doing what she swore she would never do—turning the girls over to nuns and their more capable hands.

I said a thousand *Hail Marys* and sang *Ave Maria* at the top of my lungs all the way to Corinth. My prayers were finally being answered. I just wished it hadn't taken Him so long. I wasn't the only one praying, however. Yep, I know it is hard to believe, but just when my faith in God had been restored, He slapped me with another miracle. On that lonely highway, Genevieve prayed for the first time since the day she took those tiny babies home with her fourteen years ago.

Lord, I tried my best. She whispered so softly I hoped God had His hearing aid on. *But I can't do anymore. It should have been Willard who raised these girls, my girls—not the other way around. Just please, Lord, don't let her figure it all out. You gave that baby to me. Reverend Mother said that I was Your Plan. Don't let her take them away from me now. They are the only sane things in my life.* Knowing that she hadn't done a very good job of wording her prayer, she remembered a stray verse from Chapter 8 in the Book of Romans in the Bible that had somehow lingered in a dusty corridor in her mind. *The Spirit comes to the aid of our weakness; for we do not know how to pray as we ought; but the Spirit himself intercedes with inexpressible groanings.*

This shocked me more than anything she had done. But I was happy that the recollection gave her some peace. I was so elated to hear her admit fault; however, I had to hold tight lest I get blown out the back windows of the van. I had to catch myself, too, in another way. If I wasn't careful I might slip and think this monster had a conscience. I knew better, I thought, but one prayer in fourteen years . . . major soul searching must be going on.

We rode along in silence while Genevieve raked herself through a hot bed of guilty coals. She was a professional wallower. It wasn't that she didn't know her own despicableness. She had just never figured out where her righteous boot straps were, or a way to pull herself up by them and out of her own guilt-ridden stupor.

Anna Beth's nervous chatter snapped Genevieve back to the

present. Rattled off questions Genevieve had heard every weekend, every summer for years on end, filled the stale air of the van.

"Moody, why haven't we ever gone down to Aunt Willard's before this? I mean, you grew up in Iuka. And, I know we lived there, but since we moved to Memphis, we've never been back." Silence answered. "You never even took us there when we were up at the lake. I remember Madson, though, and his cooking. And the lawn torpedo and the front porch."

Genevieve's otherwise pretty face pinched as it always did when the girls started in with these questions. She glanced out the side window and then back at the road. She wondered how children could understand the ghosts that haunt people who grow up with abuse? *Madson's cooking, humph*, Genevieve thought. She changed the subject without giving Anna Beth the benefit of an answer. Finally, she said, "Well, you're going there now, doodle-bug. Close enough, anyway. You won't be seeing much of the old home place or Madson either, but after Louisa's baby . . . " She cleared her throat. Emotions threatened. She scooted her girdled hips farther back into her seat. "Just you don't worry about a thing. We'll figure out what else to do later. But for right now, everything will be okay. I'm sure of that now."

*

Willard's 1953 Chevy pickup rumbled into the Dairy Queen parking lot about five minutes after we arrived. I was so glad to see her. God is good. God is so good. We peered out the window from our booth as her slight figure climbed down from the cab. She disappeared behind the vehicle for a few seconds before reappearing around the front of its dully-polished blue hood. The comical sight of her drew unbridled laughter from the girls, in spite of the circumstances that had delivered us there, and unbridled joy out of me.

Willard's wild hair, braided and twisted with such precision around her tiny head, crowned her with a silver tiara fit for Queen Elizabeth herself. Her white, ruffled peasant shirt and multi-pleated skirt dated her to a Woodstock wannabe who'd lost her way and ended up in rural Mississippi instead. Nervous keys jingling preceded her appearance from behind the trashcan. She wore the grin of a contented hippie. A silver crucifix the size of a fist hung around her neck.

"Well, I see ya'll made it. Oh, just look at you girls. How you've grown." She stuffed her keys deep inside her Indian rug handbag, twirled its long handle a time or two, then pitched it on the floor next to Louisa's feet. "Sorry I'm late, but I had a delivery out in the boonies near Burnsville that took me longer than I'd expected." She slid into the booth next to Louisa, legs dangling a foot off the floor. She grabbed Louisa's hand off the table, kissed the back of it and laid it in her lap, fingers entwined. Louisa's eyes teared up all over again.

"Nope, none of that," Willard commanded. "No weeping or worrying. Everything is going to be just fine. Now, what's for lunch? Five a.m. was eons ago."

Anna Beth said, "I hope nobody will expect us to get up at that hour. We'll never survive that kind of routine."

Genevieve poked her in the ribs to shut her up.

Willard smiled weakly across the table, and said, "Don't worry, sugar. Everything's gonna be okay."

Willard's dainty hands fingered the menu. I wondered if mine would have looked like hers. It's a wonder how such delicate features could stand a flower shop's rose thorn and wire-tearing abuse. But my mother's hands looked like they'd never seen a day's work, while Genevieve's were split and blackened from hardly working for years. Even all her lotions, pumice scrubs, wax baths and manicures couldn't help them. Anna Beth was taking notes right along with me. She looked down at her own hands, pink and soft as a bunny's tummy. They resembled Willard's. But they'd never seen more work than making puffs and tying a bow or ten.

Genevieve and the girls had already ordered, and after the waitress delivered their meals and took Willard's order, Genevieve finally found her voice. "Thanks for doing this," she told the tabletop. Funny how she never spoke directly to anyone, eye to eye, unless she was blessing them out. A sullen shadow had fallen over her. The possible consequences of sending the girls anywhere close to Willard were falling into heartbreaking place.

"They'll be fine. Just fine. There's no need to fret."

Thick air clogged them all like cold molasses, immobilizing them into sticky statues glued in their seats. Louisa moved her silverware around her plate, staring out the window for a minute, then daggers at Genevieve and back again. Anna Beth dipped and re-dipped French fries in ketchup for the fourth and fifth time without ever taking a bite.

"They will behave themselves." Genevieve addressed this to Willard, but it was really a warning to the girls. "They will do whatever the nuns say and neither one of them will venture off the Home's property unless they're told to do so. Is that understood?"

"They know how to act," Willard said with one of Anna Beth's fries in her mouth. "I'm sure you've instructed them well. And when the baby comes, well, I guess we'll all just chip in and change diapers. You know they can come stay with me at the home place, if they'd like."

Genevieve's face grayed markedly at the words '*baby*' and '*diapers*.' Obviously Willard had not listened to Genevieve's plans for the future very well. But her teeth almost fell into her plate at '*stay with me*.' It was just like Willard to go against her wishes and to put ideas in the girls' heads about keeping the *mistake* and coming to live in Iuka, she thought.

Louisa burst into tears.

"Okay, ladies," Willard almost shouted, "it is time for us all to just get a grip. I'm not having all this wailing and such, so get over it. I know you girls aren't exactly thrilled at the prospect of moving to the boondocks to live at a convent with nuns." She glanced in Genevieve's direction. "But it won't be that bad. I promise. You can be sure of that."

Louisa wrapped herself around Willard's neck and bawled in her ear. The rest of the meal was consumed in silence. They finally finished playing with their food and walked out to the truck like they were headed for the gallows. Anna Beth sat sandwiched in the middle, thankful that the old truck's gearshift was on the steering column and not between her knees. She struggled to keep her tears from rolling.

Willard gunned the pickup, and yelled, "Wave to your momma, girls." She spun us out of the Dairy Queen parking lot and drove as fast as the angels would take us, buckity-buck into a new life. "Hang on, girls. This might just be fun if you can see your way clear to letting it."

The girls couldn't see how, but I had my suspicions.

Anna Beth looked back once, just to see what Genevieve looked like in a cloud of gravel dust. She was surprised. Genevieve didn't even fan the chunky air. She just stood there next to the van, looking like she'd sold her last cow. She almost lifted her hand to wave once, but must have thought better of it and stuck it into her skirt pocket instead.

*

The domed mushroom tops of ancient oaks came into view long before the main house did. Ah, the splendor of home.

"But this isn't the Home for Unwed . . . ," Louisa started to say when the *Livvie's Heavenly Bouquet* sign appeared beside the road. She swallowed the lump in her throat and continued, "I thought we were going there."

The truck turned off onto deeply grooved gravel. Willard chanted, "Home again, home again, jiggedy-jig." She looked sideways at the girls and grinned the most deviously sweet smile we had ever seen. I broke out into another chorus of *Ava Maria*. "Your Moody turned you girls over to me. I guess I must have been mistaken about that Home for Unwed Mothers. There is no such a place. Not around here anyway." We rumbled down the mile-long driveway lined with a graying picket fence. "We'll just act like a bunch of daisies. Daisies never tell, you know. We'll make it our little secret—that is, until Genevieve forces us to throw up the truth." Willard slowed to ease over a hole in the driveway big enough to swallow the truck.

"That's fine with us, Aunt Willard," Anna Beth said, relieved. After a moment she asked, "But Moody told us that you don't even live in the big house. She says you live in the shop. Why's that?"

Willard gunned the engine, and pellets pitched out from the tire treads sprayed the pox-marked fence. The driveway opened up into a gravel clearing between the big house and the building behind it that housed the flower shop.

"Ghosts, that's why." Willard answered like it was the most normal of things to believe. "And because I rented it out."

The girls' eyes widened as they remembered Genevieve's stories about the place as we slid to a stop in front of the double-decker carriage house. A cloud of dust enveloped the truck, then dispersed. "We're here," Willard chimed. The old pickup shuddered when she cut off its juice. She kicked open her door with her foot and slid down from her perch. The girls followed suit from the passenger side and met up with her at the tailgate to unload.

Willard paused for a moment, staring back at the main house, transfixed on the old Victorian structure. "I left this place once, a long time ago. And when I came back and ya'll moved to Memphis, I just couldn't convince myself to move back in over there." She gazed thoughtfully at the old house like someone might wave from a window or call out to her from the porch. "Your great-grandparents, Grandma Olivia and Grandpa Clancy, were both ornery old biddies—especially Grandpa. Mean as a yard dog that man was. Renting it out just made more sense to me somehow. That place gives me the creeps."

"Who lives there then?" Anna Beth asked.

"Friends. Some dear old friends."

The girls took this to mean that an elderly couple had moved into the big house, but I knew what my mother meant. The nuns had moved into the house. They had closed up the *Beaver's Auto Parts and Shop* convent and now spent their days praying right there across the driveway from *Livvie's Heavenly Bouquet.*

Willard, however, had reason to get the woollies. I wondered if anyone could see what I saw. Ghosts from ages past had gathered in the front yard to welcome us, the friendly ones, and those other souls, so sad and pitiful, whom I prayed for relentlessly, but also steered clear of. Without being too rude, I shooed them away. The bad ones dispersed quickly, thank goodness. I didn't want the girls to sense them and be afraid to be back here, back home. The remaining lot waved and went on about their business. They were spirits like me, guardians without wings, and had loved ones to attend to, but had stopped by just to welcome us home.

In the meantime, Anna Beth had climbed up into the truck bed and was pitching luggage at Louisa.

"Gives me the creeps, too," Louisa murmured, but only I heard her.

They unloaded all their belongings, and Willard left her ghosts behind. Some people have ghosts who only exist in their minds. This was the case with my mother. She didn't mean and had no knowledge of the real, haunting kind that Genevieve dealt with on a regular basis, or the ones that gathered to wish us well on our return home. She meant simply the sorrowful spirit of aching that walked the lonely corridors of her heart and echoed its maternal longing through chambers with no doorways out.

This yearning for her children made moving on with her life a difficult task. She wanted so much to put her grief behind her, to lay her sorrow to rest, but she didn't know how. Watching the girls now sparked a fantasy, a tug deep within her that caught her breath. *What if they are mine?* she thought. *What if Reverend Mother gave Genevieve my children?* She grabbed her chest. But the image faded into a mist of ridiculousness.

How silly of me, she thought. She had known all about Genevieve's pregnancy, of course. There was no way her fantasy could have happened. No way at all. She believed that her babies were gone, had been given to a good, Christian home, and knew she had to accept that fact. She and the Reverend Mother had remained close friends and the good nun had reassured her time and again that she should, "Trust. Trust that the Lord knows what He is doing and that He led me to make the right choices for you. Trust, dear Willard, as I have had to remind myself perpetually for all these years."

Both amused and saddened by the tricks of her imagination, my mother draped her arms across the girls' shoulders and led them to the smaller and plainer of the two front doors of the carriage house. One door sported a fancy green awning with script letters reading, *Livvie's Heavenly Bouquet*. Only paying customers ever used that door. The door they stood in front of, however, resembled an arched mouse hole in a wall. "Watch your heads," Willard warned, not having to duck to keep from hitting her head on the low doorframe like Louisa and Anna Beth did.

Anna Beth almost scurried on ahead, but restrained herself and waited at the foot of the stairway so she wouldn't appear too eager. It felt so good to be back here. We were all thrilled that Willard had hoodwinked Genevieve, but the girls weren't quite sure what to make of this deceit. How about my mother, huh? She was one sly bird. And for the first time, I knew my girls would feel safe and be cared for with ordinary love.

Inside, they paused for a few seconds to let their eyes adjust. A staircase ascended immediately inside the door. All eyes followed it upward. The place smelled like old wood and varnish with the faintest hint of roses. They clomped up the stairs, banging suitcases along behind them. Halfway up, Anna Beth sidestepped someone she could not see.

Guess who? She had the urge to say, "Excuse me, Olivia," but stifled it, worried that Willard and Louisa might think she was nuts. It was the first time my name had taken shape in her thoughts. Hearing it echo there thrilled me so much that I wondered how any of them could miss seeing my glow. It was as if being back here held a magic all its own. For the first time in many years I felt like my place in their lives held the promise of a purpose. Like my mother and the Reverend Mother, I, too, would have to trust God to reveal it to me in His time.

At the top of the steps a long dining room stretched out to our left, the kitchen beyond it. To our right a room met us with tall twin beds in its corners and an upholstered sitting area with a TV over to one side. The space seemed not to be able to make up its mind if it wanted to be a bedroom or a living room. The girls certainly weren't going to ask. Walls, floor and ceiling were cloaked in dark wood paneling, Jesus dripped from a half-dozen crucifixes hanging on each wall and angels, saints and the Blessed Mother peeked out from every nook and cranny like eavesdropping kids.

Anna Beth wondered why Willard would want Jesus and His holy friends and family staring down on her and watching her every move. I knew, of course. Who wouldn't want good friends around to keep you company, especially in times of need?

"This is my room," Willard announced, sweeping her arm. "We can all watch TV in here, play games and whatever else. Your room is through here."

Ducking again, we followed her through a tight passageway that led to a junked up room with five doors, one on each wall, and no windows. It was a convoluted and confusing house, especially for girls used to a typical two-story box. Odd-sized doors and windows linked mismatched rooms together in the apartment Willard called home.

"This is the hesitation room," she explained. "We're standing in the rafters of what used be the barn. All these rooms around you used to be hayloft, but when they turned downstairs into the flower shop, all this up here kind of got added onto and fiddled with so many times it got befuddled. I renovated it when I moved home. You have to 'hesitate' here just to figure out which way to turn, which door you dare to open and go through—kind of like life, I guess, huh?"

Anna Beth squeezed Louisa's hand and swallowed her apprehension. Maybe her hopes for normal were a little premature.

We stepped over a rolled-up rag rug and bypassed a stacked set of antique wicker chairs. A door half the height of most doors opened into a room overwhelmed with a massive poster bed at its heart. The room must have been built around it because it couldn't have fit through that tiny door. The bed was draped in gauze, cream satin and antique needlepoint, and little steps waited beside it to boost them up into its eiderdown.

Louisa hadn't said much all day, but finally opened her mouth with her foot not far behind. "Aunt Willard, this is too . . . too nice." She glanced around the room as if searching for another door or some way to sneak out. Not finding any, she said, "Just give us the twin beds out yonder. We'll do fine out there in the other room."

Willard smiled, knowingly. My mother was no fool. "Now, Louisa dear," she said, moving closer and encircling her with both arms in a wrestler's bear hug. "Until this baby comes, just call me Aunt Guard Dog. If you want to sneak out of this house, you're gonna have to come past me, honey." She brought her fingers to her cheek, thoughtful like. "Or, I guess you could climb out that window over there and onto a screened porch swarming with blood-hungry bees. They live in these walls, you know. Hundreds, maybe even thousands of them. I suspect—if you survived them—you could climb down the most unstable stairway ever to hang off the side of a house."

She picked up a loose strand of Louisa's hair and tucked it behind her ear. "But you wouldn't take the chance of hurting yourself or your baby, now would you, darlin'?" Louisa looked down at her hands. "No, I didn't think so. That's a good girl. Now, help me with these bags."

They hoisted the suitcases onto the bed as Anna Beth walked

over to the window and looked out. She wondered why on earth anyone would build a screened porch up so high, on a roof and off a room with no doorway out.

"Come on, now. Let's go on downstairs," Willard said. "You can unpack later. I've got to check on things in the shop."

Louisa caught Anna Beth's eye as we followed Willard back through the strange house. She winked, mouthing, "Just you wait. I'll get out."

Anna Beth rolled her eyes. It never ceased to amaze us how Louisa could disregard the direct orders of authority figures with such dispassionate ease.

Willard gave us a brief history lesson as we descended the stairs. "My great-grandfather—your great, great—Cornelius Alexander Clancy, built this place back in 1898. It was a lovely plantation with livestock, especially horses, and a variety of crops back then." She didn't tell them that the two subsequent generations of outrageous taxes and money-dumb relatives had almost ruined the place. "By the time Grandma Olivia, the renegade that she was, opened the flower shop, most of the crops had been lovingly replaced with flowers of every variety, color and scent. Our family's been in the flower business ever since. And after Genevieve moved ya'll to Memphis, Madson and I managed to pluck a lucrative business out of the place."

At the bottom of the stairs, we turned right through another dwarfed door into a dark parlor blanketed in red velvet upholstery, heavy drapes and three inches of dust. Willard didn't even bother to turn on a light. Louisa uttered a little cough of distaste. She held her arms close to her, being careful not to alarm the mountains of dust. Anna Beth seemed not to notice, although she did move in closer to Louisa and didn't dawdle. They remembered that Genevieve had always kept this room closed off.

I had been here many times, but even in my situation, the place emitted an otherworldly attitude. In the chair in the corner, the ghostly presence of Grandpa Clancy watched us pass. His bushy eyebrows did little to conceal the hate in his eyes. He had died in that very chair, although no one here knew that fact, except me. He'd thrown a blood clot to his lung and suffocated just weeks after my mother had run away and only moments after one of his rages in which he beat the living daylights out of Genevieve for no reason at all. She had watched helplessly as he collapsed, gasped for breath and cursed her at the same time, his lungs and heart convulsing in a violent last effort to remain live.

I shuddered just thinking about how awful it must have been. God had a way of revealing tidbits of information in the most unexpected and disturbing ways sometimes. *Poor Geneveive*, I thought. *She's blamed herself all these years. It is no wonder she turned out the way she did.* I pointed my finger in Grandpa's direction. *Stay away*, I warned. He acknowledged me by baring his rotten teeth.

"Let's just say the business needed refurbishing after your mother's creative management for all those years," Willard was saying, her words dragging me back to the present. She stopped in the center of the room and wrinkled her nose like what she'd said smelled bad. "But don't you worry. I'm holding onto the Clancy heritage for posterity's sake. We've got over a hundred acres of chrysanthemums, gladioli, baby's breath and iris, and six greenhouses stretch out as far as you can see behind this old carriage house."

Anna Beth guessed that "posterity" meant she and Louisa since Willard had never married. It made her wonder even more why Genevieve had evacuated them from the place when Willard moved home, and why she had never moved them back to Iuka to lay her claim.

Willard stopped before we reached the other side of the parlor and turned back to look again at the room we'd just crossed. "We never spend any time in this room really; I'm not sure why," she explained. "Just pass through it as quickly as we can." Her sad eyes scanned the bleak space, then she dropped her chin to her chest as if in mourning before she turned back and opened a door leading into the shop.

A huge workroom opened up before us. Florescent light brighter than God flooded the room. An extremely thin woman with a crooked nose manned two telephones that blinked and buzzed hysterically. She smacked a mouthful of bubble gum as she jotted notes on an order form.

"Loretta, these are the girls," Willard announced without giving names.

The woman greeted us with a yellow smile.

The greenness of the workroom made Anna Beth wonder if anyone realized that other colors exist. Green walls covered with green shelves stacked with green boxes full of green foam outlined the space. Even the gray concrete floor was green, strewn with discarded greenery and broken green wooden picks used to support flimsy green stems. Behind one of the six green worktables, a wiry black man in a green apron ferociously crammed spiky greenery into three mammoth centerpieces at the same time. At least he wasn't green. A dozen wedding bouquets encroached upon him from all sides.

"One of Iuka's elite is getting married tomorrow," Willard explained, moving closer to the man. "Madson, can you believe these young ladies are Louisa and Anna Beth?" Then she exited stage left, leaving them standing alone in the middle of the room to fend for themselves as she disappeared into the storage room.

Madson looked over at the girls, shaking his head in disbelief. "Ya'll were just little girls the last time I saw ya," he said loud enough for Willard to hear in the adjoining room. "Good Lord, look how you've grown. Good to see ya'll. Welcome back, or I should say, welcome home."

Willard reappeared with her own green apron and a large sheet of green Styrofoam. "If any of ya'll see either one of these girls out prowling about when they ought not to be," she said to anyone within earshot, "I'd call it a great favor if you'd snatch them up by their drawers and bring them straight to me." Willard eyed Louisa as she said this. Madson's smile grew bigger. He nodded in agreement.

As if real twins, Anna Beth and Louisa thought in unison, *You couldn't catch me if you tried, so don't look so pleased at the possibility*. My girls had trouble written all over them.

Louisa stood there speechless for a few moments, in disbelief that fate had delivered her here. Then she shoved her hands deep inside her jeans pockets and wandered off to check out the greenhouses behind the shop, leaving Anna Beth to chit chat and lend a hand wiring white roses and spider mums for the wedding's candelabra sprays.

Madson stood behind his worktable studying Anna Beth. His hollow eyes twinkled, down deep inside somewhere, youthful mischief playing havoc with his duty to behave like an adult. He sucked his teeth, shaking his head like he knew something good to tell but had sworn not to divulge it. Finally, he fished around in his toolbox with hands as broad as bed slats, and joined Anna Beth at what would become her table. He presented her with a broken-in pair of wire cutters, a roll of green floral tape and a stem-striping knife.

"Well," he said, struggling not to smile, "since you girls are going to be around awhile, you might as well learn you something while you're here."

Anna Beth looked up at him weakly, accepting the odd gifts without a word. She remembered him so well, but it felt strange to see him now, after so many years. She tucked her head and busied herself wrapping stems with the green floral tape to keep her mind off of our wayward Louisa and the desperation we saw in Louisa's eyes.

Burning Love
Top 20 *Billboard* Hit Single

Just when I thought my link to Genevieve had been cut for eternity, God jerked me up by my wispiness and hurled me back to Memphis. I hated it when He did that. It was hard enough keeping up with everyone when they were in the same city, but zipping back and forth from Iuka to Memphis like a chipmunk on diet pills had the potential to give me vertigo.

She had crossed back into Tennessee four hours after dropping off the girls, after pissing and pilfering around on her way home, stopping at every junked-up antique shop along the way, in no hurry to begin life alone in the house she could never call home.

But amazingly, when the Memphis city limits sign whizzed passed the van's window, a metamorphosis took place. In that instant Genevieve ceased to be herself. The transformation took only seconds. A persona she'd almost forgotten settled in on her, softening her pinched face, relaxing her shoulders and easing her breath. By the time we pulled into her parking space in front of her flower shop—still named Flowers by Ned—Genevieve Clancy Hersh had been reborn. Moody Baxter was dead.

"People snap all the time," she said aloud to her dashboard Elvis altar in some kind of warped justification of her decision to send the girls away. "I should know; I've snapped more times than I deserve. Now, I have a chance to snap myself back into place."

She strutted into the shop, to the surprise of every employee.

"To what do we owe this unfortunate pleasure?" Mildred Minniver asked. She watched Genevieve out of the side of her face.

"Oh now, hush, Mildred. I'm here to work. It is my shop, you know. What's wrong with that? Have my roses to Elvis gone out yet today? They'd better not be late arriving. See to it, will you?"

Mildred just shook her head.

Genevieve hadn't gotten her apron on or her purse put away good when the tinkle of the bell over the front door made her look up. "I'll take care of this one," she said, heading back up front to help the customer, as if she did it all the time. Mildred let her go, shaking her head again.

Genevieve fluffed her hair and bit her lip for color as destiny in a three-piece, vested leisure suit strode past the houseplants and potted mums.

"I'd like a dozen roses—delivered," the man said. "How much will that be?"

Before reaching for his wallet, he slicked his hair back with his hand like Elvis always did. Genevieve almost swooned. Her neck warmed. She couldn't answer right away. She was trying on her new-old Genevieve smile, the one that used get her in trouble with the boys and stopped traffic on Iuka's main street when she was young. It had been so long since she'd worn it she'd forgotten how good it felt to have it on.

"That depends," she finally said in a husky whisper that almost startled her. She looked down for a second, then back up and directly into his eyes. "Are they for your wife, lover, mistress or girlfriend?" She batted her eyelashes like a strip joint slut, leaning so far over the counter she almost poked the poor man in the eye.

He leaned in too, propping his elbows on the counter. Before his smile completed its trek toward his ears, he whispered, "Lover," and winked a wink that a blind woman couldn't miss.

She touched her neck, fingered the little indention at the base of her throat. "With thorns or without?" she asked, taking a deep, chesty breath.

"They wouldn't be any fun without thorns, now would they?"

She rocked back on one leg, stretching her arms out to the counter for breathing room. Then she couldn't stand the distance and leaned in again. "Well, in that case, how much do you want them to be?"

He looked like a man who'd just handed over his gun.

Moody Baxter was dead, gone and buried. Genevieve Clancy Hersh was back in rare form and headed for heartbreak—again.

After the man left with his thorny bouquet, Genevieve grabbed her purse, threw kisses to Mildred, and dashed out the door. I wasn't

sure if she was going to stake out Jack Bland or Elvis. It didn't matter.
All I could think was: Lord, deliver me. Please!

*

Madson finished loading the rest of the wedding flowers into the
walk-in refrigerators on the far side of the workroom, and then pointed
Anna Beth in the direction of Louisa's hiding place.

"Yeah, she's found her a good place to fester," he whispered so
Willard wouldn't hear. "Just go straight through the first greenhouse
and out around back of the shed. Those big ol' trees out back called
her. They'll keep her company in her mourning. I'm sure of that."

Anna Beth followed his directions and found Louisa sitting statue-
still in the elderly rope swing suspended from the thick arm of an oak
tree.

"Whatcha doing?" Anna Beth asked as she rounded the tree.

Louisa jumped out of her mental solicitude. "How'd you find me?"
The rope groaned under her delicate weight. "Leave me alone. I'm
not coming in, and I'm certainly not staying here in the God-forsaken
boonies with an aunt I hardly know."

Anna Beth marched over to her, fisting her hips like Genevieve
always did, her long curls bouncing off her shoulders like Slinkys
tumbling down a flight of stairs. She was on the verge of oxidation;
swelled arteries coursed angry ropes of blood up her slender neck.
"Get over it, Louisa. We're here, so get used to it. And thank the
Good Lord it's not that Home for Unwed Mothers, where Moody
thinks we are. You got us into this mess, so live with it. Aunt Willard is
a saint compared to what we came from."

Louisa twisted her tether in tight circles, then let it spin itself out. It
wasn't until she finally stopped spinning that Anna Beth noticed the
tear stains on her cheeks. Crocodile tears wouldn't deter her from
this mission. She grabbed the swing and held the ropes so Louisa
couldn't twist away. "Louisa Marie Baxter, you listen to me and listen
good. Is there no sense in your head? Being here is gonna be a lot
better than with Moody. Don't you realize that? You got yourself into
one heck of a mess and brought me in with you, but Aunt Willard
seems willing to help us out, if you'd just let her try."

She forced Louisa's chin up and struggled to keep her own from quivering from both anger and upset. *What a tough little daisy mum she is.* Lord, she'd been that way since day one. She figured out the who's, why's and what for's of every situation, and then stood up strong for everyone else, but seldom considered standing up for herself. Looming over Louisa now, she sucked in her heartache and held it there, hoping it would make her stronger, make her last.

Louisa pushed through Anna Beth's arms and walked over to hug the tree. "You don't understand, Anna Beth. I can't live without him. And he doesn't even know about the baby, yet." She stared into space with the desperation of an addict. "I have to be with him. This is his child. He loves me and I love him." She kicked the dirt like a two-year-old. "Oh, what's the use? You can't understand."

"I understand more than you think, you ninny. I know, I know a lot. You're just so stuck, lollygagging around in fantasyland on your own personal cloud nine hundred, that you can't see what's going on. You don't listen. You don't have a clue."

"What do you mean? If you know something, spill it." Louisa wiped her nose on her sleeve and panic rose. She grabbed Anna Beth's arm. "What? What do you know?"

Anna Beth jerked away, "I heard the two of you at the lake. I was swimming that night under the dock."

At first, Louisa didn't get it. Her head cocked to one side like a basset hound. She didn't understand what dock or when, but her face slowly melded into a growl as her night of splintered sex under the stars rewound itself in her memory. Anna Beth still believe that Little Spec was the father, but Louisa didn't know that and thought Anna Beth had recognized Jack Bland.

Finally, Louisa's jaw clinched and she pinched Anna Beth so hard she howled. "Does Moody know?" Louisa shrieked. "Good God, did you tell her? Did you tell anyone?"

Anna Beth wondered why Louisa was so upset. Oh, why couldn't the women in this family tell the truth about anything? "No, no, but she's not stupid. Good grief, Louisa, I'm your sister. I love you. I want to help you. Can't you see that?"

Louisa sank onto the oak's feet.

"I won't tell. I promise," Anna Beth said. "I wouldn't ever, but the whole world isn't butt-dumb like you think. Everyone will figure it out. You've got to grow up. You know Moody. She'll see to it that you'll never be together. It doesn't matter who he is. She won't have it. She won't let the world know she had a daughter pregnant out of wedlock—period. End of subject. She'll die first. It's not in her plan. Don't you know that's why we're here?"

Anna Beth collapsed cross-legged in front of Louisa, took her hands and explained Genevieve to her sister-of-very-little-brain. "Moody's had our china patterns picked out for eons, our life all planned out. We'd marry proper, respectable society boys, and their families would deliver her out of middle-class working motherhood and into women's luncheons and garden clubs. She'd attend our children's recitals and riding lessons in Germantown. All that hotsy-totsy crap.

She was gonna sponge, Weesa. Sponge off you, off me, off our husbands and whoever else she could soak it up from. She had it all figured out, and the Bland family was her favorite mark—if you just could have waited. But you slipped around and screwed all that up for her. In a weird way, I'm kind of thankful. I won't have to worry about breaking away on my own now."

Louisa looked up with suddenly hopeful doe eyes. *Maybe it could still work out*, she was thinking. The clueless Ferris wheels set to spinning in her love-crazed head.

Anna Beth could read her as well as I. "No, stop it. Stop thinking," Anna Beth shouted, hoping to scare it out of her. "It won't work. Moody has already talked to Jack Bland. I overheard her on the phone talking to him. He swore to her upside down past Sunday that Little Spec is not the father of your child." She looked away and did not notice the look of relief on Louisa's face. She hated having to hurt Louisa like this, having to burst her pretty bubbles all at once. But she had to make her see the truth. Sometimes that is all you can do for folks who can't see the two-by-four before it breaks their nose. "Look, I know what I'm talking about. She's been yammering to somebody else for the last few days. Heck, it could have been Elvis for all I know. But after Jack Bland convinced her that Little Spec had nothing to do with you, she admitted that she didn't know who the father is— and that you're not telling. She said you'd ruined her hopes for the

Bland reunion she'd always dreamed about.

"'Reuniting the Blands and Hershs,' she called it. The way our families were supposed to be, in her mind, a wholesale/retail dynasty. You know she's so full of bull."

Yes, but it was Genevieve who wanted to be reunited, not for the girls to be. There was no way for Anna Beth to know about Genevieve's delusions.

Anna Beth could talk all she wanted, but Louisa didn't hear. She was lost somewhere off in love land, swimming in murky waters with her lover and their baby. Anna Beth knew, right then and there—and I had known for a long while—that we'd have to watch Louisa like a bird dog, keep track of her wandering mind and spirit, but especially the wandering of that body of hers.

*

Genevieve had never been good at being alone. Her flirting at the flower shop the day she returned from droppin g off the girls had renewed her sense of self and convinced her—again—that there was hope for her and Jack Bland. If she could just make him see that, he might remember the love they'd shared. They had talked on the phone more than usual lately, mostly about Louisa's "dilemma." His reassurances that Little Spec had had nothing to do with Louisa gave Genevieve great relief, and also gave her hope. With that encumbrance out of the way, Jack Bland might actually come back to her. He was just what she needed. He could help her with Louisa. They could be a family, just like Genevieve had always known they should be. Why could she never make him admit his true feelings for her?

A few days later, she drove to the wholesale house, hoping to catch him alone, but was told by the manager who was locking up that he had left hours ago. When she pulled onto his picturesque Chickasaw Gardens street, she was met by a line of fancy traffic, all inching toward the Bland's house, which was decked out with lights and finery for what appeared to be a grand society event. Orchestra music floated through late afternoon air as uniformed staff helped sequin-clad ladies from cars with glowed hands. Recognizing with a frown that Genevieve was not an invited guest or from the retail florist that had been commissioned for the event, another uniformed staff member motioned for her to "move along."

What a fool I am, she thought, as the house disappeared from view. *What a sad, sad fool I have always been.* It seemed that her obsession lived in the front seat of the Mid-South Fair's famous rollercoaster, *The Pippin,* cycling between heights of euphoria to depths of despair, and never knowing the peace of horizontal tracks.

Now, stretched out on her bed, she realized that she could stand not having the man she loved—she had managed on hope for almost fifteen years, after all—as long as the girls were around to keep her ghosts at bay. And, yes, she meant the real, dead, haunting kind—not me or something metaphorical.

She already missed the girls in the worst of ways. Where had she gone wrong? Better yet, where had she not gone wrong? With the girls away, the walls held their breath each night. The house echoed more. Night sounds hung around, making her jumpy, making her worry, making her wonder if the rattling skeleton of Grandpa Clancy was prowling around.

It was, of course, but I had no way of making him go away anymore than she did. She couldn't stand the darkness. It dredged up all kinds of nightmares, both imagined and those closely reminiscent of her youth.

I took the opportunity, since ghosts were on her mind and I was feeling sorry for her, to offer her a little comfort, however, my effort backfired. I accidentally kicked over her life-sized cardboard cut-out of Elvis, which fell face first into the bed with her. My tactic didn't get me the response I had hoped for. She grabbed him close to her for a hug and wept onto his lifeless chest.

I wished for a miracle, but would have settled for a very large pair of scissors to snip my spiritual umbilical cord. I pitied her, really I did, but her convoluted life exhausted me. I was over being ready to cut myself loose.

*

The carriage house moaned and lamented like an arthritic old woman, but after only a couple of weeks, Anna Beth had learned which noises came from age and which ones came from Louisa. I'm sure my screaming in her ear also helped to rouse her, although I could never be too sure. Her eyes shot open, and she felt for Louisa in the bed. She sat up, but Miss Preggers was gone.

"Weesa," she whispered to the darkness. "Don't do this to me, pleeeease." Throwing the quilt back, she stepped into her shoes as she pulled up her jeans. She stuck her legs through the opened window while still buttoning up her blouse. The cool night air raised pimples on her arms, and she prayed she wasn't allergic to bees.

She had hoped Willard's warning about the bees in the walls was just to scare them, to keep them from climbing onto the porch and sneaking out. Now, she realized that Aunt Willard had told the truth. The walls and floor hummed with vibrating life. She tiptoed across the warped floorboards, sweet honeycombs and their vengeful owners resting uneasily below her feet. Of course, I was never far behind.

The screen door squeaked when she pushed it open, but she breathed a little easier when it closed behind her without a sound. She started down the rickety outside steps, hanging onto the wobbling rail. A fig tree slapped her in the face on the way down, but she forgave it, hoping it had slapped Louisa, too. I smiled to myself. It had. I'd made sure of that.

"Knock some sense into her. That's what she needs," Anna Beth grumbled, jumping off the last step into moist grass. I agreed, I agreed.

Nothing but greenhouses stretched out in one direction, the old garage/stable in the other. *Where on earth is Louisa going,* she wondered. *Better yet, how's she gonna get there with no driver's license, no keys, no car?*

She headed in the direction of the stable and yelled softly toward the lean-to just as its bare bulb lit and answered her plea. She picked her way through a bed of faded Iris stalks and jumped a mud puddle. Her jeans hems got soaked. At the opening of the stable we found Louisa, standing on a stack of crates with one leg in the air and fighting to mount the bare back of an old nag who had no desire to be ridden— ever—especially at this ungodly hour.

I realized the need of my services. I grabbed that horse's attention and had him staring straight ahead, transfixed and not daring to look away. I managed this feat of genius by threatening to turn him into a bottle of glue. He believed I had the power to do it, I guess, shook his head and sputtered, stomped his feet a few times to hang onto his dignity, but he didn't move. That sucker was going nowhere.

"What do you think you're doing?" Anna Beth asked, blocking the gate in case Louisa actually managed to climb onto the beast.

I took care of that possibility. The horse snorted and reared his head. He stomped again and stepped sideways on cue. Louisa hit the dirt and came up cursing words Anna Beth didn't have the courage to say out loud.

"Damn it, I'm going to see him," Louisa griped, standing up. "He's up at the lake and I mean to tell him about his child, our child."

"Not that way, you're not," Anna Beth commanded. "Have you lost your ever lovin' mind? You're almost three months pregnant, and you've never ridden a horse in your whole life. You're not starting now."

The horse backed away a few steps, staring down his would-be rider as if making sure she didn't try anything else.

"I'm going. You can't stop me," Louisa said, brushing off her pajama pants. "I'll walk if I have to. I'll find a way. You just watch me."

Anna Beth shook her head and held up Willard's extra set of truck keys. "Come on, dummy. What else are sisters for?"

I could think of a lot of other things. Fourteen-year-olds driving without a license was not one of them, but no one ever listened to me.

Moments later, we climbed into the driver's seat of my mother's pick-up truck.

"I'm driving." Louisa snatched the keys from Anna Beth's hand, but her elation was premature. "Oh, no!" she exclaimed, defeated again. "It's a four-speed."

"What? Miss Know-It-All can't drive a stick shift?" Anna Beth moaned, not believing Louisa's unlimited list of incompetencies. "But you just said you could drive, Weesa. Good Lord, how were you gonna pull this off? You're worse than Moody. Didn't you even think to think ahead?"

She dragged Louisa over her into the passenger seat as she scooted in behind the wheel. She'd visited it often enough lately while helping Madson with flower deliveries. She just hoped his driving lessons on the dirt roads behind the greenhouses had taught her well.

"You can't drive either, you ninny," Louisa squealed.

"Oh? You don't think so? I haven't spent my days moping around, like someone I know. Madson is a great teacher, and I probably look every bit of twenty-one, give or take a day."

Oh, how children delude themselves. She was glad Madson had parked behind the greenhouses because there was no way to restrain the rumble of a Chevy—especially one with a hole in its muffler. "Just watch me," she said, grinning as we rolled slowly out of the back drive, headed toward Pickwick Lake and Louisa's rendezvous with Lover Boy.

Anna Beth was afraid to look over at Louisa as she drove for fear we might wreck and have more expensive things to explain when we got caught. But it was hard to keep her eyes on the road with Louisa bouncing to the Bunny Hop and the Slide at the same time as she hooted and hollered like a two-year-old on her first bike ride, dancing in her seat to no music with the wind blowing her mile-long hair smack-dab into Anna Beth's face.

I was a nervous wreck, to say the least. Keeping them from mounting a horse was one thing—or actually two things, I guess—but driving off the road was another thing all together. If I had had sweat glands, I would have been dripping rock salt.

"Calm down," Anna Beth warned. She squinted into darkness blacker than even I imagined a night could dish out. The dim headlights did little to help. "Look for the turn off. I don't want to miss it and have to find a place to turn back."

Louisa tossed herself about like a wild cat. "No, no," she squealed, "Keep going. We're meeting him up on Goat Island. He's coming by boat."

Anna Beth's foot compressed the brake with such force Louisa slid into the floorboard. She couldn't believe Louisa had planned it all ahead of time. She thought they were just taking the off chance that Little Spec, the boy she suspected was the father, would be at his daddy's cabin for the weekend and that they'd be able to rouse him somehow without waking up the whole house.

"Goat Island! You conniving little so-and-so." Anna Beth screeched so shrill Louisa's teeth vibrated. "And what, pray tell, do we do if the water's up? I'm not about to wade up to my butt in pond scum to get you over to that tiny patch of land. And I'm not gonna swim it either, not at this time of night and with you acting like you've been smoking dope." She threw the truck into first and started down the road again, grumbling.

Louisa shoved her shoulder. "You worry too much, Anna Beth. Just get me there and my whole life will be complete, everything will be right with the world."

Anna Beth would have rolled her eyes, but with loose steering, she was afraid she'd lose control and end up in a ditch, smart girl. It warmed my heart when she whispered a little prayer that whoever the presence was that hung around them all the time was riding shotgun. She needn't have worried, but I will admit, we needed all the help we could get. Even if I had to make a deal with Lucifer, I wouldn't let my girls wreck the truck.

We drove along going thirty for a few minutes, until Anna Beth collected herself enough to ask, "So, how are you gonna tell him?" Silence answered. "Just gonna tell him flat out, I suppose? 'Oh, Little Spec darlin', I'm preggers, so marry me please and save me from myself.'" She over-dramatized her wording, even without the use of her hands as swooning props.

Louisa stopped bouncing abruptly and sat very still, staring at the side of Anna Beth's head like she hadn't heard her right.

"Or will you call him Spec-tor, like you did at the lake?" Anna Beth went on. "I thought I'd choke. Where'd you come up with that one? I wanted to laugh out loud. I almost drowned right then and there." She stopped talking long enough to realize that Louisa wasn't in a joking mood all of the sudden. She looked over a couple of times. It wasn't like Louisa to lose her steam so fast. Could it be something she'd said? She figured she had just surprised Louisa by calling Little Spec by name. It had become kind of a game with them—not attaching a name to the father of Louisa's child. Kind of like not naming the dead, I suppose. But, for the first time, Anna Beth also realized that she might be wrong about the identity of the father.

Louisa finally settled back into the passenger seat, pouting. "Why do you say it like that? You make it all sound so tacky, like I'm some pitiful little girl and just need him to rescue me. Like we don't even love each other and we'd only be together because the baby forced us to be."

Anna Beth should have known better than to joke about something as serious as Louisa's version of true love. "I'm sorry," she said, trying to mean it. "I know you love him, but I just hope he's not leading you down a path of daisies like Moody says every man she knows has ever done."

"He's not like that. He wouldn't do that to me." Louisa crossed her arms over her ever-fuller breasts. "We love each other. We'll work it out somehow. I'm certain of that. The way he looks at me, the way he touches me. I know it's real, Anna Beth. We were destined to be together. You'll see."

Anna Beth hoped she was right, but not in the way Louisa was counting on. If rich people were anything close to how Moody described them, she thought, the ignorant Louisa would be birthing and raising her unfortunate baby alone. Still, Anna Beth couldn't help but think that if Jack Bland, the man she still assumed was the soon-to-be grandfather, ever found out about his son's philandering and Louisa's plight, he would do something to make it right.

She hoped he wouldn't put a barrel of buckshot to his son's head— or any other part of his anatomy—and threaten to blow it off if he didn't take responsibility and marry Louisa to give a proper name to the child.

*

Quiet draped the breakfast table like a funeral shroud. Earlier, Anna Beth had wondered if she had underestimated Willard when she wasn't standing in the driveway, waiting for us when we pulled in around four a.m. Anna Beth and Louisa had sneaked back into their room through the window, piled back into bed and acted sleep-dazed when Willard came to wake them up at five-thirty a.m. Now, in spite of the mournful silence, breakfast with Willard and Madson in the dining room had stuck to its normal routine. If the townspeople could see Madson at our table like this, they'd shun us at the very least and probably burn the house down, at worst.

Everyone munched through the meal, looking up from their plates rarely, only long enough to ask for the pepper to be passed, before resuming a silence so thick you could stir it with a spoon. Willard read the newspaper while Madson served up eggs over-easy, homemade angel biscuits, sausage, fig preserves and, of course, fresh honey on the side. Oh, what I would have given to have taste buds.

Maybe Willard and Madson are as dumb as the rest of my family, Anna Beth thought.

No, I wanted to tell her, *they are the only two, besides you and me, with any lick of sense in their heads.* She didn't realize that last night's escapade had been discovered until she helped Madson clear the dishes. He cornered her in the pantry.

"I just thought you should know that we know about your little trip last night." His husky whisper caressed the air like a velvet warning as he handed her a canister of flour to put up, but his expression was as serious as a wide-eyed corpse at a Requiem Mass. "I had to tie Willard to the bedpost last night to keep her from runnin' out in the dark after ya'll. But, God love her, she knew she had to let you girls go on and get it told."

Anna Beth backed up against the pantry shelves. She was a bad liar. Always had been. Now, she was caught with nowhere to run. "I just did the driving, promise, honest," she admitted, thinking death would come soon enough. "I couldn't let her go out there alone, being as stupid as she gets sometimes. And in her condition . . . I had no other choice, Madson. I was looking after her, that's all."

A tan-toothed smile played across Madson's face as he squeezed her shoulders with hands the size of waffle irons. "Aren't you just the little momma, now? Fussin' over your sister like your Moody Momma should have done all these years." He leaned back against the canned goods. "We're just praying that that boy'll do the right thing, be responsible for what he's done and be a man about it." He paused, staring her down like he wanted facts.

Sure, Madson had always been a part of the family, but she wondered for the first time who this man was exactly. Why, he seemed to always be with us, from breakfast till lights out and every moment in between. Madson's constant presence and intimate knowledge of our family's goings-on made her question how he had achieved that status, how a middle-aged black man could fit so neatly into Willard's home life, business life and middle-of-the-night life while we were out gallivanting around.

She rearranged the spices, biding her time and wondering just how much she should tell. She hadn't actually heard what Louisa said to Little Spec. After all of her much needed assistance, Louisa had made her wait in the truck while she wandered out onto Goat Island to talk with him alone. Louisa was gone for over an hour though, so she had plenty of time to tell him about the baby and work things out. But Anna Beth was a little shy on the facts.

Louisa's secrecy made Anna Beth doubt even more that Little Spec was the real father. There was just something about the way Louisa acted on the trip back home that made her rethink her assumptions. I had a lot to do with those doubts, of course. She couldn't ponder the possibilities too long now, though. Madson wanted something concrete to tell Willard, something to offer her a brighter end to this predicament than the one they faced now.

"Louisa seemed a little more chipper on the way back," Anna Beth said finally, without turning around. "Not as sad and depressed as she's been. That must mean something good. But that's all I know, Madson—honest." His breath warmed her collar. She knew he wanted more. She turned and gazed up into kind eyes. "She's secretive, like Moody—hard to read, ya know? But she told him. She would've told me if she hadn't. I'm sure of that."

A hint of rust darkened the whites of his eyes, adding warmth to his otherwise chiseled face. He squeezed her shoulders again. "It'll be all right," he said. "All we have to do now is wait and see. A few prayers won't hurt either, I don't suppose." He handed her a few more items to put up and she busied herself with them until she felt his presence leave her. When she turned, he had retreated back into the kitchen to scrub the sausage skillet and put up the eggs.

Louisa was just coming back out of the bedroom from getting dressed when Anna Beth reentered the dining room. Willard still sat at the head of the table, fingering her rosary beads and whispering prayers. Madson shadowed Anna Beth. She sank into her chair, ready for World War III to begin, and he rested his hands on its back. Finally, Willard looked over—first at him, then at Anna Beth. Willard's lips turned up weakly. Then, as sweet and understanding as can be, she gave Anna Beth a sad wink.

"You girls—Louisa, come on over here and sit for a minute," Willard said softly. She patted the table beside her. "We need to have a little chat."

Louisa's blood abandoned her face as she eased herself down into the chair farthest away, stiffly ready and as defensive as a linebacker.

Anna Beth thought, *Oh no, this is trouble. I can feel it on my shoulders.*

I just smiled and settled in for the show. Lord, my mother was good.

"Your momma called last night," Willard began.

Louisa almost collapsed onto the table from relief, thinking that maybe they hadn't gotten caught after all. Her body postures reminded me so much of Genevieve's when she had sat in Mother Superior's office that cold winter morning over fourteen years ago. Louisa's mind had already raced to the edge of reason and shuffled through excuses so lame they wouldn't get an innocent man out of jail, only to realize in that remarkable instant that she might not need any of them.

"She knows that ya'll are here instead of at the 'home,' and she's not a happy camper—not a happy camper at all."

"Is she coming to take us back to Memphis?" Anna Beth asked, in a voice etched with worry. Then, she clarified, "I mean, we like it here just fine . . . better than . . . well, maybe not better than, but well, uh, you know . . . It would be nice to see her, though. She hasn't come to visit and she *is* our mother. Maybe we should . . . " Poor dear, she felt torn between liking the stability of Willard's and the guilt that gnawed at her for not wanting Genevieve too close at hand.

"It's okay, dear, I understand, but no, not exactly. She's not coming here. Best I could figure out, she's up in Nashville, camped out on the sidewalk outside Elvis' recording studio. Been there over a week, or at least that's what she said. What a way to waste a perfectly good life. Although, she could have been calling from a jailhouse somewhere, but I doubt she'd use up her one phone call to call here. She knows I'd never bail her out. What in our Savior's name has gotten into her? I surely don't know. I guess we'll just hold out and see how long it takes her to bust a gut. You know how she lets things fester until she's ready to self-combust. I'm sure, when her rock star is off on some ten-city tour, she'll have time to get all riled with me. Or when her money-man takes a hike. Of course, he and Elvis could be one in the same, for all I know."

Willard stopped herself suddenly, her hand covering her mouth with embarrassment, and realized that she shouldn't be saying these things to the girls, and that she was on the verge of becoming a gossip. She shook her head and stared at her rosary. "Fact is—I didn't do what she wanted. I'm sure she's peeved to no end and will make me pay in spades. We'll just worry about that when Elvis' Vegas escapades hit the fan, if you know what I mean."

She dropped her rosary into its little lace pouch. "But for now, you girls need your lessons. It's time for you to be back in school." The girls blanched. Scowls accompanied their groans. "I've decided—you start today. My good friend, Reverend Mother, has agreed to tutor you both." Louisa's head fell—kerplunk—onto the table. "And I expect you to study hard for this saintly woman, learn all you can from her, because you're both gonna need it, no matter what you might think now."

Madson still stood behind Anna Beth. His fingers touched her shoulder in a strangely comforting way.

"So, where is this school?" Louisa finally asked without looking up, as she rolled her forehead back and forth across the mahogany tabletop. "Or is it a convent? Moody said something about a convent somewhere close by." She strained to lift her head and rested it in her palms.

Willard didn't answer for a moment. The lines in her forehead wrinkled with puzzlement, as if Louisa's question was the dumbest thing she'd ever heard. "Why, yes, there was a convent that Genevieve knew about, but the Sisters have moved from that place. They now rent the big house, the one across the driveway. I realize that you couldn't have seen any of the Sisters around, them being cloistered and all, but I assumed that you had seen the Reverend Mother coming and going. She doesn't get out much, but she leaves the property once a week or so to pick up their supplies and groceries and such."

Anna Beth and Louisa gawked at Willard like they'd been slapped with a wet dishrag. They couldn't believe it. Nuns right there under their noses? How could that be? They'd been all over the property, explored every hiding place, shed and greenhouse for the past few weeks and they had never seen a movement, heard a whisper, prayer or cough from the house just twenty yards outside the carriage house front door. They had seen an old black car parked on the far side of the house, but figured some elderly couple rented the house since no one ever seemed to come and go from the place. And they had been a bit distracted, with all of Louisa's drama and Madson keeping them busy working in the shop.

"You've got to be kidding," Louisa finally whooped, slamming her hands down on the table. "Nuns rent that house from you? Well, ain't that just the cat's pajamas? Where are they? Where do they hide themselves?"

"I have seen packages on the front porch a few times," Anna Beth said, searching her memory for any hints she had missed. "And there were some flowers left by the door, too. I just figured the old couple couldn't make it to the door."

"I still don't believe it," Louisa said.

Willard scooted back in her chair, uncomfortably affronted. She reached inside her shirt collar and readjusted her bra strap, then folded her fingers around her rosary pouch. "Well, like I said, they don't get out much," she explained in a mild huff. "They're a small sect, living a consecrated life. They pray mostly. Reverend Mother is the only one who can speak freely, as a matter of fact. The others took a vow of silence, you know. She handles all their business interests, takes care of their other necessities. She's a dear, dear woman. I've known her since, since . . . "

Mist flooded the corners of my mother's eyes. She glanced up at Madson for support and clamped her jaws shut, forcing the words and emotions to stay put. She couldn't go back in time and explain how she knew the nuns, how dear they were to her, how much she relied on their support of her decisions in life, of their prayers and friendship. She got real still and glanced around the room like she wanted to escape. Finally she almost stuttered, "Well uh, I've known her a long time, a long, long time. I'm surprised that you haven't at least seen her around."

The girls were both still shaking their heads, unwilling to consider the possibility that they'd missed something as unusual as black habits moving about in that old Victorian house. They had wondered about the inhabitants, but since Willard had seemed so frightened of the place on their first day home, they had steered clear. It was true that the gloomy façade of the house conjured up scenes from *Psycho* and *Rosemary's Baby* in their overactive imaginations and dreams—especially Louisa's. They remembered, too, Genevieve's warnings when they were little girls about being blown to Kingdom Come by some ghosts and how Grandpa Clancy roamed about. But nuns? Right there across the driveway? It seemed impossible that they could have missed such a thing. It made them wonder what else they had missed.

Anna Beth turned sharply to face Madson. Unasked questions popped into her head faster than she could put them into words. "And you still live over there in the basement like you did when we were little," she said, pointing her finger. "You still live there. *Under* the nuns?" Her words trailed off as the second twin bed in Willard's bedroom came to mind.

Madson took a step backward and craned his neck. "Why Lordy girl, sure I do. I've lived there my whole life and plan to die there, if you don't mind. Thank you very much."

She leaned over the back of her chair, resting her arms on its spine for support and to keep herself from falling out in the floor. Madson nodded, smiling one of the best 'I'll-be-damned' smiles I'd ever seen. She collapsed back against the table. "Well, I'll be a monkey's uncle. I feel like you've just blasted me off to the *Twilight Zone*."

"I'm right there with ya," Louisa said, rolling her head back and forth against the back of her chair.

Madson shook his head and grinned so big it crinkled up his eyes and plumped his hazelnut cheeks. He turned toward the kitchen, but didn't leave. Leaning on the doorjamb to support his laughter, he buckled at the waist and said, "You girls are worse than your mamma. You've got some kind of imagination and some kind of way of not seeing things that are right under your nose."

One Broken Heart For Sale
Top 20 *Billboard* Hit Single

Louisa and Anna Beth stood on the front porch of the big house that once could have summoned up visions of genteel ladies in taffeta gowns—that is if they hadn't known its history and hadn't been as nervous as cockroaches in daylight. They looked at each other and swallowed hard. Anna Beth rang the bell and held her breath. She fidgeted and glanced over her shoulder with the strangest feeling that someone was skipping up and down the porch behind them like they used to do when they were kids.

She remembered taking swan dives off the porch and swooping down to land delicately beside the now faded pink lawn torpedo. She could almost feel herself doing that now, arms stretched wide, or walking the lawn torpedo like a balance beam. Her arms felt weightless, as if extended in an arabesque, a pirouette, a back-flip dismount. The sensation made her dizzy and a little giddy.

"What's with you," Louisa asked, staring at her like she'd done something stupid. But before Anna Beth could reply, the empty swing that Genevieve used to sit in moved, drawing the girls' attention to the far end of the porch. It swayed back and forth like someone had pushed it lazily with a foot.

The girls looked, startled by the sudden motion, but saw no one. I danced my fingers up their arms, just funning with them. Louisa turned a kind of pasty white and squeezed Anna Beth's hand, who then smiled and relaxed a bit, knowing I was there, watchful, always watchful.

They didn't hear the footsteps approach from inside the house, and jumped when the front door creaked open. A woman dressed from head to toe in matte black stepped back to let us in. She never met their eyes or uttered a word, gazing downward instead, and didn't seem to sense my presence either. Reluctantly, the girls stepped inside, but not before Louisa took one last look at the swing—now perfectly still.

The woman led them down the long central hallway toward the back of the house; her heavy shoes echoed on the hardwoods. Airborn dust floated like magic snowflakes through the front rooms and out into the hall. Light from the front windows sprinkled the motes with the iridescence of fairy dust. Anna Beth closed her eyes as we walked through it, as if it held some kind of magic that could save her, and wondering all the while how many nuns lived there. She still couldn't believe a group of them lived within yelling distance.

She gazed up at the tall staircase as we passed under it. Familiarity stroked her memory like the touch of an old friend. All evidence of Genevieve's Elvis obsession was gone, replaced by walls adorned simply with artwork representing a more reverent kind of worship. Anna Beth had never understood why Louisa and Genevieve were affected so adversely by the place. Still, she glanced into each barren room as we shuffled past, checking for signs of life—or death.

The silent woman pushed open the door to the kitchen and stepped back. Anna Beth turned to thank her, but she had vanished, disappeared into the ancient structure. The kitchen now brimmed with bookshelves laden with Bibles, pamphlets and bottles of holy water, Mason jars full of peaches, tomatoes, pickles and okra stacked high. There was enough canned food to feed the Confederate army stationed at Shiloh before the 1862 siege.

In some ways the room reminded Anna Beth of an Italian pizzeria, minus the red-checkered curtains and tablecloths. Twenty-pound bags of flour and sugar almost blocked the back doorway. Huge cookie sheets, piled even higher, were stacked on top of the flour sacks. A deep sink and three wide-mouthed ovens lined the far wall as monster cans of pure virgin olive oil—what other kind would a nun have?— stood sentry upon heavy wooden shelves above. Anna Beth pulled Louisa two more steps into the room. A strong twinge of vanilla, mixed with mildewed lace and rat bait, mingled together in the air.

And there she was, the woman who was present at all of our births, the woman who had prayed for guidance about what to do with my sister and received Genevieve as her answer. She truly believed that Genevieve was God's divine plan. I still didn't understand it, but God kept trying to teach me that some things were out of my

control. Now, I was so glad to see her. Her dark form on the far side
of the room hummed softly in front of the sink. Yards of black fabric
fell from hunched shoulders. White triangles were folded across her
back, revealing her veil's underside. The whiteness stood in sharp
contrast against the black of her robe. Louisa cleared her throat to get
the Sister's attention, but when the woman turned the girls stepped
back, grabbing each other's hands and struggling not to wince.

Sister Mary Howard, a.k.a. the Mother Superior who helped
bring my sister into the world and ushered me into death, had the face
of a fright-night goblin, zit-scarred and reddened around the nose,
chin and cheeks. So ugly to most, but beautiful to me. Errant hairs,
long, black and curling, popped forth from large pores, most likely
swollen from adolescent pimple popping. The largest, blackest mole
they had ever seen protruded from her wrinkled forehead. It rested
precariously on the frames of her oversized spectacles, almost dangling
off her left eyebrow. Pity shivers pulsed up Anna Beth's arms. She
prayed to the Blessed Mother for help to keep a pleasant face.

The now middle-aged Sister moved closer to them and Louisa's
clamp on Anna Beth's hand gritted Anna Beth's teeth. "Hello Sister,"
Anna Beth said, forcing her lips open through the pain. She looked
down and away, anywhere but at the woman's face. "I am Anna Beth
and this is my sister, Louisa. Our Aunt Willard sent us for torturing, um
uh, I mean tutoring, but if you're too busy, we could come back later
or some other day." Louisa started to move toward the door for a
quick escape, but Anna Beth held her in place.

Reverend Mother's white-fronted shroud was close enough to
touch. Anna Beth's eyes darted about, not wanting to revisit the
woman's multiple deformities, but Sister reached out and touched her
shoulder. Morning light from the window glanced off the crucifix hanging
around the woman's neck. Anna Beth forced herself to look up.

"Your aunt has told me so much about you both." Kind eyes,
bluer than a robin's egg, peered out through magnifying-glass lenses.
Sister's thin lips drew up into a pink satin bow of a smile. "I'm so glad
to see you both . . . again. Oh, it has been so long, so very, very long.
Welcome. Please, please, come in and sit down." Her voice fondled
the air.

Anna Beth jiggled restlessly. She needed to talk to fill the still air with something besides her shock and confusion. She wondered when and where they had met before. Surely, she would have remembered this woman. Who could ever forget that face? She wondered, too, how someone so unsightly could seem so angelic close up? She shuffled across the room, dragging Louisa behind her.

"What's all the flour for?" she asked, struggling to think of something to say. She pulled a chair from under the mile-long table at the room's heart. "Dar-nation, er, uh, I've never seen so much cooking stuff in one place. I mean, Jesus, oh, sorry, I mean, uh, gosh, or uh, golly. You've got enough canned stuff crammed in here to feed the hungry, but then, that's what you do—feed the hungry, the poor people, I mean. Nuns do that. You help others, charity, or charitable stuff . . . "

Reverend Mother waited for Anna Beth's nervous jabbering to relax, smiling that luminous smile the whole time. When Anna Beth finally came up for air, Sister said, "We make Scottish shortbread, and we ship it all over the world to raise money for our cause."

"What cause?" Louisa mumbled, drumming her fingers on the table and looking everywhere, except at Sister's face.

"Why, prayer, of course. That's what the Good Lord called us to do. We pray night and day, every day, for all those who need the extra assistance—living and dead—or those who cannot pray for themselves." She let her words sink in for a moment, then said, "But today and for the next few months it is my pleasure to instruct you fine young women in your studies. Shall we get to work?"

Anna Beth opened the only spiral notebook she'd brought with her from home, but she could hardly keep her eyes off Sister's face. She had learned in their religion classes at school in Memphis that God gives everyone something special, something original that only they can claim, something only they can do. She had always hoped that was true, even though she had yet to figure out what her own special gift happened to be. Well, God gave the Reverend Mother peacefulness, a calming effervescence that obliterated all efforts to find fault with her looks. It radiated from her like an eternal flame, fueled by the serene voice of Saint Gabriel himself.

Sitting in the cold isolation of that kitchen, Anna Beth got from this blessed woman exactly what I had hoped she would gain. She suddenly felt whole. She felt loved. It took only seconds for Sister's disfigurements to fade. They dissolved from frightful to holy, into the unique look of serenity only Reverend Mother could carry off. Anna Beth realized for the first time what she wanted from life. She wanted that look, that peace. She doubted, however, that she would ever get it.

I also had a revelation that day. I recognized that I, too, wanted assurance of my special gifts. Despite my unique perspective, despite my beyond life abilities, I owned all the doubts and needs and insecurities these humans felt so deeply. I wanted to know the why, the how and the purpose of my existence. And I wanted to know it all on my terms, to call the shots, to have some lasting and recognizable effect on the things that escaped my control. But what I wanted more than anything was to live. With life I could have all the rest. With life, my death would make sense. And, like Anna Beth, I doubted my hopes would ever be realized.

*

There is nothing quite like the scent of a gardenia or the petal-softness of an old English rose. Is it any wonder people give gifts of fragrant blooms to celebrate their happiest occasions like births, weddings and holidays, or that they veil their tragedies with flowers, sending loved ones off to the hereafter in fine style? My great-grandmother's flower shop, *Livvie's Heavenly Bouquet*, had taken this job seriously for three generations, presenting its customers with the very best for all occasions, cheerful or somber alike.

Each year, Christmas was the main event. A good Christmas in the flower business means surviving another year to do it all again.

As the girls tended the waves of potted poinsettias that covered the greenhouse floor one afternoon in early December, promises of the blessed season, new life, peace, hope and good will drew carol hums from our tone-deaf Louisa. Anna Beth couldn't believe it, or keep herself from joining in. It was good to see Louisa happy and hopeful for once. The Bland-Hersh truck from Memphis backed up to the delivery door like it always did. Right on time, eleven a.m., three days a week, and Louisa's hums sprouted into full-bloom melodies.

"No shortness of spirit around here, I see," the driver commented between her choruses of *Jingle Bells*.

"Yep, life is wonderful, ain't it?" Louisa said.

Anna Beth almost dropped a thirty-pound box of floral wire on her foot, astonished by Louisa's sudden mood swing. The three of them unloaded the truck. They hauled out boxes of long-stem roses from South America; cymbidium and phaleonopsis orchids from Hawaii; red, white and peppermint carnations; Christmas greens and supplies that Willard had ordered for the pre-Christmas rush. When they'd emptied the truck bed, Louisa pulled up a flat cart full of poinsettias to fill the order Bland-Hersh had ordered from them.

"Here, let me help you with that," the man said, and lifted a huge tray off the dolly. He slid it into the truck bed, then jumped up to join it, pushing it as far back as he could. "You shouldn't be doing all this heavy work in your condition."

"No, I'm fine. Really," Louisa said. She leaned down to lift the next tray up to him so he wouldn't have to jump down off the truck. Anna Beth rushed over to help. She shot Louisa one of Willard's 'Behave yourself' looks. She'd memorized that look. Willard had used it a lot lately in regards to Louisa's devotion to breaking house rules.

Today, Louisa's mood was better than it had been for months, probably because we'd sneaked out for yet another meeting with Louisa's unwilling-to-commit lover. She was well into her seventh month of pregnancy and usually disgruntled. With good reason, I supposed. In all practical ways, her pregnancy had been an easy one from the get-go, except to hear her tell it.

She had complained *ad infinitum* of pains in odd places, nasty indigestion, swelling and seepage since we arrived at Willard's in late July. The doctor always reassured her and gave her a clean bill of pregnant health at every monthly appointment.

Anna Beth and I had done our best to put up with it all. As a last resort, after listening dutifully to Louisa's moaning for longer than most could tolerate, our only choice was to nod when appropriate and ignore. Anna Beth thought it was high time the father 'fessed up and claimed responsibility for their child, however, her suspicions about Jack Bland being that man had intensified, so she also wasn't surprised that he hadn't. Louisa, on the other hand, seemed immune to her predicament, unaffected by the certain and impending husbandless motherhood that waited just a couple of months down the road.

They finished loading everything into the truck and the driver settled up with Aunt Willard in the shop. Louisa scurried up to the truck cab just as the driver was pulling out. She stepped up onto the running board, tapping on the window, and fumbled in the deep pocket of her green apron. She palmed an envelope hidden there, and while looking over her shoulder, handed it to the man. They exchanged a few words that Anna Beth couldn't overhear. Then, smiling, Louisa jumped down and waved good-bye like he was some long-lost friend.

"What did you give him?" Anna Beth demanded, with her hands poised once again on her hips. "And what put you in such a good humor today?"

Louisa smoothed her apron over her big belly. "He's a delivery man, isn't he? I just asked him to make a delivery. That's all." With an uncharacteristic lilt in her step, she paraded back into the greenhouse to hum carols again like a merry housewife.

Anna Beth stood there for a moment, then plodded back into the greenhouse, realizing again that she would never understand Louisa. She was glad that she and Aunt Willard had worked so hard on the nursery and getting everything ready for the baby's arrival. It was obvious that Louisa would forever live in dreamland.

*

The next day it rained, and the day after that, and the day after that. That cold, icy kind of rain that chills to the marrow and makes folks glad they live in the South, where it happens not too often. The shop was always closed to customers and employees on Tuesdays, but it never closed for the girls. There was work to be done, Willard's cure-all of anything that ails you. That morning Willard and Madson left separately before dawn to make deliveries.

They put Louisa and Anna Beth in charge of filling the centerpiece orders marked for delivery the next day. They had both become adept at floral design, not necessarily from inbred talent, but by osmosis and proximity.

Anna Beth could read the signs, the signs of good fortune as well as the signs of trouble. I guess my ethereal tutelage did get through to her sometimes. At about noon, she went upstairs to fix lunch. I had been sending her vibes all morning, trying to warn her, but this morning her spirit antenna must have shorted out. She seemed oblivious to any presence, still upset and ruminating on the screaming fit Willard and Louisa had had the night before.

Willard was fed up with Louisa's catting-about late at night to meet up with 'the father of that baby,' But felt helpless to stop it. She still assumed the father was Little Spec and had done her best to reason with Genevieve about how to handle the situation. She had also talked to Jack Bland, who denied everything having to do with his son, without making any headway. Since no one else seemed concerned about Louisa, Willard had decided to take care of things herself, by preparing for the new arrival and praying constantly for direction and grace.

Anna Beth was fed up, too. She did her best to buffer and defend Louisa, but the stress was getting to her. And Louisa seemed to not care about anyone but herself.

Anna Beth was on the steps coming back down with lunch when she heard Louisa's calls. The yells sounded more tired than urgent, but Anna Beth dropped the tray anyway, covering the stairway with tuna fish salad and potato chips as she took flight.

"Help me, help."

She rounded the corner into the shop and searched the worktables for sight of Louisa before realizing that the walk-in refrigerator muffled the howls. The huge door stood open with its long sheets of heavy plastic hanging to the floor to hold in the chilled air. Heart pulsing in her throat, she burst through the translucent shield, looking about, eyes wild with panic. "Weesa?" A pink liquid trail led her past metal buckets overflowing with roses the color of blood. And there, sprawled on the floor, holding her stomach, Louisa lay on the damp floor behind peppermint carnations and baby's breath.

"I can't get up," she whispered, not looking up. "Something's wrong. Help . . . please." She struggled to pull herself up, but couldn't. She leaned against the wooden bleachers overflowing with crushed garlands and upended floral sprays, holding her red-blotched dress high between the legs.

The shop had never felt so empty, the big house never so far away. "Don't move. I'll get Sister." Anna Beth said, and bolted. She paused just long enough to dial "O" on the telephone, stretching the long cord with her as she kept moving toward the front door.

"Operator, send help. *Livvie's Heavenly Bouquet* . . . the old Clancy place . . . off Highway 25 . . . need an ambulance . . . Dr. Crowder . . . Hurry, hurry, please."

Rain pelted her as she raced across the driveway, screaming. The mud and water felt surprisingly warm. She bounded the pickets and the lawn torpedo. Dormant azaleas cushioned her fall. She exploded through the front door of the main house, panting. A black-and-white flock of nuns met her in the entry hall, alerted by her screams, and they scurried across the yard, habits fluttering like startled birds as dark clouds rumbled overhead.

"Let's get her out of this cold," Reverend Mother commanded when they burst into the refrigerator. She stood over a semi-conscious and moaning Louisa. Anna Beth pleaded again into the phone for help as the bevy of saintly penguins surrounded Louisa and eased her into the workroom, where she lay in a sea of crushed Christmas greens.

"Ambulance is on its w-way," Anna Beth stammered, struggling to catch her breath.

Louisa's disheveled clothes dripped crimson. Her hair was strewn about her like tangled tentacles of a monster squid. Anna Beth rounded Sister to see what had transfixed her between Louisa's legs, and her eyes widened at the sheer volume of congealed blood. She thought she might vomit, but swallowed hard, willing herself to be strong.

"My baby, my baby. " Louisa's pleas washed away from her in a tide of unconsciousness as her eyes closed, and she drifted into the silent prayers of her guardian penguins.

"Do something," Anna Beth begged. "Do something, please!"

Sister gave orders like she knew what she was doing, and her silent assistants worked feverishly as Anna Beth stood frozen in a soundless vacuum. We watched as the tiny body left its mother, oozed out with a giant gush, but no living breath. Sister snatched the child up by its ankles much like she had done with me so many years ago and manhandled the slippery bundle, fighting to pound life into it, breathe breath into it, willing it to live. I screamed and wept. *Don't let this happen. Please, Lord, let it live*! But I got no response.

I nudged in close to Anna Beth and grasped her hand. She felt me as surely as if I owned flesh. I wanted to do something more, but couldn't. Then, a stirring motion caught our attention. We both watched it develop, a glow, a calm. Our eyes drifted upward, in awe, as our little niece's spirit left its body, ascending, lifting, swirling happily into the Light that only we seemed able to see.

Oh, this is what it should have been like for me, I thought. Anna Beth wasn't sure if it was real or imagined, if her mind had concocted this spectacle because it was what she wanted to believe. I wondered, too. Why? If this is what happens when you die, why hadn't I done the same? As if our minds melded into one, we both longed to join this child, to follow her to heaven, or wherever she was headed.

Neither of us had any assurance of our purpose—in her life, in my death. Why couldn't we just tag along and be done with it? Anna Beth could be free of her chaotic childhood. I could relinquish my guilt for not being able to do more. She trembled. Tears soaked her shirt. She glanced around at the others. They all stood there, staring down at the lifeless child, stricken with sorrow, helpless to do anything but pray. Only Anna Beth seemed to know there was nothing else to fear. The child was safe now. Her purpose was fulfilled. A door of Light opened above her, and the tiny spirit's tether drew her in to a realm that I had only visited in my dreams.

The nun closest to Sister gathered up her apron, but with her veil, bib and coif to reckon with, she was unable to get it off and over her head. She offered the tail end of the lily fabric as swaddling to Sister, who accepted the linen with silent reverence and gently wrapped it around the lifeless body of the child.

Turning, she then placed the tiny parcel into Anna Beth's arms, who clutched our niece to her breast and wept, both now joined to the nun by a linen umbilicus. The woman herded them back into the refrigerator tomb to get them out of the way, and flooded eyes muddled our view as ambulance attendants swarmed into the shop and whisked Louisa away. Anna Beth wasn't sure what happened next, how Sister and the attendants saved Louisa or when it was that Willard and Madson arrived and crumbled at the news of our loss. But there, perched on a frozen bleacher, Anna Beth stroked the dead child's face, drew circles with her finger around the relaxed lids of unseeing eyes, kissed limp fingers, so tiny, so frail, each one perfect, each one still.

"What song should I sing to her?" she asked me. Did choirs of angels already herald this child? "*Jesus Loves Me?*" she asked. "But does He, really? Does He love you, little one? Does He love you, Olivia? Or me?"

Yes, she said my name. After so much time loving her, she finally knew me for who I am. She buried her face in soft linen, and her tears washed our niece's unresponsive little hands. "Who couldn't love such a sweet little thing?"

She rocked the baby for several minutes, surrounded by inaudible prayers, until the ambulance attendant came to take the tiny body away. She sang softly to the little bundle, even though she knew her sweet spirit had already gone. And she pleaded for God to swoop down and lift her to heaven, too. She wanted to believe in goodness, in glory, but her whole life had been a happenstance of loony living and confused attitudes. *How could this happen*, she wondered? *Why? Oh, why?* The dull melody of the refrigerator fan accompanied her tunes, and a chilled halo enveloped them both as Anna Beth relinquished her agony, poured out her pain into the once-white apron of a nameless nun.

Then, as if wiped fresh with a cool rag, peace relaxed her face. Who delivered this reassurance, she wasn't sure, but it calmed her, settled over her like a handmade shawl of tranquility. How else could she have cradled a dead child and sung praises at the same time?

*

Anna Beth woke up late that same night. I had poked her and tousled her hair until her eyes opened.

"Is that you, Olivia?" she asked.

Yes, I said. *Yes, dear one, it's me.* And my essence soared.

She lay there for a few minutes, silent in her empty bed, listening but not hearing. She reached out for Louisa, then remembered she wasn't there. House noises roused her from her mourning; muffled sobs echoed softly across the hesitation room from down the hall. They called her to investigate, begged her to overhear. I urged her to go and she got up, her bare feet numb to the chill of the oak floor planks as she eased down the hallway, knowing she'd never experience cold again like she'd felt today.

At the door to Willard's confused room, Madson's voice was the only one she could hear clearly. She hunkered down behind the door, squatting with her knees under her gown, hugging them, and listened.

"Now, Willard, don't do nothing hasty," he was saying. "I know how much you love her, Sugar. I know you want to tell her, how much you want her to know."

"It might help her, comfort her somehow." Sobs garbled Willard's words.

"With all she's been through, it just isn't a good time. Let her heal. Sometimes sharing isn't what's called for. Please, don't go digging up old ghosts and getting yourself all upset."

Willard said something back to him, but Anna Beth was in such a daze, she couldn't be sure what. Then Madson said, "Those are old wounds, Willard. They're best left alone."

He said something about forgiveness, how God forgives even the most horrid things when they are done out of love, but Anna Beth couldn't fathom what he meant. No rational explanation of what Willard might need forgiveness for or why she'd want to share it with Louisa came to mind. She slumped against the doorjamb, too spent to put her mind to work. There was so much she didn't understand.

After a long while, Willard's cries eased softly into whimpers. The lamp went out and left only dimness thrown from the kitchen to illuminate the room. It became still and quiet. Anna Beth waited to make sure she wouldn't be heard or seen, then she stepped out from her place behind the door, peeped around the doorjamb and took two steps into Willard's room. There Willard and Madson sat on the sofa together under the Crucified Jesus with Blessed Mother and all the saints and angels looking on. Madson's arm encircled her shoulders, comforting her in the most caring and intimate image Anna Beth had ever seen.

If a stranger had witnessed this scene, horror and disgust would have been their impression at best, public retribution and lynching at worst. But Anna Beth had grown accustomed to this man's presence in their lives. She wondered now if their love for each other was really something innocent, benign. Close friends sharing compassion? Or could this private display of affection be what it looked like, what first assumptions might lead someone to believe? Two lovers in a comforting embrace. Her grief buffered her from judgment, at least for now.

After Anna Beth returned to bed and dosed off, I returned to my mother's room. She was asleep, her head resting on a bolster. Madson had covered her with a quilt before he left to go back across the driveway to his basement apartment. An understanding settled upon me as I watched her. I realized that, yes, she and Madson did love each other. Why God had not let me know this before was one more mystery for me to acknowledge. Maybe I needed to evolve to this place of acceptance. Maybe I needed to grow accustomed to the idea, too. Maybe I couldn't recognize the truth until I was ready to appreciate it for the goodness it held.

*

Madson drove Anna Beth down to Tupelo to see Louisa in the hospital the next day. She didn't say a word about what she'd heard or seen the night before. She wanted to forget the whole day, to put all the tragedy and bafflement out of her mind. She decided, too, that she had imagined all the good parts, the vision of the baby rising to heaven, the light, the peace, the closeness she felt to me. She had imagined it all. It didn't happen. God was too cruel. He took Louisa's baby and let something good be untouchable, invisible, so close, yet so very far away.

Her sneakers squealed on the pea-green linoleum of the hospital hallway. What would she say? How would she comfort Louisa? How would we get through this loss? She remembered last night—Madson in Willard's room.

His soundless paces beside her now made her wonder what else they were hiding, what else was concealed in the silent grace of this man. Too many things about our family didn't add up for Anna Beth. Our people didn't own logical histories. Nobody ever talked about the past.

shoulders back, and his head pivoted slowly to stare her squarely in the eye before he spoke.

"There are lots of people in this world with only pieces of what they ought to have. And some of y'all have much more than you think."

His words resonated through the hollowness of the cab and echoed in Anna Beth's mind like shouts into a tin can. They didn't make sense. *Some of y'all have much more than you think.*

What does that mean, she thought? Pondering, she drummed her fingers on her knees, but she never made heads or tails of what he'd meant. Finally, her thoughts reverted back to the image of Madson on the sofa with Willard. Until last night, he had done nothing to make her doubt his loyalty to the family, nothing to make her question his character, but she wondered now how it had all started. How had the *hired help* managed to get so close? Just when had he and Willard come to care for each other enough to snuggle up together?

She didn't have anything in particular against black folk. I'd made sure of that. But she wasn't stupid. Unlike Louisa, she paid attention when she watched TV. Most importantly, we had grown up in the South. All the colored people she'd ever known—mostly employees at the flower shops—had been kind and generous, as far as she could tell.

But Genevieve made no bones about it—Madson was okay, but the rest of the black population ranked somewhere far below the pedestal that kept her shirttail from getting wet. Still, seeing Madson hold Willard with such tenderness, forced all sorts of questions to the forefront of her adolescent mind.

Am I imagining it all? Or do they really love each other, she wondered? If so, she could see why they wouldn't want anyone to find out, especially in Iuka. The stories she'd heard about the Ku Klux Klan and what they did to black folks who mixed up with whites curled her toenails. If Willard and Madson were doing what she thought they were doing, they could get burned out, strung up, or even something worse.

Anna Beth told herself that maybe she was just worrying for nothing. After all, it was almost 1971. The riots in Memphis, when Dr. King got shot dead, happened over two years ago, way back in '68. That event had changed people's thinking, shocked them into understanding that blacks are just the same as whites. Right? No, she was too smart to believe that.

She squirmed in her seat, trying to get the unpleasant consequences popping into her head to settle down and go away. She didn't need anything else to worry about. Louisa had just lost her baby, and from the looks of her, she'd lost herself, too. And then there was Genevieve, who'd always been our top-ranking fret. *Where is she,* Anna Beth wondered. *Why hasn't she come?* Having to add Willard and Madson to her anxiety plate would overload it for sure. She shook off the temptation to fester. Worrying was a sin. She vowed not to let it smother her. She got out her panic shovel and buried her worries deep, down there with her anger.

Madson parked the truck in front of the carriage house and kicked open the door, but Anna Beth grabbed his arm before his feet hit the dirt. "Tell me everything's gonna be okay."

He leaned back in, one leg still hanging out the door. "Yep, but it's going to take time, a whole lot of time."

"So, where's Moody, huh? She should be here. Louisa could have died. Why hasn't she come?"

"Well, Sugar, I'll be damned if I know." He looked away and fingered his shirt.

Fresh tears stung her eyes and she screamed, "That's a pile of crap and you know it. She's off with Elvis, traipsing after him so she can throw her panties on the stage at his feet. Or, better yet, she's in jail again. One of these days the police are gonna wise up and keep her."

"I don't know anything about that, child. I don't want to know."

"But she ought to be here, Madson. Doesn't she care at all?"

He didn't answer, only shook his head. There was no way to explain Genevieve. He turned and stroked Anna Beth's cheek with rough fingers. "Ease up on yourself, child. It's gone be all right." But his caress felt more like a warning, a physical understanding of just how tough life can be.

*

We found Willard in the work room stabbing Calla lilies into a miniature casket cover for a coffin the size of a boot box.

"You can't do this," Madson hollered, rushing to her. He eased the knife from her white knuckles. A box of metal picks slipped off the table, crashing like needles to the concrete at their feet. His tan arms encompassed her, and dwarfed her even more, as she fought to climb up him and hang on. Sobs ravaged them both while Anna Beth watched and failed to figure out life, love and pain.

"Her baby, my babies," Willard wailed. "I have to do something. Where's Sister? She needs to be here. I can't do this alone."

"Willard, hush now. I'm here," Madson warned. He pulled her face back from his chest and gazed into her eyes; his own fogged up blinking back tears. He glanced up and noticed Anna Beth standing there, staring. His face softened as if it didn't matter.

Willard beat her forehead against his shoulder. "I don't care anymore, Madson. Everything's changed now and I don't care about the secrets. Let's just let them out, give some fresh air to this family, to this place."

The words puzzled Anna Beth, and her mind raced around in a panic trying to piece it all together. It was Louisa's baby, not Willard's. *Why is she wailing and befuddled like that*, she wondered? And which "sister"? Moody? Or Reverend Mother?

But Reverend Mother had been here all along. If it hadn't been for her, Louisa would have died. *What have secrets got to do with anything? What secrets? Arrgh*! A thousand questions thundered through her mind, pounded the inside her skull, confounded everything she'd heard, everything she'd seen. Finally, she exploded, "Who gives a damn? I hate this family. I hate you all."

She ran across the work room and burst through the back door. Willard's voice called after her as she bolted through the greenhouse and waded knee deep through the poinsettia sea. She fell into the swing of the old oak tree, Louisa's favorite place to hide, her jeaned knees dangling in the mud like a cast-off rag doll.

Teardrops fell to earth and vanished into the moist ground, disappearing like they never existed. Never there—like our little niece, a momentary sorrow, an interruption in the more important lives going on all around us. Never there—like Genevieve, the maniacal mother obsessed with the gyrating hips of a rock star, only concerned with herself.

She hadn't had the decency to even show up and comfort Louisa. And now, Anna Beth worried about Willard and Madson. And I couldn't seem to ease her fears.

"They think it's a blessing that Louisa's baby died, Olivia," Anna Beth told the mud and me. "One less embarrassment for Moody to handle, one less excuse to make up, one less kid to put up with."

Twisting in the wind to the moans of the old oak, a bitter sadness grabbed hold of Anna Beth and wouldn't let go. She gazed deep into the rich earth. "Are you there, Olivia? Are you real, or am I crazy? Oh, that sweet little girl. Why'd she have to die?" Her words stung her, too, but she pretended not to notice, choked it back. "I'm sorry, you deserved better, little baby. You, too, Olivia, whoever you are. But I should know. Louisa and I deserved better, too. Maybe you both really are better off. Nobody knows how to love here."

"You're wrong."

Willard's voice didn't prompt her to turn around. Anna Beth tried to convince herself that she didn't care what Willard had to say. But really Willard's opinions had been the only ones she could count on, the only ones so far that had ever made sense.

"We all loved that child," Willard whispered, "but there's more to it, more to it than you can know right now."

Anna Beth sat back on her heels, knees sinking deeper into the soft earth. She talked to the tree. "Go on and keep your old secrets. I don't care. I don't want to know. But what I *do* know is this: you're in love with Madson." She spun around and glared right into Willard's eyes, threatening to tattle like an angry child. "And if people found out, it would be bad, really bad."

Willard slumped against the rough trunk, gathering up the hem of her peasant skirt. She hiked it as she squatted to sit on a root. "There's more to it, Anna Beth. Life's more complicated than just whether we love each other or not—or how we love each other. Life has rules. When you break them, there's hell to pay. This family has been breaking rules for a long time and we're all paying now, it seems."

"I don't care about what ya'll do." The swing twisted as she leaned into it. "Love him if you want. Makes me no mind. I'm just worried about Louisa and the baby . . . "

Willard joined her in the mud and pulled Anna Beth from the swing ropes. She cradled her like she had wanted to cradle her own daughters for so many years. I cradled them both. "Louisa will survive this. We all will. We'll be here for her. We're here for you, too. And the baby, well, she's safe with God. That's what we know, what we trust."

I stroked my mother's hair and wondered what it would have been like to feel her stroke mine. Would it have been curly and unruly like hers? I suspected that, yes, unruly hair would have suited me just fine. She was some kind of a special woman. I was so proud to call her my own.

*

Genevieve showed up twenty minutes late for the funeral, looking like she'd just fallen out of bed with a snake. The van spit her out of its driver's seat. She hit the ground unsteadily, righted herself and patted down her hair.

Everyone had already gathered at the back of the property in a garden chapel Willard had built not long after she moved home and now waited impatiently, teeth chattering from the cold. Lipstick trailed off the edge of Genevieve's lips and searched for its proper place. She stumbled around vehicles, parked this way and that on the side lawn. She yanked at her slip that had ridden up and tugged at those new-fangled pantyhose, all bunched up, crooked and twisted in her crotch and cutting circulation off to her upper thigh. She cursed, waving her arms in frustration. She'd have to fix them later, if she survived the day, the ordeal, if she survived being back at the home place and burying her first grandchild amid the public glare of gossip. As usual, her mind only had room for thoughts about how she would deal with the situation. She had no idea what the rest of us had been through.

She moved down the grassy slope, chatting to herself like a schizophrenic bag lady. Her pointed-heel boots sank into the earth. She fought with her gloves. She hated this place, couldn't believe she'd ever stayed here or come back, even for this. Ghastly memories of belt buckles, locked doors and frayed rope flooded her mind as she passed the big house and headed down toward the clearing out back.

"Get away from me, Grandpa," she growled at the wind, still waving about. "I got no time for you, hear? I'm all grown up now and I'll knock your lights out. I'll bite you in the butt like a rabid dog and never let go. Swear I will." She stopped in mid-stride and wheeled around, the crazed look of a cornered 'possum in her eyes. "I mean it, ya hear?"

Six spirits that I was glad I had never seen before had gathered around her, each wearing the gruesome face of torment, twisted with misery, deformed beyond recognition by the hideousness of their sins. They taunted her, "Join us, come on."

She ignored them. They poked at her with bony fingers draped in rotted flesh, and took turns spinning around her like bullies picking on the weakest kid on the playground, while Grandpa Clancy stood off to the side, staring and grinning. He never approached her, never spoke a word. He didn't have to. He just watched. That was enough.

She stood her ground remarkably well, head erect, chin out, eyes forward, disregarding them the best she could. But I sensed a crumbling within her, a subterranean shift below the surface of her stamina. I had never seen her so rattled, so emotionally off the charts, and I realized how worried I had become for her. I couldn't be angry with her now. She was too pitiful, too afraid.

As she struggled down the hill, she grumbled incoherently to herself, ignoring all else. She mumbled something about Grandpa, "the old buzzard," how she never should have stayed here on the home place after he died and with Ned in Memphis all the time. She guessed it was her way of standing up to Grandpa, her way of not letting him ruin her life from the grave, not letting him run her off from the only home she had ever known, but his reach was too long.

Finally, she stopped to catch her breath—not from exertion, but from a more innate fatigue, a numbing exhaustion from years of running away from her life. She turned to face her tormenters, but they had vanished. Her eyes swept the landscape and settled on the house. Now, something else played on her nerves. Shivers rippled over her, spooky and cold. She could feel eyes upon her, human eyes. Someone had been spying on her as she descended the slope. Her breath caught in her chest and she pulled her coat around her. After a moment's pause, she turned again and hurried on.

Ancient oaks lined the walkway that wove its way down and away from the house, craggy tree branches loomed above her, and twisted shadows lay on the ground. "Deliver me, Lord. Deliver me," she prayed. The scent of moist earth and dead leaves permeated the air. "Damned place. I hate this damned place." The path parted with waves of spiky monkey grass sewing a complicated labyrinth around hundred-year-old trunks. She knew these paths well, too well; they haunted her dreams.

This grove had once been her playhouse, her magical world of fairytale princesses and happy endings as a young child, but as barely a woman, it had morphed into a dark cave for hiding, an eerie sanctuary and morbid refuge from unspeakable harm.

The clearing opened up in front of her before she was ready. Everyone was already seated. Thirty eyes turned to stare. She stood breathless, clutching herself. Reverend Mother looked up from her prayer book.

Genevieve straightened her shoulders, took one deliberate step into the little copse and tripped over a root. She warbled a minute, unsure what had happened and searching for something to grab for support, then stumbled to the right, to the left, as if God himself was now tossing her about, a soiled rag doll thrown to the public in disgrace. Her heel caught in a knot of grass and she pitched forward, but made a good save and managed to right herself just before she tumbled into the crowd.

Her gyration over, she stood frozen for a moment, only her eyeballs still swimming, scanning the concerned faces around her. Then, stiff and exacting, she smoothed her skirt with great effort and walked gingerly down the grassy aisle, hands out for balance like a toddler on a balance beam.

The open-air chapel had been cleared a few years back and was used often in good weather for Mass. A rough wooden arbor, swathed in barren wisteria and supported by old columns culled from a decaying plantation house nearby, sheltered a concrete altar at center stage. Saintly statues stood guard inside a low boxwood hedge, keeping watch over a marble Virgin Mary who cradled her crucified Son in her arms.

It was warm for December, but last night's frost obliged its chill to the standing-room-only crowd. I was overcome and quite touched by the numbers who came out to show their respect, customers mostly, and Iuka townsfolk who had known the family for decades at least, if not centuries. No need for secrets here. They'd all gotten to know the girls, either through Willard's proud introductions or through the lively grapevine that broadcasted the girls' escapades far and wide. The lay people were dressed warmly, but the nuns, lined up on benches in neat rows, trembled either from cold or sorrow that would not ease.

About the time Genevieve made her way to her seat behind Willard and Louisa, she realized that she was surrounded, a prisoner on all sides by black-draped nuns.

"Where have you been?" Willard whispered over her shoulder, glaring. She had finally gotten in touch with Genevieve the night before. She held Louisa close about the shoulders. Louisa didn't turn around or look up.

"It couldn't be helped," Genevieve said, leaning so close she almost touched Willard's ear with her icy lips. "I'm here now." Willard's head dropped to her chest.

Reverend Mother stood at the podium. She had led everyone in prayer while we'd waited. We were on the fourth decade of the Glorious Mysteries of the Holy Rosary when Genevieve interrupted us with her entrance. Sister had planned to pray only the Joyful Mysteries—send this child off in happy style—but Genevieve's tardiness forced Sister to drag it out and we chanted right on through the Sorrowful Mysteries, and luckily had time to get into the Glorious Mysteries before Genevieve showed up.

Anna Beth sat up front next to Sister since she'd volunteered to do the Bible readings during the service. She was just a child, scarcely fourteen, but looking at her there, so stoic, so resolute, a stranger could easily mistake her for a grown-up. She fidgeted uncomfortably with the black woolen skirt she'd borrowed from Willard. It was too short, just barely covered her knees, plus she rarely wore skirts or dresses, preferring jeans and baseball caps to any other attire. She shifted on the cold stone bench, perturbed, twisted her mouth into a sour sneer, and fixed angry eyes on Genevieve. She had watched her stagger out of the van and fumble her way down the hill through the naked woods, and Anna Beth's impatience had risen to an unpleasant level.

Poor, Louisa was hunched over in Willard's lap, looking more like a toddler than a child old enough to suffer such a loss. Darkness hooded her hollow eyes. Another teenage mother might consider this loss a blessing, but in Louisa's fantasy, motherhood was going to deliver her, grant her the love she'd longed for and transform her life. She hadn't eaten at all and had hardly spoken in the four days since the baby's death. I wondered if she would ever be all right again. Her hands fumbled with a handkerchief Willard had given her. She twisted, folded and re-folded the sad keepsake from decades of mourners before her, and I wondered if Mother had worried that same handkerchief as she lay alone in her room after Sister whisked my sister and me away.

After everyone settled down again, Father Kennedy, the priest from Corinth, stood up and moved in slow motion to the podium for his abbreviated version of the traditional funeral Mass, but as he began the liturgy, Anna Beth's eyes wandered toward the house. Something had caught her attention and drew her away. No one seemed to notice, except Genevieve and me.

Genevieve's eyebrows puckered. *What's Anna Beth looking at,* she wondered? The porch was at least two-hundred-yards away. Even squinting, no one could make out the details of someone that far away. She remembered her feeling of being watched as she descended the hill and glanced around the congregation as inconspicuously as she could muster. She counted heads.

No nuns were missing, far as she could tell. She turned ever so slightly—maybe in the kitchen window?—but met eyeballs with the stern glare of Sister Sabrina, a woman Genevieve had hated since she was ten. Genevieve smiled weakly and faced forward again.

Did Anna Beth feel it too, Genevieve wondered? She pushed the thought from her brain. *Of course not. That's silly*, she thought. *Why would she sense the ghosts that haunt me?* She shrugged, tugged at her gloves, mumbled to herself, and pulled her coat closer as the pall of transgression clawed at her heart.

Father Kennedy wasn't the most engaging priest we'd ever heard. His voice droned on and on, just like Genevieve remembered from every Mass she'd ever endured. This guy must not have gotten the word about the new rules of the Mass. He murmured along in Latin, not having the good sense to follow the new vernacular regulations set down by Vatican II. Hard as I tried, even I couldn't keep up. Genevieve gave up before the *Gloria* and focused her attention on Anna Beth instead, who was obviously distracted.

When Father finally sat down, everything became still and expectant, until Anna Beth jumped up with a start. She'd missed her cue. She coughed, shuffling through the pages of the *Lectionary* to find her place as she stood behind the podium. Finally, she raised her head to read the passage, but another movement from the house caught her eye and she froze, mouth gaping, in a stare. Veiled heads turned in unison to see what transfixed her, and there, there.

Genevieve craned her neck. Is it him? Little Spec? *Sure as the world*, she thought. Watching the whole proceeding from the kitchen window stood someone tall and blonde. She squinted, trying to make sure. The window screen and curtains made it difficult to tell, and before certainty could crystallize, the café curtains fell back and concealed his face. Who was it? *Living or the dead*, Genevieve wondered? She fought the urge to jump and run to check it out. "Well, I'll be," she whispered, reassuring herself.

An exasperated Willard slapped her on the knee before turning back around to face front again.

*

Madson was such a dear. He had chopped and hacked his way through pine roots as big around as his bicep to hone out a grave as close to Louisa's ancient oak as he dared. He worried that the pine might not survive the damage, but thought losing it would be better than taking the chance of hurting the oak's roots. She had refused to bury her baby with the other Clancys, where, now that I think about it, I should have been laid to rest, too.

Louisa had said that 'her tree with her swing' was the only place, the proper place. I suppose she was right. My grave was also under an oak tree, behind the old convent just a few miles down the highway. Since I'm not buried there, only my discarded flesh, I guess it suited my bones just fine. But yesterday Louisa had marked the spot for Madson. "Dig there, right there," she had said, and she'd watched as he lifted each shovel full from the ground.

She hadn't understood why he was being so nice. He had always been kind, of course, ever since we moved back less than five months ago, but Louisa was never the least bit concerned about him. She saw her world only in shades of black and white, no sepia or gray tones allowed. And Anna Beth hadn't divulged her new suspicions: not the right time, not important in light of all this. But there he had been, in the razor-cold digging a proper grave for Louisa's child.

Louisa had leaned down and grabbed the handle of his shovel. He looked up and she forced him to rise. "Will you carry the casket tomorrow, Madson? Will you do that for me?"

He coughed into his hand like a wad of cotton got stuck. "I'd be honored," he whispered, tears brimming.

Now, standing underneath the trees, he leaned down and lifted the small chest. Willard's casket flowers and errant tears tickled his cheeks as he led the somber processional to the spot. Louisa walked behind him, staring at the ground, unconcerned if anyone else came along, as we shuffled past the greenhouses, around back of the shop, wading through knee-deep hay grass and across dry Iris beds. Dead stems poked out of the ground like arthritic fingers frozen in pain. Finally, Madson knelt under the arms of the great oak, hugging the white box to his Sunday-suited chest. He eased it to the ground, crossed himself with a trembling hand, and backed away.

Anna Beth had been clutching Reverend Mother's hand this whole time. They'd trailed along behind the others, Anna Beth not feeling comfortable in the crowd. Sister squeezed back and held tight to shore her up for the hardest part to come, and when we rounded the last greenhouse and the empty swing came into view, Sister was there to hold her up.

Louisa stood erect, too shell-shocked to have enough sense to fall apart. She faced the eternal home of her child's body and all she could do was wring her hands and weep. Father Kennedy sprinkled the tiny coffin with holy water, said another prayer, made crosses in the air. So many dull and complicated rituals to send off a spirit who left this earth on the breath of God the second she had died.

I realized then that I had to do something. I wanted to help, wanted to lighten everyone's spirit, to give them a sign that all was not lost. In a flash of black and motion, a flock of birds took flight from their perches in the tree. Lifting higher and higher on my cue, their wing beats echoed through the crystal-still air and fluttered like a child's heartbeat, soothing and calm. Everyone gasped—except Louisa—and looked up, astonished, and watched until every bird had risen toward heaven and vanished.

Anna Beth felt me there beside her. She smiled weakly, winked and whispered, "Thanks."

When silence resumed, Louisa fell to her knees and grabbed hands full of dirt. She threw one, then the other; tears choked back. She stretched out over the grave and shoveled earth into the hole, into her lap, with white woolen arms. "Good-bye, Baby," she said softly, her voice ragged, so parched. "Rest, Baby, okay?"

Willard collapsed beside her, patting and shooshing, "It's okay, love. I know, I know, it's okay."

But Genevieve, oh, Genevieve. Where had she been all this time? She hung out on the fringes, an outsider with no one to hold, no one to hold up. She wavered on the outskirts, wrestling with her ghosts and her fears. Seeing Louisa comforted by Willard was almost too much to take.

And Anna Beth in the arms of the woman who had put her in this situation in the first place, all the years, all the sacrifices, all forgotten by this one tragic event. But no one cared about *her*, no one needed *her* any more. She couldn't take it; it wasn't fair. She glanced over at Anna Beth and saw adoration in her eyes. Not for Genevieve, no, for Willard! Anna Beth loved her; it was so easy to tell. How had it come to this?

Of course, it was destined from the start, this outcome, this twist, but Genevieve knew she had caused it to happen now. A wave of anger washed over her. She had brought this reckoning to premature fruition by sending her girls here, by placing *her* children in Willard's loving care. A maternal jolt pierced her as if God Himself sent lightning to strike her down. It shot through her like labor pains and, in that instant, time compressed and Willard reclaimed not only her child, but Genevieve's baby girl, too.

Pulse thumped in Genevieve's neck, flushed her face, her neck stiffened to a point just this side of rigor mortis. She had to get out, to get away. She shoved through the black wall of habits, staggering toward the sacred clearing, to the ragged woods beyond it that held only terror from her distant past. Panic gathered her momentum and her trot bloomed into an all out dash to escape.

Anna Beth watched Genevieve's flight unfold, not knowing the why of it, but certain of its finality. "She's gone," she said out loud to no one. Willard and Sister looked up and followed Anna Beth's eyes to where Genevieve ran. "She's leaving us here and she's never coming back." A tree branch snapped somewhere close by, brittle and dead. It fell to the frozen earth and disintegrated on impact with the ground.

*

Later that afternoon, while mourners still filled the house and everyone was busy consoling themselves, Anna Beth slipped out the back door. She had changed into her uniform of bellbottoms, a *Memphis State* sweatshirt, Keds, and a baseball cap. None of the mourners heard the pickup rumble down the driveway and out onto the highway headed west.

"I'm going to kill her," she whispered to me after a few minutes of ragged breath. "I hate her. She won't hurt any of us ever again." She glanced over at the passenger seat as if expecting to see me. She knew I was there. And, if I could have materialized, I would have. I thought about touching her hand. She would have felt me, I'm sure, but instead, I let her drive for a while and think.

And then, just inside the county line, she noticed a sign on the side of the road that she had never seen before. It was old and faded and kudzu had grown over part of it, obscuring its edges. She slowed to a stop in the middle of the highway to get a good look, and she read the faint words: *Beaver's Auto Parts and Shop.*

A red arrow pointed the way. *This must be the old convent building that Reverend Mother always talks about,* she thought. She switched on her blinker, obeying vehicular laws, glanced over her shoulder, and turned left onto a dirt road that hadn't hosted tire treads in years.

That's right, go on, girl, I whispered. *You've so much to learn.* The deeply rutted passage bounced us, and about a hundred yards into a jungle of twisted branches, naked honeysuckle and mounded kudzu so thick it blanketed everything in shades of deep green in spite of the winter's chill, there it was, the shabby site of my death. I was a little surprised by the decrepit look of the façade. When the sisters had moved to the home place, they'd offered the run-down relic as a storage building to parishes close by.

Since then, however, people had used the abandoned property as a dumping ground for things they wanted rid of but didn't have the heart to throw out. Over the years, refuse had made its way to the weedy parking lot: iron beds with no mattresses, broken stoves with no eyes, fence posts with mismatched pickets, frayed trunks with no lids, automobiles without motors and their seating innards ripped out. Everything was missing a part of itself.

Anna Beth pulled into the lot and eased around back, careful not to run over anything that might leave us stranded with a flat tire. Then she cut the engine and climbed out. Waist-high grasses grew in patches here and there where the gravel had lost its battle with chickweed and Johnson grass.

In the late afternoon shadows, the yard's junk pieces seemed to take on lives for themselves. Anna Beth's creativity saw everything in a unique way. The old park bench welcomed brightly dressed paint cans to come over and sit a spell, wire bed springs became trampolines for any chipmunk that might happen by, empty flower pots took on the shapes of puppies with weed tails, doorknob noses, Coke bottle eyes, and a farm table with no legs became a theatrical stage for muffler actors and commode dancers in lily white.

Anna Beth picked her way through the happy menagerie, touching things here and there, introducing herself to the inanimate objects. Then she worked her way to each doorway, tried the windows—all locked. She was almost ready to give up and leave, but noticed the bricked recesses below ground level where basement windows hid out. *That might be a way to get inside*, she thought. It just so happened that one window stood open just a crack. Imagine that.

She climbed down and forced the metal frame open all the way with her foot. Then, without thinking, she jumped, and *poof*, she was gone.

Spinout
Film, Metro-Goldwyn-Mayer, including
the songs, *Spinout, Stop, Look and Listen*
and *Never Say Yes*

Well after midnight the next day, I took a little trip to Memphis to check on Genevieve. Anna Beth had conveniently decided, with my influence, that murderer was not the proper career choice for a fourteen-year-old girl—at least not just yet.

I was feeling pretty good about that. I liked being able to direct her, liked her openness to me, and how her free will seemed to listen to my common sense. So, I left her and Louisa in Iuka and floated along on currents moving in from the west, headed toward the bluff city and Genevieve's Memphis blues.

It was nice when God allowed me a moment's peace, time to explore on my own. At first I followed the highway. Car headlights glowed below me like a silent string of jewels. They reminded me of our Virgin Mary statue at the home place, votive candles flickering at her feet. Then I remembered that no bounds of asphalt could hold me. I took a sharp right and soared higher, venturing out over cotton fields that, come summer, would resemble clouds that the land had decided to keep for itself.

I was in no hurry to get to Memphis, even though God's nudge seemed sharper when I slowed my pace too much. I was happy for a little time to myself. I must have tarried too long, though. A sudden and swift kick in the backside propelled me sixty miles in two seconds. Even God's patience wears thin when He knows He's being ignored.

I wasn't the only one who had dawdled. By the time I arrived at the house, Genevieve was just pulling into the garage. It had been thirty-six hours since she'd fled the funeral. She couldn't remember where she'd spent all that time. The van shuddered when she cut the engine, and she followed suit. She climbed down from the cab, and the harsh beam of the streetlight accentuated the shabbiness of the house. She hated this place. She turned the key in the door. It took almost more effort than she could muster. Shuffling across the living room, she flipped the switch on the phonograph—*You'll Never Walk Alone* from Elvis's gospel album—and fell into the couch without turning on a light.

She had turned down the heat before she left, and now it felt colder inside than out. Or was it just her? She wondered how her life had become so vacant, so remote. Had it always been this desperate? Or did this paralysis creep up on her without her knowing? Did each day, each month, each year drop her a few degrees, stiffen her a bit more, so she didn't recognize herself anymore?

An old afghan that Grandma Olivia had crocheted for Grandpa Clancy lay over the back of the couch. She pulled it over her, but then threw it across the room when her childhood tormentor materialized before her in the dark. Grandpa Clancy, in spirit form, stood over her. She had teetered so close to the edge of reality for so long, she wondered if she had finally slipped and fallen off the edge.

Was this vision a hallucination concocted by her mind? Or something more, something real? Her psyche had played all kinds of tricks on her lately. Minds do that when people are fractured or confused about right and wrong. She wasn't sure. But I was. I tried to shoo him away, to protect her, but he refused to go. He existed in that other realm, that slice of misery that rests uneasily in a disjointed space below anything good. The absence of hope resides there. Its only fire is visceral loneliness. My goodness held no persuasion against him. He bore only disdain for me, and anyone who owned this precious link to Paradise that he would never know. He was as mean an old buzzard in death as he had been in life.

"What do you want?" she screeched at him.

His eyes bulged. Spittle dribbled down his chin from a mouth of rotten teeth.

"You've ruined my whole life," she whimpered. "And now you follow me here? What more could you want?"

She scanned the room for means of escape, her eyes red from longstanding rheum. Maybe Elvis could save her. She had flicked on the record player on her way to the couch, but all she heard now was the *swish, swish, swish* of a needle reading the rim—no music to soothe her, no melody to hold reality fast.

shoe out.

"Hey you," Louisa hollered. Anna Beth looked up. "Stop daydreaming. We've got work to do out here."

Anna Beth turned her nozzle off, staring down at her hands. "What's it like, Weesa?"

"What?" Louisa was on the other side of the greenhouse, not paying much attention. "What's what like?"

"Being in love. You know, sex and stuff."

Louisa paused, holding the hose in front of her. Water puddled around her feet. "It's the most wonderful thing in the whole wide world," she said. She took a few steps toward her sister. "It's confidence, Anna Beth, that's what it is. No matter what happens, things'll work out. Nothing can hurt me. With him, I can do anything, be anybody, and say anything I want to say. And nobody can do a dad-blame thing about it."

This was Louisa, all dreamy and irrational. She was a romantic and falling in love had softened her head even more to the consistency of marshmallow cream. It made her thick and oozy with nonsense.

Anna Beth barked, "What do you mean? He let you go through losing the baby all alone. He never agreed to marry you, never even stood up and said, 'This is my child.' I'll swear, Louisa, sometimes— no, most of the time—you don't make a lick of sense." That's my girl. At least one of them had some common sense. She had also curbed her cussing since our recent trips to the convent, I'm proud to say, but maybe her language still needed a little more work.

"You don't know what you're talking about. He's always been right by my side. Plus, you need to lighten up, sis." Grinning, arms spread, Louisa tiptoed down the concrete aisle like a ballerina on a psychedelic trip, swinging the hose back and forth, and spewing water high in the air so it rained down on her and soaked her through. "It's love. There's no sense to it. You won't understand till you feel it. You're too closed off and shy. You gotta get out and raise a ruckus, make some friends." Tulip pots within ten feet of her got drenched in the unnatural rain. They sucked up as much as they could, then overflowed, their soil washing down the sides of their pots and into the drains in the floor. Louisa took the nozzle and stuck it down her shirt, just standing there with her hands on her hips, the hose dangling, and water streaming down her body and into her drawers. "Have you ever in your whole life had a friend other than me? You need to find yourself a man, sister, and try love on for size. It's the best thing in the world, being all grown up and in love."

She was really starting to get on my nerves, talking like Susan Hayward in one of those movies that Willard said was bad for them to watch.

Anna Beth mumbled, "Yeah, you're really grown up, humph!" Then she yelled, "You've gone mad, stark-raving-and-ready-for-the-loony-bin mad."

Amen, girl. You tell her!

She aimed her hose at Louisa and loosened the nozzle. A hard stream shot across the greenhouse, hitting Louisa in the face. "But we're not all grown up, you ninny. We're barely even fifteen."

"Eeeeewww!" Louisa screamed, ducking and weaving, throwing up her hands and laughing. Then she stopped abruptly with the grin of the devil lighting up her eyes, and turned her weapon on Anna Beth for a full-out water war.

"You're not kin to me!" Anna Beth hollered, dodging one way then another. "You're the most illogical girl in the world." She stepped in a flat of hyacinth, stumbled and knocked them over.

"Yeah, ain't it great?" Louisa squealed back. "You should try it sometime."

When their water play slowed, they broke up into giggles. I was sad to see it end. They'd never been so carefree, so childish, so free. It saddened me, too, that I couldn't participate and join in the fun, but my place in their lives was more fulfilling than I ever dreamed it would turn out to be. They shook off the excess water, their clothes sticking to them, revealing panty lines and pointy white brassieres. Louisa motioned Anna Beth over and they collapsed together on an empty bleacher, wringing out their clothes.

"No really. I'll probably never know for myself. I want to know what *it* is *really* like." Anna Beth was squeezing out her hair.

Louisa blew a drop of water off her nose. "Just the facts or the mushy parts, too?"

Anna Beth smiled big.

"Okay, let's see. Where to begin? The first time he kissed me, his tongue slid into my mouth, soft and warm, playing tag with mine. It made Fourth of July fireworks seem like sparklers, I tell you. I got all melty inside, like caramel sauce. Nothing mattered. That was all it took. I was a goner from that moment on." She looked up at Anna Beth who wore the sour face of a kid who'd just tasted collard greens for the first time. "Don't look that way, girl. You haven't heard the good parts. I'd better skip ahead or you'll never survive the juicy stuff.

"Remember when we were kids and we saw Johnny Hoopersmith's pickle? You know, that boy down the block in Memphis? The one who dropped his britches and tee-teed in our yard? Well, let me tell you girl, it ain't nothing like that teeny-weeny, little shriveled up thing. Nothing at all. When boys get our age, or maybe a little older, they grow when they see a pretty woman. They get hard as a rolling pin and almost as long. It's true, it's true. I have a hard time walking down the street now, just imagining all those men looking at me and their privates getting big and bulging out of their drawers while they watch me walk along. I'm telling you, girls, or uh, women, especially pretty ones like me." She looked Anna Beth up and down. "And you, too, I guess. We have power, honey. Power like you can't hardly believe. I hate to say it, but Moody is right about at least one thing or ten."

Anna Beth sat engrossed, holding her slack jaw up with both hands propped on her knees. She couldn't believe she hadn't asked this stuff before. How dumb was that? She'd wasted a whole season, maybe more, when she could have been putting accurate pictures into her otherwise boring fantasy life. She had a wealth of experience and practical education right there in front of her in Louisa, and she hadn't managed the nerve to form the questions and delve into her sister's expertise. "So, what do they do? It must be uncomfortable with all that going on."

"Well, what do you think?" Louisa raised her eyebrows and looked southward into Anna Beth's lap. Well, that was all it took. Anna Beth clasped her hand over her mouth like she might barf any minute. Her eyes bulged out of their sockets. She shook her head, NO! Louisa just nodded like a school teacher explaining long division, then said, "And let me tell you, missy, it is a wonderful thing when it all comes together. You don't think so now, but you should try it sometime. It is pure-dee magic with a real man like I've got."

They sat there, quiet for a moment, Anna Beth shaking her head in disbelief. She couldn't figure out how she'd missed out on all this excitement. Here she was, already turned fifteen years old, and she didn't know the first thing about life. She'd always thought that *she* was the smart one. Never dreamed Louisa would be on top of things—in more ways than one. She'd checked out every one of Genevieve's naughty magazines, but now they all seemed tame. Heck, they were about as exciting as a *Field and Stream* in comparison. If she hadn't been so thrilled about finally getting this information, she might have gotten depressed about her lackluster life.

Miss Frances, the part-time shop help, stepped into the greenhouse on her way to smoke a cigarette and sneak a snoot of Jack Daniels from the flask she kept hidden in the potting shed. The girls were hunkered together, giggling and whispering. Miss Frances surveyed their sopping clothes and the ravaged plants, but just shook her head and went on, without saying a word.

When the coast was clear again, Anna Beth grabbed Louisa's arm, hell fire and damnation coming to mind. "It's still a sin. I mean… it's not right to do those things. I've never heard the specifics like you tell them, but this stuff ranks right up there in the top two or three of the 'Thou shalt not's'."

"I don't know, Anna Beth. I think grown-ups tell us all that no-no stuff to keep us in line, to keep us doing what they want us to do. All I can tell you is that me and my sweet honey made that beautiful little baby that grew inside me. Now, how on God's green earth can something so sweet and innocent come from something that's wrong?"

Anna Beth thought about this for a moment. Louisa had never been a real smart girl, but she just might have a point. Here it was the 1970's. The black people were moving up in the world and she'd heard stuff about the sexual revolution, women's rights and birth control. Maybe all the women in the world (black and white) were getting wise to the fact that they'd been missing out on a whole lot of fun.

Genevieve always said that it's really women who run the world. "Women just let men think it's them so their over-inflated egos won't explode and cause an atomic blast," she'd said. She might just be smarter than Anna Beth thought, too. Still, this pregnancy thing was a drawback. Louisa might think she was ready for a baby, but Anna Beth wasn't so sure motherhood was all it was cracked up to be.

Louisa stood up and stretched, bringing an end to her life-lessons class. "I'm hungry and it's getting chilly out here. I think I'll go in, change clothes and get Madson to whip up some mashed potatoes and gravy, cornbread and turnip greens. You comin'?"

Something about the way Louisa turned, the way her wet skirt clung to her caught Anna Beth's breath. "Oh my God!" She stood up and grabbed Louisa by both arms, still staring at her tummy. "Oh my God, Louisa," she said again. "How could you? Have you lost your mind for real? You're pregnant again."

Louisa's grin went slack. "So? What if I am? Besides, who do you think you are? Saint Elizabeth or something?" She shrugged away, reached down and snatched up the green snake of a hose from the floor at her feet. "Just because you were named after her doesn't mean you can see into my womb." She squatted, pretending to fiddle with a plant. The too-sweet smell of young hyacinth and wet dirt saturated the air.

"But why, Louisa? Why? I know it's fun, but you've got to stop this. Why would you let him do that to you again?" The automatic fans kicked on. The sudden "whirrrr" drowned out her last few words, and the instant suction of air pulled at their wet clothes.

Louisa shrugged and started rolling the hose up neatly around her arm. She hung it on the bracket by the back door while Anna Beth just stood there, staring, waiting for some logical explanation, but knowing none would come. As Louisa passed her on her way back into the shop, she said without stopping, "Love, Anna Beth. Pure and simple. I do it for love."

*

Anna Beth didn't even bother to dry off or change clothes. She stomped out the back door, climbed into the truck and, within a few minutes, she was pulling into the junkyard in front of *Beaver's Auto Parts and Shop*.

Part Three

Girls! Girls! Girls!
Film, Paramount
Top 20 *Billboard* Album

"I can't believe you're going away to a nun's college," Louisa griped at Anna Beth as they crammed the stems of two-dozen roses into individual water picks. It was late in the summer of 1975. They had both managed to pass the tests that said they were as good as graduated from high school, Anna Beth with A+'s across the board, Louisa with shallow C's. Reverend Mother had assisted in getting Anna Beth accepted into college, but was sad and worried about the fact that it was located in Memphis, too close to Genevieve for anyone's taste.

Louisa had miscarried yet anther baby, making a total of three, but blindly continued her devotion to Jack Bland, in spite of everything.

I had become quite content with my place in this world. I felt needed and beneficial, at long last, almost accepted by Louisa, and certainly by Anna Beth, and that, even if God never let me in on the good stuff in heaven, I just might make it fine for eternity in limbo. Of course, being close to my mother, and not having to deal with Genevieve on a daily basis for the past few years would lighten anyone's mood.

As Louisa arranged leather-leaf fern in the bottom of a cut flower box, Anna Beth placed the roses in one at a time. They layered the delicate fronds of greenery between each row of roses in descending order, and salmon-colored buds peeped out above the greenery. Anna Beth sneaked a sprig of baby's breath from the bucket on the floor— nice name for a flower, I thought—and added it to the box just before enclosing the flowers with a cardboard lid.

An amused smile played over Louisa's mouth. "You'd give away the clothes on your back if modesty would let you." She had kept her hair long, hanging well past the middle of her back, and had the habit of swinging her head from side to side so it swished behind her with the undulating rhythm of windshield wipers.

Anna Beth smirked. They weren't supposed to add the delicate sprigs of baby's breath without checking with cost-conscious Madson first, but she got away with it all the time. She pulled off about three yards of cream satin ribbon and twisted it into a bow for the box. She'd made so many in the four years we'd lived with Willard, her sturdy hands worked without supervision while her mind concentrated on other things. "It's not a nun's college," she quipped, aggravated that Louisa was once again making fun of her choices in life. Who was she to taunt, after all? Her life choices had been one disaster after another.

"What other kind of school would you call The Women's College of the Immaculate Conception of the Blessed Virgin Mary?" Louisa stuck her nose in the air as she said this, talking through it, then she caught the bow Anna Beth threw in her face. I knocked a couple of Styrofoam balls off the shelf beside her. They landed on Louisa's table, dropped off the edge and hit her toe. She kicked them away.

"See, even Olivia agrees with me," Anna Beth said, smiling up to where she knew I'd be.

Louisa tied the bow into place on top of the box, looking about. "Well, it sure isn't a wild, party school," she said, and thrust the box into Anna Beth's arms to put away. "And stop talking about that Olivia girl. I know you like her a lot, but people are gonna think you're nuts."

I had to laugh.

When they returned to the subject of school, Anna Beth jumped back on the defensive. "Well, of course, it's a Catholic school, but that doesn't mean they'll recruit me into the Order. Sister's friends on the faculty just helped me get accepted. That's all there is to it. I am *not* becoming a nun. I think I may major in art."

"Art? You haven't sketched in years. And with your grades, you could have gotten into Harvard, for Goodness sake. But who is ever going to teach you how to loosen up and have some fun? You're eighteen and you've never been kissed. You've never even been out on a date. Now, you listen to me for once and I'll fix that. I think you should . . . "

Anna Beth disappeared into the refrigerator to put up the roses. Its plastic flaps and cooling fans drowned out Louisa's tirade. She hoped that, when she returned, Louisa would have moved on to less abrasive topics, not that these two ever dabbled in light chit-chat about fashion magazines or pop stars. Bigger monsters to kill. But when she came back out, Louisa was still yapping over her shoulder and walking toward the doorway into the parlor.

"Yep, Sister took your soul the minute we set foot inside her kitchen. And she's used every one of my miscarriages to draw you deeper and deeper into the fold, the old bat."

So much for a reprieve, Anna Beth thought.

Sure, I had hoped she would find a nice country boy, have a normal teen life, fool around a little in a back seat of a car or two, learn the art of making out *without* going 'all the way'. But it wasn't happening *my* way. All the time we spent at Beaver's was the main reason she had no obvious personal life. But that was time well spent.

I was glad she loved spending time there, but it had almost become our second home. Not many people knew about the place, especially since the nuns had moved out and it had become a storage building, and no one suspected that Anna Beth was going *there* when she disappeared each evening. Nope, we skulked away every night after dinner, and any other time we could get away, and didn't return until she was good and ready.

Once we stayed gone for two days. That went over real big at the home place. Oh, how Willard had fussed and fumed over Anna Beth's clandestine life. As much as she believed Anna Beth was a 'good girl', she also feared that Louisa's example might be detrimental at some point. Often she'd be waiting for us with hands on hips and a good talking-to written out on paper so she wouldn't forget to cover everything. She threatened every punishment imaginable, but Anna Beth just smiled, and said, "I love you, Aunt Willard, but I have to go. You'll have to trust me on this," and walked out the door.

When Willard took away the keys to the truck, we walked. She even tried tailing us a time or two to see where we went. But we were too smart for that. Nope, trying to get Anna Beth to toe the line was like being dragged by an elephant. All it got you was sore ankles from the heel ruts you left in the stubborn ground.

The girls walked through the spooky room on our way upstairs. We passed through that room every day, but never stopped long enough to turn on a light or stir up the dust that now stood so thick on the furniture you couldn't tell what color anything was.

Louisa stopped at the bottom of the steps. "Sister thinks I'm a major, hardcore sinner, doesn't she?"

"What do you mean? No, no, she doesn't," Anna Beth lied. "So, maybe you've made mistakes here and there, but . . . " She paused and decided it would be to her advantage to redirect this conversation yet again and toss it back to Louisa. "Why would she use your tragedies to manipulate me? That's ridiculous."

Louisa stopped cold in her loafer tracks on the third or fourth step and turned. The dark staircase ascending behind her added a sense of drama to her stance. "Mistakes? Ha! You mean my *sins*. My *sins* are keeping me from fulfilling God's plan. Right? Is that what she said?"

Anna Beth deflated and shrank back under Louisa's dominance above her. One of these days she'd learn to choose her words more carefully.

Shaking her head, Louisa continued up the steps, stomping as hard as she could. "You are such a wimp, Anna Beth. A naïve little wimp. The only way to escape our childhood is to grow out of it. And you, sister, are way behind in that class." She stopped again at the top of the stairs, hands on her hips. "I've watched the way Sister maneuvers you. How that woman comforted you with holy mumbo-jumbo about why I can't carry a child to full term. Why, she can just kiss my foot, better yet—my ass."

Anna Beth's mouth fell open and she threw up her hands. *Where is all of this coming from?* she wondered. Guilt talking, she guessed. With as much guilt as Genevieve had spewed in my direction, I could tell it a light year away.

"Oh, don't look so shocked," Louisa continued. "I know better. I know God is just punishing me. What? Does Sister think I'm dumb? He's making me pay for giving myself to a man I can't have. God is a mean old buzzard, like Grandpa Clancy was. And a cruel one to boot."

The way Louisa twisted common sense into a panty wad amazed me. It reminded me of someone—oh, who could that be? But I guess, with what she had to go on, she was doing the best she could do at the time. She strode through the hesitation room and into the bedroom, and flung herself across the bed. She rolled over onto her back and crossed her arms over her voluptuous chest, waiting for Anna Beth to catch up.

When she darkened the door, Louisa shifted gears yet again. "You do realize that going to school in Memphis, right there under Moody's nose, is gonna make her think you've come home to be close to her. She is gonna bug you to death, and you know it. Do you really want that?"

"I can handle Moody. I'll steer clear."

"You know, she's been calling Aunt Willard a lot lately. I guess it's about time again for her once-a-year guilt trip. She'll get over it in a day or two, but if you move there, no telling what will happen. You should just come to New York with me instead. We could have a great time. I'd take you on as my protégé. I'd have you footloose and scandalous within a month, guaranteed." I didn't doubt that.

"Since when are you going to New York? Or, is this another one of your schemes to get back at him?" Anna Beth sat down hard on the vanity bench, with her back to Louisa. She stared at Louisa's reflection in the large antique mirror as she raked a silver-handled hairbrush through her short-cropped curls. We couldn't for the life of us figure Louisa out. All these years and three miscarriages. Louisa had wasted her whole young adulthood, mooning and moaning over a man who took pride in taking advantage of her stupidity and misguided devotion. Anna Beth vowed never to be that butt-dumb, and I hoped her resolve would stick.

"Today! I decided to move to New York today, right this very minute, if you want to know the truth," Louisa said. "And I think it's a fine idea. Inspired, in fact."

"And what, pray tell, are you going to do there?"

"I don't know yet, but at least I won't be giving up living to be on my knees ten hours a day, mumbling boring prayers for people I don't even know, like Sister thinks I should do."

Little furrows around Anna Beth's eyes pinched together, giving her the stern look of a Mother Superior. Louisa laughed out loud. "Sister's even taught you how to scowl like a professional saint."

Anna Beth ignored the remark. She had long since figured out that Jack Bland was Louisa's lover. Little Spec getting married had been a defining clue, since Louisa had no reaction to the event. Anna Beth recognized that Louisa would never come to her senses about Jack Bland. The man had put Louisa under some kind of spell from which she couldn't escape, even though she protested often that she was going to 'change her life.' "I'll bet he won't think much about you running off?" Anna Beth said without thinking, then felt bad for using his jealousy to make Louisa read the writing on the wall.

Louisa sat up abruptly and snatched a pillow from under the covers. She hugged it to her chest, sitting cross-legged in the middle of the bed. "He doesn't know. And I don't think I'll tell him."

Jack Bland was twice Louisa's age, married with no intention of leaving his wife, had gotten her pregnant three times, but she would break every rule and commit every sin to be with him. I didn't understand it, and neither did Anna Beth. God had granted me a wealth of knowledge, and, thanks to my time with Genevieve, I had witnessed lots of illogical reasoning, but this beat the band. I would never understand the ways humans entwined down-and-dirty horniness with real, abiding love. It didn't make a lick of sense to me.

"Well, that's the first rational thing I've heard you say in years," Anna Beth admitted. "Make a clean break. It will be the best way for the two of you to get on with your lives."

"I'm so glad you think I'm finally sane," Louisa groaned.

Anna Beth walked over to the window that looked out onto the screened porch. Louisa had climbed across it and down those rickety steps innumerable times. Not even blood-hungry bees could keep her from flying off to meet her lover—or from Willard's wrath. And Anna Beth and I were never far behind, protecting her on her excursions and defending her to Willard and Madson on our return. Someone had to help her; Louisa certainly wasn't looking out for herself.

But when Anna Beth left to delve into her secret life at the abandoned old convent, she used the door. She announced to Willard, "I'm going. I'll be back after while," and walked proudly out. She explained to Willard that she wasn't doing anything *wrong,* but that she just needed time to herself. She asked for Willard's trust. Honestly made the difference. Anna Beth wanted Louisa to be able to do the same, but doubted that Louisa would ever understand the concept.

"So, you've finally given up on His Highness? I hope you stick to it this time. He's been using you from the start. It's time to give up this fantasy of yours and move on."

Louisa scooted off the bed and wandered over to the closet to choose an outfit for her evening out. I wished that Anna Beth's sermon—rattling on and on in the background like a repetitious litany—would finally sink through Louisa's thick skull.

"You know, I give up on you," Louisa said, not turning around. "Explaining the ins and outs of true love to a girl who wouldn't know it if it bit her in the butt is a waste of my time. You'll never understand."

Anna Beth bit down hard on her bottom lip and straightened the seven rings that adorned her trembling hands. What could she say to that?

*

The pay phone rang and a young woman yelled down the dormitory hallway. "Anna Beth? You here? Phoooooone!"

"Not again," Anna Beth grumbled, shuffling to the phone. The ragged bell bottoms she had thrown on as she slid out of bed dragged across the mustard-colored linoleum, making a whooshing sound around her feet. Even though she had just awakened from a deep sleep, her amber crown of curls danced atop her head like velvet corkscrews. "Louisa was right. Moody won't give me a moment's peace."

We had been at college for several weeks now. What a life. I had no idea school could be so diverse, so fun, so different from our existence at the home place. I was learning, however, that my loved ones weren't the only strange balls bouncing around this world. Anna Beth might actually have the opportunity to make a friend here, and that was a good thing. I was pleased that she seemed to fit in. She lifted the receiver to her ear and, without giving the caller time to say hello, groused into the phone, "No, I'm not coming to visit you. And, no, I don't know where Louisa is. And no, you may not come to see me . . . "

"Anna Beth? Sweetheart, is that you?" Willard's voice interjected.

"Oh, Aunt Willard, I'm so sorry. I thought you were . . . It's just that . . . ."

"It's okay, honey. I was just calling to check on you. Need any money? Are you eating right?"

"I'm fine, thanks. Just tired."

"Genevieve's been calling, I suppose? Now you just listen to me, honey. Your mother may be a lot of bad things—I'll save you the list—but she's never stopped loving you girls, in her own way. What I would give for this family to mend itself somehow."

"I'm sorry, but I can't, Aunt Willard. We've been through this all before." She slid down the wall into a heap on the floor.

"I know, but I'm telling you anyway. I can't believe I'm saying this, but give her a chance. She's messed up big time, over and over again. I'm sure she knows it. Just up and leaving you girls with me the way she did must have been the hardest thing she ever did in her life. But I'm sure she realizes what horrible mistakes she's made by now. Talk to her, sweetie. That's all, just talk. Keeping things inside you like that'll eat away at that beautiful heart of yours. I should know."

Anna Beth sighed, knowing Willard was right. It had been almost five years since Louisa's first baby's funeral. Five years since she'd seen Genevieve. But was five years a long enough sentence for abandoning your own kids? Anna Beth wasn't so sure herself. Life without parole seemed more appropriate to her.

"I'll try, Aunt Willard. Lord knows, she hasn't given me a moment's peace since *someone* told her I was here."

*

Crouched down behind a neighbor's fifty-year-old azalea bush, Anna Beth parted the thick foliage, and we peered out towards the house. The curtains were drawn, except those in what had once been her room on the second floor. One shutter hung cock-eyed off its hinges. Anna Beth swallowed a lump the size of Montana in her throat. It resisted being shoved down. I patted her on the shoulder, and that seemed to settle her a bit.

We'd gotten off the bus at the corner of Highland Avenue and Central. She'd left the truck on campus—Willard's gift to her for good grades—because she didn't want it to be recognized, and she'd walked up and down both streets, looking for landmarks, searching her memory for glimpses from the past. I helped out in this regard. Lord knows, I knew my way around Memphis and had been there plenty of times.

When she finally stopped fighting my urgings and found the familiar side street, the pit of her stomach contracted, threatening a diarrhea attack. "What'll I do if Moody spots me?" she had whispered, and wondered how she would explain her presence there, especially after she had refused rather loudly to see her, screaming into the phone, "I never, ever want to see you, ever again," before slamming the receiver down.

She hadn't thought of the consequences of being detected until now. What reasons could she use to explain her wandering around the old neighborhood? "Moody will think I came to see her," she told me. But no, she was only there to see the house, right? She had never thought of this place as *home,* just a house, a place with no lasting impression, at least none holding warmth.

The flower shop van was parked in the driveway. It had lost its back bumper. Rust tarnished its dented back doors. We glanced up and down the street. It was idle, vacant, like everyone was either away or hibernating in their brick-and-mortar caves with the blinds drawn.

Anna Beth unwrapped an Almond Joy bar she'd brought with her, tucked the wrapper into her windbreaker pocket, and sank her teeth into the rich chocolate as the sun sank below the horizon, allowing a chill to set in. That's one thing I'd always wondered about—eating. Everyone seemed to enjoy it so much, but then got mad at themselves for savoring the pleasure. Explain that.

Okay, so now what, she wondered? *Just sit here in the dirt and stare at the decrepit old place*? She was stooped down in the next-door neighbor's side yard, her back and bottom sticking out onto the sidewalk. If a car came by, they'd think she was casing the joint. She looked around. No one in sight.

She'd lost track of how long we'd been watching the house, and ducked behind the neighbor's station wagon when the across-the-street neighbors came home from work. *What good is it doing, just sitting there, staring at the place*, I wanted to know? *Take action if you're going to, but don't just sit here on your heels*. She pulled her jacket in closer and didn't hear the car pull up behind us until its tires crunched over a branch lying in the street not ten feet away. She turned and stood up, startled, and we stared into the unlit headlights of Little Spec's yellow Mustang Mach One, the same car he'd driven that summer at the lake, five years earlier. Jack Bland had given it to her when Little Spec got married and needed a new vehicle.

Louisa yelled out the driver's side window, "Just as I thought. You couldn't stay away. Get over here, girl." She motioned for Anna Beth to get into the car. I beat Anna Beth to it, leaving Anna Beth on the sidewalk, and settled myself into a backseat so tiny and confined I wondered how flesh and bones would ever squeeze in.

Anna Beth's head tilted at a distressed angle. She still hadn't budged. Instead, she stood there by the bushes, hands raised in frustration and praise, mouthing, "What? How?" Finally, she shuffled around to the passenger seat, flung open the door and climbed in, ducking down. "Hush up, Weesa, do you want her to hear us?" She motioned for Louisa to slump over in the seat, but Louisa ignored her, of course. "And just what are *you* doing here?"

"Me?" Louisa squealed. "What in the Sam Hill are *you* doing here? I went to your dorm room and some brainy girl with a bad haircut told me you'd gone to 'explore the city.' I know you better than anyone. It didn't take me long to figure it out. And sure enough, here you are. If Moody sees you, she'll reel you back in and have you stalking Elvis by the weekend."

"If you don't hush and get us outta here, she *will* see us. Plus, you aren't supposed to be here."

"I'll swear, you can't do anything without me." Louisa threw the car into drive and gunned it, tossing up a tornado of autumn leaves in her wake. "I should have known. It's a good thing I came here. If I'd gone to New York, Moody would have been all over you like Aunt Jemima syrup, too sweet and too sticky. You'd never wash her off." She paused only briefly at a Stop sign and hung a left, headed in the direction of Overton Square, the favorite hangout for dope heads and hippies.

"Now, just wait a minute, Louisa. What are *you* doing here? And how did you know where I'd be?"

"Just an unlucky guess. Ha!" She drummed her fingernails on the steering wheel just like Genevieve used to do. If she'd had a Lucky Strike between them, no one could have told them apart. Smacking chewing gum to beat sixty, she wove through traffic with all the dexterity of a remedial juggler with ten balls in the air. I held on tight and prayed.

"Yeah, I'll bet. You never really planned to go to New York. I may be naïve, but I'm not stupid. And how did you get Little Spec's old car? It figures—leftovers for Louisa."

Louisa swerved through traffic in a zigzag motion that threw us this way and that, slamming us into the doors and sliding me across the rather bumpy back seat. My most extreme assistance techniques were put to the test to move other cars out of our way and keep us from snatching off bumpers or scraping paint chips from all the cars we passed.

Understand now, I couldn't make anyone do anything against their free will, but I could assist in the steering of their vehicles, as long as they didn't catch on and decide they wanted to go the other way. I had never worked so hard or been so exhausted in my death, not even when working my blessings on Genevieve.

"And where's he got you put up? The Peabody? Or did he get you an apartment? He didn't buy you a whole house, did he? Oh, Louisa, you can't do this. Have you lost your ever-loving mind?" Anna Beth was on a roll, and I was proud to hear it.

"Well, I never." Louisa slapped the steering wheel, trying to look aghast. She took her eyes off the road ahead which caused her to veer into oncoming traffic before correcting just in time and moving us back to the proper side of the yellow line.

"You never, my foot. You had this all planned out from the start. New York City, my eye. You knew you were coming to Memphis all along. You didn't want to listen to me tell you how *wrong* it is to be the kept woman of a *married* man. Oh, Louisa, when are you ever going to get it through your cotton candy head? Your Bland man is *married!* He keeps you the way he's always had you—his obedient little whore."

Louisa stomped the brake so hard in the middle of East Parkway that smelly black smoke billowed up from the asphalt behind us, then wafted into the car when it caught up. As the tires squealed, tears filled her eyes, and when our forward motion ceased, she beat the steering wheel with her fists, screaming, "Stop, stop, stop, stop! Do you hear me? Just stop it."

Now it was Anna Beth's turn to tear-up and squall. She covered her face with her hands. "Oh, now look what I've done. I'm so sorry, Weesa. Forgive me, forgive me, please." She reached out and patted Louisa's shoulder, not even caring about the traffic bearing down of us from all sides.

Louisa slumped over and sobs raged through her as horns blared behind us. I don't know about most other folks, but my family members could cry at the drop of a hat. Cars passed on both sides of us, their drivers yelling, cursing and flipping us so many *birds,* as Louisa called the hand signal, I was sure we would take flight.

"I can't take it. Do you hear me? I love him. It's all I know. I'm a big nobody without him. I don't know what else to do, how else to live."

Anna Beth sat back, silent, and spent. She stared over at Louisa, thoughtful for a minute, studying the signs. There had to be another reason for this outburst. Her ranting and raving couldn't be the only cause. It wasn't in Louisa's psychological makeup to get this upset; she usually just shut down. "You've lost another baby, haven't you?" Anna Beth said, more like a statement of fact than a question.

She reached over and took Louisa's hands in hers, but Louisa's head jerked up like she'd been slapped, and I promise it wasn't me. She stared straight out the windshield, not blinking, not saying a word. A few seconds ticked by and her tears stopped as abruptly as they'd begun. Finally, she pulled loose from Anna Beth's grasp, grabbed the gearshift, threw the car into drive and eased ever so slowly down the road. "I'm hungry," she said after a block or two. "What about you?" She wiped her arm across her face.

Anna Beth knew better than to push. Louisa was never going to confide in her. She might as well stop expecting that miracle. She dropped her chin to her chest as if in prayer, and whispered, "Yeah, sure. Whatever. Let's eat."

Louisa eased into a parking space behind the T.G.I. Friday's at Overton Square, and they moved in slow motion toward the restaurant, not speaking, shuffling along like two escapees from a nursing home. Inside, we sat at a window table and watched a menagerie of tourists and drug addicts mingle together on one of Elvis's favorite streets of Southern dreams.

*

A few months later, Louisa's arms were loaded down with packages when we stumbled out of the Casual Corner store at Poplar Avenue and Perkins Road. I had seen a little more of her lately, as they were trying hard to act like sisters again. Anna Beth had given up trying to talk sense into Louisa. What was the point, after all?

Shopping is so much fun; I had no idea. Anna Beth hurried up to hold open the door. They glanced around like they always did, still uneasy that we might run into Genevieve. With Louisa living all the way out in Germantown in her swanky new and fully furnished condo, she didn't usually have to worry about it too much.

But the college was only a few blocks away from *Flowers by Ned* in midtown, so Anna Beth dodged disastrous mishaps at every turn, or so it seemed. We had escaped a near-collision with Genevieve coming out of Seessel's Grocery Store just last week. Anna Beth actually hid behind a potted fern until Genevieve had passed. But we'd been in Memphis over seven months now and had managed to avoid her pretty well so far.

Louisa unlocked the trunk of her Mustang and dumped her purchases in—paid for with a limitless credit card imprinted with her name. Anna Beth snatched the keys away and climbed into the driver's seat, feeling good about the afternoon and spending time doing normal things.

We had tried to get together with Louisa whenever Anna Beth's studies allowed, which wasn't as often as Louisa would have liked because of our frequent trips to Iuka to spend time at *Beaver's Auto Parts and Shop*. Being away had taught Anna Beth one thing, though: *home* was the old carriage house and *Livvie's Heavenly Bouquet*, not Memphis. Willard, Madson, Louisa, and me, of course, were the only family she would ever need. She wouldn't allow herself to feel anything for Genevieve, or to ruminate on why Ned had up and left them.

She cranked the engine and turned on the radio. On WRVR FM

104.9, the Doobie Brothers sang about Mississippi moons. She sang along. She always drove when they were together, ignoring Louisa's protests, thank goodness. She liked the feeling of being in control, and didn't trust Louisa's driving after the little traffic jam she'd caused a few months ago.

I didn't think I could handle another one of Louisa's wild rides. Neither could Anna Beth. Besides the fact that her driving scared Anna Beth to death, it almost made her sick to her stomach. In the intolerable heat, it wouldn't take much to make Anna Beth vomit everywhere. Summer was not even in full swing, and Anna Beth looked out at the simmering, hot pavement and wondered why it was already so dad-blamed hot.

Louisa climbed in beside her and flipped down the vanity mirror to investigate her face. I'd gotten used to my place in the backseat. Anna Beth watched her, and memories flowed over her like a hot shower. She flushed, remembering when we drove Louisa out to Goat Island that first time—the first time of so many.

They were just kids then, but it seemed like a hundred years ago to them, and only an angel's blink to me. Watching Louisa primp now reminded me that nothing had really changed since then. We were still carting Louisa around to do things that dug her deeper into her grave of regrets with the wrong man.

Her brain was still stupidly disabled, her heart still muddled with misspent love and paralyzed with grief. I'm not sure why, but Anna Beth felt responsible somehow. Maybe she was just living out her own fantasies through Louisa, her own longings for love. Maybe that's why she had helped Louisa go see him all the time, and defended Louisa against Willard's protests, and why she got so angry with Louisa, but never really did anything to make her stop.

Maybe her cooperation and assistance enabled Louisa to remain fickle, while filling her own existence with voyeuristic excitement once in a while. *Louisa might have let go of him long ago if it wasn't for me*, she thought now. She laid her forehead against the scalding steering wheel. Hot tears streamed down her face.

"What? What's all this?" Louisa asked, turning with her mouth still puckered, ready for hot pink lipstick. "What's gotten in to you? You don't cry. You never cry."

"I'd like to hear some funky Dixieland," echoed around us. But the sudden rap of knuckles on the window jolted them both. Anna Beth straightened up in the seat and turned. Louisa bent over the gearshift to see who it was, and Genevieve's face appeared in the window, grinning like a circus clown, her hands waving about like she'd just done a magic trick.

"Yoo-hoo, girrrrrls. It's meeeee, Moody. I haven't seen you since the Fall of Rome." Her fingers tapped the window like a secretary doing ninety words a minute.

The girls sat motionless, gawking, too stunned to react. The car door swung open and Genevieve dove in, headfirst and sprawling, her body stretched across Anna Beth's lap as she grabbed and pawed, hugging and kissing air, shoulders and hair, whatever happened to fall in front of her mouth. Her high heels dangled out the door as she patted and smoothed all at the same time.

"Oh, please forgive me, girls. You have every right to hate me, but don't turn me away. Please, don't turn me away."

Anna Beth squirmed under the weight, shoving Genevieve against the horn that yelped out a high pitched staccato, *Help-a-elp-elp-elp.*

"Get off me, get out," Anna Beth said.

She spanked the tight butt in her face, while Louisa flailed about, lipstick smearing everything in its path, and they pounded and fought off Genevieve's body, hands, kisses, and pleas. But they also struggled with the foreign emotions that consumed them. As their fists pummeled the mother they despised, their hearts realized they were beating a beloved foe.

Strike after strike the force lessened, yells of anger became wails of sorrow, shoves of hatred became loving grasps, fists relaxed into open palms, clutching, holding on and the skirmish diminished into a weepy mess as they pulled Genevieve close. Anna Beth sobbed into girdled hips, Louisa into rat-teased hair and me into that space between compassion and disgust.

"It's okay. It's okay, babies," Genevieve whined, turning to get her arms around them both. She maneuvered her rump around to rest on the hump between them. She gripped Louisa around the head so tightly, her hair got tangled in Genevieve's blouse buttons and it yanked open to reveal Genevieve's living bra. What a sight to behold. Still stuck in the stylish hell of the sixties, strands of her disheveled beehive stuck to her cheek.

Her legs pinned Anna Beth's arm painfully to the seat. They wiggled and jostled a bit, but couldn't get anywhere close to comfortable since they refused to let go of each other. Finally, Genevieve pulled back, looking into Louisa's eyes, then Anna Beth's. She grinned. "Hey, babies. Good to see ya'll. So, how've ya'll been?" Hot pink streaks smeared her teeth and crisscrossed her tear-marred face.

"We've missed you," Louisa admitted, spitting hair out of her mouth. "We hate you, but we've missed you just the same."

Anna Beth yanked her arm out from the vice of Genevieve's grip and flexed her fingers to make sure they were all present and accounted for. "Yeah, I guess, but it's not okay." She wiped her face with Genevieve's skirt hem.

"I'm so glad to see you both." Genevieve readjusted her position again.

Then we all noticed the strangers. People gathered on the sidewalk in front of the car, gaping at the sprawling, squalling spectacle taking place in our yellow Mach One. After a few more uncomfortable moments of us looking at them and them looking at us, Genevieve slid out, over Anna Beth, onto her knees and into the parking space. She sat back on her spiked heels just inside the door, smoothing down the front of her skirt and fluffing her hair.

"Oh dear me, what a mess I must be. I must look like some old crazy woman. A fright, I must be a fright." She brushed her finger across her teeth, her white breasts still bulging from her open blouse, and then dug deep inside her pocketbook for a mirror so she could fuss with her hair. "Nice lipstick color, Louisa dear," she said, gazing into her compact and wiping the smears from her face. "What shade is it, honey? I'd like to try it sometime." Then she braced herself against the doorframe and hoisted herself up to her feet.

As for the survivors left in the car, we all took a minute to regroup. The girls straightened their clothes and I fortified their resolve, but no one got out of the car. Louisa had been watching the crowd of oglers and decided it was now time for her to stick out her tongue and flip them one of those *bird* signals. Genevieve had noticed them, too, of course, and was now pointing at the girls and mouthing, "It's okay y'all. These are my girls. Honest, it's all okay." I was not surprised when the crowd whispered behind their hands as they dispersed.

Anna Beth looked up at Genevieve, who was still busy putting herself back together. She had aged markedly. Lines made deep parentheses around her mouth and her once-azure eyes seemed as dull as hobnail glass and just as thick. Her overdone make-up looked just the same, a replica of the mask she'd worn when they were kids, perfect except for the runny mascara and messy cheeks and chin.

She'd left most of her pancake foundation on Louisa's blouse, replaced by smeared lipstick now. She seemed thinner, too, more fragile. Anna Beth's heart reacted by closing ranks. She was almost to the point of forgive-and-forget when she noticed something silky hanging out from under Genevieve's shirt. She reached up and grabbed the smooth fabric, giving it a sturdy tug, and a silk scarf, price tag intact and dangling, unfurled itself like a magician's sideshow handkerchief at a kiddie carnival.

"And what have we here?" Anna Beth's voice screeched, her vocal chores tensing to a high soprano's range.

Genevieve's wide-eyed expression of long-awaited absolution slid like an avalanche into the grimace of disbelief and shock. "But, but . . . no now, Anna Beth, dear. It, it, it's not what it seems."

"You haven't changed a bit. You're nothing but a liar and a thief. And I was so close, so close. Aughhh!" She gunned the Mustang and threw it into reverse, and she started backing out with Genevieve still stuck between the door and the car.

"What, what is it?" Louisa screamed.

"I can't believe it. I almost let myself . . . " Anna Beth slapped at Genevieve with one hand while steering with the other. "Get away from me, Moody," she wailed through clinched teeth. "I hate you. I hate you. I never want to see you again."

Genevieve stumbled and staggered, but finally broke free from the vehicle and fell to the pavement as Anna Beth swung the car around and sped out of the parking lot, leaving Genevieve on her knees, pounding with scraped fists and sobbing on the asphalt into her stolen scarf.

get the conniving wheels rolling again. "You know, darlin', that car sure looked familiar. Yellow Mustang—now, who do I know with one of them?" She remembered that Anna Beth was driving, though, and she knew better than to think that *she* could have finagled a car out of anyone. So, what would Louisa be doing with Little Spec's favorite Ford?

Another few gulps from her cup sent possibilities reeling, and the more she thought about it, the hotter she got. Answers finally came to her in a blur, like most things lately, and she wondered how she had not guessed it before, despite all of Jack Bland's denials and even though he didn't confide in her much these days. Just wrote the checks to the lawyer to bail her out, mostly, which, in her mind, gave her reason to believe there was still hope. And despite the fact that she had heard that Little Spec got married. And despite the fact that Elvis had been her chief concern of late, not the girls' welfare. Maybe it was time to refocus her attention.

So, if Little Spec was fooling around with Louisa, if it had been him all along, that must mean . . .

She smiled, then frowned, then smiled again. Curiosity and speculation presented her with a new purpose in life, and like a spoiled child on Christmas morning, she squealed with a new-found energy of renewed spite. She sat up straighter in the chair and sloshed down the last sips of her vodka. Now, all she had to do was prove her suspicions right.

She jumped up, steadied herself so she wouldn't fall out in the floor, then made her way upstairs to freshen up, all without thinking ahead far enough to see how her schemes and lies might affect her own flesh and blood.

*

The wholesale house was just closing for the day when Genevieve pulled into the parking lot. I knew trouble was brewing and was glad I was there to witness the fireworks. She waved at one of the employees as he walked out to his car.

"Sorry, Mrs. Baxter, we're closed."

Genevieve cringed. She hated it when people called her that—

especially after all these years. She wished she could erase all traces of *Baxter* from her life.

"It's okay, Wes," she hollered back, not slowing her pace. "I'm just here to see Jack Bland for a minute. He's in his office, right?"

The man nodded and walked on to his car. She knew he wouldn't stop her. He and everyone else in the Memphis floral industry had heard the rumors about Genevieve's shoplifting and how his boss bailed her out all the time. She pushed through the doorway, her gait struggling to stay upright with the concrete wobbling below her feet. Jack Bland's office faced the main sales floor. Sliding glass doors separated it from metal shelves stacked with oasis, a sea of plastic flowers, rolls of cellophane and ribbon rolls in every width, color and sheen. She paused in the wide opening to his office, leaning against the doorjamb in what she hoped was a provocative pose. Metal funeral spray easels stood beside her, propped along the paneled office wall like a hundred soldiers guarding the door.

"Working late again, I see," she sang, tapping her foot to music only she could hear. She was wearing a curly hairpiece left over from the sixties. Most of her fashion statements proved she was stuck in that unfortunate era of fashion hell. The mound sat lopsided on top of her head, its corkscrew tendrils varnished into place with half a can of hair glue. A flat, black bow perched, wackerjawed in front, and dangled from bobby pins ill-placed. I had half a mind to rip it right off of her head and set fire to it in the floor—that would have stripped her naked—but I stifled the urge since Jack Bland was at hand.

He didn't look up from his ledgers at first. "How much do you need this time? Or should I just call the lawyer and tell him to deal with it again?" His smooth hands fingered his fountain pen as his face tilted upward to meet her eyes.

She had memorized his features, still so youthful, so tanned. He hadn't aged a bit. Only the slightest hint of gray kissed his honey-colored temples, adding the dignity she knew he'd always dreamed of having, but never owned. She quivered noticeably, longing to stroke those sideburns again.

"I'm not here on business." She referred to her legal and financial affairs with him as *business*, her way of separating the unpleasant aspects of their relationship from the fantasy only she believed to be

real. "I'm here about Little Spec and Louisa." His eyes registered
only the faintest alarm. She teetered across the room to perch her
behind on the edge of his desk. "So, I see you're ready to admit
they're fooling around. That figures, I guess. But you allow it, Mr.
Proper and Upstanding? Little Spec running around on his wife is
okay? But, darlin', it never was with us."

"I don't know what you're talking about." He leaned back in his
chair and entwined his fingers over his chest. The chair moaned and
his jaw tensed only slightly.

"Why, Jack Bland, I'm surprised at you. You buy him a pretty
little society wife, and then let him fool around? That's not like you. I
think I just might be appalled."

"Nothing of the kind is happening, I assure you," he said, turning
back to his books. "Now, run on home, Genevieve. You're drunk and
I'm busy. I haven't got time for your tall tales and fantasies tonight."

She *tsssked* at him, shaking her finger, then dragged an office
chair over, stopping right in front of his desk. She sat down and leaned
forward at the waist, resting her chin on red lacquered fingertips perched
on the edge of his desk. "You've been so good to me over the years,"
she whined, looking up at him with puppy dog eyes. "Even after your
family swindled me out of half of this business."

He looked up, perturbed, but he didn't egg her on.

"Well, you know it *was* rightly mine after Momma and Daddy
died. But you've taken care of me, haven't you, and made sure I
never wanted for anything. You're a good man, Jack Bland. You know
that? I love you. I'll always love you." Abruptly, she sat back in the
chair and kicked the front of his desk with her foot. "But, I'll swear on
Grandma Olivia's bedpost, sometimes you are as dumb as mud and
twice as thick."

He tossed his pen at its tortoise shell holder and slammed the
ledger shut. "Okay, Genevieve, that's about enough. Spec and Louisa
are doing no such-a thing. I heard she's in New York or somewhere."
He picked up his cold coffee, but didn't take a sip, then he set it back
down. "Oh, what's the point? How would you know, anyway? You've
burned so many bridges with your girls; I'm surprised they even talk
to you. Lord knows I wouldn't if I didn't have to." He cracked his
knuckles, something he didn't normally do, but tonight he seemed

edgy, unable to figure out what to do with his hands.

Genevieve stuck her bottom lip out about an inch and pouted. She usually loved it when he got all upset with her, but this time his words stung. "You don't mean that, Jack Bland. Come on now, say you don't. You love me. I know you do. Just look at what we've been through together. Look at what we've meant to each other all these years."

He stood up and stretched his back, rubbing the back of his neck. "Good Lord, Genevieve, what's all this about? You know I care, but it will never be like that movie reel you've got running in your dizzy head. Now, go on home. Sober up. I'm ready to get outta here. It's been a long day."

She grabbed his arm as he passed her and spun him around. "Then, just tell me why Louisa is driving Little Spec's old car?"

Jack Bland shook his head, disgusted. He pulled away from her grasp and walked out of the office and across the wholesale house to check the back doors before locking up. She was right on his heels.

"She is, ya know. I saw her myself. And you've got to stop it, honey. It isn't right for them to be together. It isn't *natural*."

He flipped switches, darkening the massive space, then disappeared inside the walk-in refrigerator. The flimsy plastic doors slapped behind him, but he wasn't getting away this time. She strode right in behind him, cold air billowing her skirt as the fans kicked on. He was standing near the back, fiddling with the thermostat.

"It was one thing when she got pregnant," she almost yelled so she'd be heard over the noise of the fans. "They were just kids back then, and we didn't know what they were up to."

He jerked around to face her and she stumbled backwards, knocked over a tall bucket of daisy mums, and icy water pooled around her feet. Yellow and white daisy faces strewn around her ankles looked up her dress as she placed her open hands on his chest. "I can't believe I'm admitting this to you, but I was so relieved when she lost that child."

Well, that did it. I was ready to dump a flower bucket over her head. I couldn't stand much more. And she had punched the last button he was going to take, too. This was nuts and she was drunk. He pointed his finger at her, almost touching her nose. "You really are crazy. I've suspected it for years, but I'm certain of it now. I'm telling you again. Go home, Genevieve. I'm not listening to anymore of your liquored-up ranting and raving tonight." He pushed past her.

Just before he hit the plastic doors, she yelled, "One of my girls is yours, Jack Bland." That stopped him better than buckshot and caught me in one of those harrowing moments that made me wonder, too. What am I doing here if nobody fills me in? He didn't turn around. "Yep, that's right," she taunted, "which one do you think it is? Anna Beth? Or Louisa? The same Louisa that's sleeping with your son, Little Spec."

He turned on his heel and marched to no more than an inch from her satisfied face. "Your children are twins, Genevieve, or have you forgotten?" he said, through his teeth. "One of them can't be mine and the other one someone else's. It doesn't work that way. Now, if you are finished with your nonsense, kindly leave here, *now.* And don't come back. I'm done with you, darlin.' I've had you up to here." He saluted over his head, spun around and stomped out into the darkened showroom.

She strolled after him, taking her time, dawdling along, weaving through the aisles of merchandise while he waited, patting his foot by the front door. When she finally made her way to him, she paused right in front of him and stared up into eyes that wouldn't meet hers. She smiled and caressed his cheek with her fingers. "They're not twins," she whispered. "One of them is Willard and Madson's girl. I just raised her as my child's twin to save Willard's butt. The other one is ours, darlin'—yours and mine. Which one do you think it is? Only I know. Are you going to trust that it isn't Louisa?"

She pushed the door open and slung her purse over her shoulder as she headed for the van. "Put that in your pipe and smoke it, Jack Bland." She swung open the van door and stood behind it, leaning into the open window. "I realize it's been done before. People do it all the time, all over the place. But are you really gonna take the chance that your precious son might be doing *the wild thing* with his little sister, huh?"

*

What was I saying about God tossing us grounders to see if we're paying attention? I couldn't believe she had been able to keep this pertinent information locked away from me in that fractured and delusional brain of hers. Lots of things she'd done had thrown me for a loop, but at this, I was shocked and appalled. Talk about bad reception. All I could think about was the girls, my poor, sweet clueless girls. I prayed there was a hope in heaven that they'd stay that way. I hated my family's plethora of secrets, but this one even I was willing to keep.

The flower shop van needed new tires, new brakes and a tune up. Better yet, it needed to be junked. Business had been slow lately, or so Mildred Minniver told Genevieve all the time, but Genevieve had no first-hand knowledge of that fact, of course, since she only showed up a couple of days a week to fill in on employees' days off and to make sure her precious Elvis deliveries got sent out. Mildred handled all the accounts and cut Genevieve a check once a week. "She's probably ripping me off blind," Genevieve said to no one, wiping sweat from her upper lip as she sat in the hot van.

The vinyl seat stuck to the back of her legs as she craned her neck to peer through the side window. She had been playing detective the last few weeks, ever since the big blowup with the girls and her personally designed run-in with Jack Bland. She figured she had to do something. It was obvious that he wasn't going to take care of the situation. Plus, after that little talk with "the only man she'd ever love," she was feeling restless with herself. Seeing him always affected her that way. It brought back all her aggravation with him for not leaving his wife. He'd had plenty of chances, but was just too good and caring to hurt the old bat, she thought. Seeing him always stirred up her hormones, got them gyrating inside her to beat the band. Hot flashes and Genevieve were the best of friends.

Now, she sat in the parking lot of the convenience store across the street from the ritzy Germantown apartment Louisa occupied. "Jack Bland must be paying Little Spec pretty well for him to afford a wife, and Louisa on the side," she told the miniature plastic statue of Elvis that had lived on the dashboard since the girls were ten.

Just about the time I thought I was going to oxidize if she said another word, her surveillance paid off. She strained and squinted into the night as the door of the apartment opened, and a man stepped out into the light.

In that instant life, as Genevieve knew it, ceased to exist.

The Trouble With Girls
Film, Metro-Goldwyn-Mayer, including
the songs, *Almost, Clean up Your Own Backyard* and
Swing Low, Sweet Chariot

"Anna Beth, phoooone."

"For a girl with no real friends, I sure get a lot of phone calls," Anna Beth griped, as she trudged down the hallway. She lifted the receiver, and Mildred Minniver's voice came on the line.

"Anna Beth, hon, I hate to bother you, but I've been callin' and callin' and Genevieve won't pick up." We hadn't seen nor spoken to this woman in years, but Mildred jumped right in with her problems like we'd seen each other everyday. "Your Moody gets this way sometimes, ya know. Don't show up at the shop for days on end. Leaves me in the lurch most all the time, but it ain't like her not to come in and at least pick up her check."

"Well, uh, what do you want me to do?"

I did everything I could to shut this woman up, but that free will God gave people got in the way again. It seemed like it was always either *His* way, or *their* way, leaving not much of an opportunity for me to ever get *my* way. How fair is that? But I did not want Anna Beth anywhere near Genevieve right now.

"I'd go over there myself. You know I would. I'd love to jerk a knot on your crazy mother's head. But I do enough around here. Now, be a doll baby and drop in on her for me. Tell her lazy Miss Highness to get her drunken butt up and tend to her business. She tells everyone she runs it, after all, while I do all the work. Thanks, hon. Well, I've got to run; we've got us a wedding this weekend that somebody's got to make umpteen bouquets and boutonnières for."

The line went dead, leaving Anna Beth standing, breathless, in the hall, and me frustrated again with the limits God imposed on me when I was only trying to help.

*

Anna Beth hadn't been back to the house since her little stakeout, when Louisa caught her spying on the place almost eight months ago. And she hadn't been inside since Genevieve packed us up and sent us to Willard's when she and Louisa were fourteen. God love 'em, but the past five years had clogged every pore of her adolescence and glued Louisa to a life of tragic love without hope. Now, Anna Beth shuddered as we stepped onto the dingy porch. Her finger paused an inch away from the doorbell, hesitant about if it should do its job and push.

I had made sure the truck wouldn't start that morning, but that didn't stop her; she got a classmate from school to drive us over and drop us off, and she now thought that getting back to campus was her only other problem to solve for the day. She wondered if she should just turn around and start walking. *Yes, go! Please just go*, I said, but either God had blocked my signal or she was too upset to tune in. I'd hoped to save her the heartache, save her the anger.

She glanced around, fidgeting, buying time. The beat-up van sat catawhompus in the driveway—again. Genevieve had misjudged the angle of the concrete strips running alongside the house, and two wheels rested in the lawn. The bumper nudged an azalea bush in the front bed, bending the branches in uncomfortable directions. She steadied herself and, even with me pulling and screaming, "No!" in her ears, she forced her finger onto the bell. She pushed once, twice, hysterically. But no one answered. *Okay, can we just go now?*

"Just my luck," she grumbled under her breath.

She pulled open the storm door out of reflex, and its suction tugged at the interior door, then released it. It gaped open just enough for her to see that it was unlocked and unlatched. She placed her hand on it, barely touching it, and wondered if she really wanted to do this, but before I could convince her otherwise, make her listen to me and object, the door opened itself. *Okay, God, I get the point*, I said.

She took two steps inside the entry hall and her sunglasses fogged from air-conditioned air so cold it could freeze the pipes. It was ninety degrees outside and thirty below in the house. She pulled off her glasses, wiping them on the tail of her shirt, and yelled weakly,

"Helloooo, Moody? You home?"

She eased farther into the dark hallway, looking about in a squint, replaced her glasses and stepped under the arch into the living room. The phantom furniture that had appeared out of nowhere while we were away at church camp still occupied the space. Nothing had changed, only aged.

"It's me . . . Anna Beth. Anybody home?" She rubbed her arms. "Think you've got it cold enough in here?" Wandering through the rooms on the main floor, she felt uneasy about being here. Instead of feeling like home, it felt more like a shrine. Elvis paraphernalia hung, sat and was perched everywhere. "This is nuts," she said, and thought Genevieve had probably been arrested again, and that they had kept her this time.

Stepping into the kitchen, she thought she would just leave a note— *Call the shop. Mildred needs you*—and we could be on our way, but curiosity urged her to look around. The cabinets gave the impression of being brand new—never used is more like it—but the table seemed tired. She slumped into a chair, and tried to conjure up one happy memory from this kitchen. This effort failed, and then she wondered what she should do. She cursed herself for coming in the first place. She should have stood up to Mrs. Minniver and yelled a resounding, "NO!" into the phone. But she was too good a girl for that.

Silence encompassed her, and her mind began to focus on the lack of sound in the room to keep herself from thinking about seeing Genevieve. What would they say to each other? They were strangers really, only held together by bitterness and mistrust. Still, she had promised Willard that she'd try. *When hell freezes over*, she thought now, recalling the parking lot escapade a few weeks back. Minutes ticked by on the clock over the stove. Should she just sit here and wait? *This is ridiculous*, she thought. She could be here all night while Genevieve was off stalking Elvis.

That's right, girl. Go on, get out of here, I urged.

The cloud of her own breath caught her attention. It seemed increasingly odd for a house to be so cold. She glanced around the room. No dirty dishes, no knickknacks out of place. *Mr. Clean is the only one who's been here*, she thought, but just the image of Genevieve cleaning brought a weak smile to her lips. She figured she must have a maid.

Her eyes scanned the cabinets and drifted across the floor. The electrical cord that lay in a puddle of water beside the refrigerator didn't jump out at her at first. Her eyes just stopped on it, resting for a second, before her brain kicked in with confusion. She stared at it. *Why is the refrigerator unplugged?* Water seeped out and dribbled down from the freezer on top. "Oh great," she finally said aloud. Whatever was in there was going to reek to high heaven. She certainly wasn't going to hang around to clean it out.

Tears welled up in her eyes for no reason, and for every reason at the same time. That was her job in life, wasn't it? Cleaning up after everyone else's messes and mistakes, always being there to take care of things, to keep things from falling apart. Genevieve's abandonment had certainly taken its toll. But why was she crying about it now? She blinked, letting the tears run, but she didn't sob or wail or bury her face in her hands and weep, she just sat there staring at the unplugged refrigerator with water streaming down her cheeks, unchecked.

When her tear ducts finally dried up, she made herself stop raking herself over cold coals and sat up straighter in the chair, feeling like a garbage truck had backed over her. *Okay, Miss Crybaby*, she thought, *you can either sit here feeling sorry for yourself, or you can get your butt up and out of here*. Maybe she was finally tuning in to me. I cheered her on.

She stomped out of the kitchen, slamming her Keds against the hardwood until her rubber soles bit back, but at the front door she stopped, and looked back toward the stairs, her determination to leave circumvented by curiosity again. She wondered about our old rooms. Had we left anything behind when we moved? Had Genevieve kept them the same all these years? She wavered for a moment, then decided it wouldn't hurt to check and headed toward the stairs.

*

I've learned that when people are desperate and hurting, all reason and logic gets tossed to the wind. Their minds take vacation from good sense, if they ever had any, and let disillusionment move in to housesit. As I watched, Genevieve Clancy Hersh Baxter's last hopes of sanity vacated her premises that evening outside Louisa's apartment. The minute she recognized Jack Bland what was left of her brain took a hike.

Getting home had taken almost more effort than she could muster. Her whole life of lies, deluded sacrifice, and deserved and undeserved guilt spun around inside her, haunting her from within. Plans gone bad and love unfulfilled mocked her. She had plodded up the front steps, certain that her last scheme would show us all. Show all of us who loved her in spite of herself that she could do whatever it took, that she would give whatever she must, to be perfect, to be lovable, to be loved. After all, it is honorable to sacrifice everything you've ever dreamed of for your kids, right? She thought so.

She stumbled through the living room, stopping to jack up the air-conditioner to full blast, and detoured through the kitchen to pat the freezer door and remember what all she'd hidden there, and in all her other hiding places around the house. Then, with a smile, she yanked its plug from the wall.

Upstairs, she cranked up Elvis on the record player. The timbre of his voice soothed her, embraced her like it had done so often in the past. Standing in her closet, she studied her wardrobe. She needed the perfect ensemble to look dignified, well accessorized. She chose a few and nodded, bits and pieces of her plan falling into place.

She was certain that, when she didn't show up at the shop to get her check, Mildred Minniver would come along soon enough to track her down. It would serve Mildred right for giving her such a hard time all these years, she thought. And if not Mildred, then a policeman or fireman, a Memphis Light Gas and Water employee coming to turn off the utilities when the bill didn't get paid. She decided on a pink angora twin set. It wasn't winter, but it would be cold enough in the house when the air-conditioner did its job. She held the sweater up to sniff the armpits. Pink had always been such a good color on her. Next, she chose a fetching polyester A-line skirt, white fishnets with high heel pumps, and a faux pearl choker. Priscilla Beaulieu couldn't have done better herself; she was pleased.

She slumped down onto the edge of the bed, her life-size cardboard cutout of Elvis by her side. Her hand didn't even tremble when she poured the painkillers into her palm. *That's the perfect name for them*, she thought. "Kill my pain, babies. Kill my pain." She laid Elvis down on his side of the bed. "You hold all my secrets, darlin'," she told him. "You can keep them forever or let them go. It's your call now, love."

I really didn't think she would do it, but she swallowed the pills in one gulp and lay down beside him, smoothed out her skirt, crossed her legs at the ankle, and folded her hands over her chest for her long, wakeless sleep. Thirty minutes ticked by . . . forty-five. She reached down to check her pulse. She was still alive.

Her small fistful (all she had left over from a four-year-old prescription from a root canal) had failed to do her in. Well, this little snafu really pissed her off. Could she not even succeed at relieving her children of the agony of having her as a mother? She had to do this for them, she thought. They would be so much better off without her. If she really loved them, she had to rid them of the shame of her. She sat up in a huff and overworked her brain for other options.

Back in the bathroom, she tucked a few errant strands of hair into place and lacquered them down with a long shot of Aqua-Net. She wondered if she should wrap her head in toilet paper to preserve the style like she did whenever she went to sleep, but decided against it. There was no telling who might find her, she told herself. It might be Jack Bland, come to ask her forgiveness for his part in this sad course of events. She could never rest in peace if she looked a-fright for him.

She stared at the straight-edged razor in the medicine cabinet for several minutes before really considering it or giving it a try. Anyone who knew Genevieve knew that she was too squeamish and self-absorbed to let herself feel real pain, and certainly too chicken to subject it on herself. She finally figured, *What the heck*. She wouldn't feel it for long. She grabbed it up. She placed towels under her wrist to preserve her outfit and hacked away on her left wrist. Her tolerance for pain astounded me. She didn't even flinch, just watched in a kind of transfixed daze as the shiny blade sliced a thin line through flesh that no longer owned the capacity to feel. Her emotional anguish dulled its bite to no more than a nibble. This would do it; she was sure. They'd be free; she'd be free. But then she noticed pulsating droplets of crimson oozing over the towel's edge, leaving scarlet blemishes on her skirt, and she stopped. I made her focus on her outfit, diverted her attention, if for only a second, to her appearance.

"Well, isn't this just a bunch of wilted roses," she said, perturbed at her never-ending string of bad luck. Stomping and strutting around the bedroom, she cursed poor old dead Ned for not buying a house with a real garage, one with a door. Carbon monoxide would have been perfect about now. Plus, she figured she could go out and buy herself that Caddy she'd always wanted. She would crank that sucker up and be a goner in a matter of minutes. It wouldn't matter about the payments, she justified.

They couldn't collect from a ghost, and she'd get to go out in style. She pondered a way to drive it into the house for a few minutes. Could she get it up the front steps somehow, she wondered? But her mind was fuzzy from the pills, so she gave up that idea.

She thought about the oven—*They do that on TV all the time*—but hers was electric. She was almost certain it had to be gas for that to work.

Finally, she cursed herself for never watching much TV. She thought, surely some detective show had broadcast *The Ten Sure-fire Ways to Kill Yourself and Not Make a Mess.* Then, she looked down, disgusted again, and revisited the closet. She didn't like the way the blood stains dried to a dingy brown on her rose-pedal skirt.

"Killing off Ned was like falling off a turnip truck," she told Elvis, while reapplying lipstick for the third time. Her left arm hung limp at her side and her right hand was beginning to shake now, making staying in the lines virtually impossible. She still believed she had caused his death, even though she had never touched the van and his own poor skills as a mechanic had caused the brakes to fail. (Elvis agreed with her on that, of course.) It amazed me how the human mind can twist reality, making truth out of fantasy and fantasy out of truth. She had given up the little guilt trips she used to indulge in for taking the girls' so-called father away from them at such an early age, though. They were better off without him, she believed. But now a nagging voice within her whispered, "Beg forgiveness. Repent."

She threw herself across the bed, arms spread-eagle and her face resting in Elvis' cardboard crotch. There was no way to forgive herself for the mess she'd made of her life. Loving Jack Bland had screwed it up good. Why on earth couldn't she just have loved Ned? Life would have been so much simpler. "Claustrophobic, but simple," she grumbled and rolled over onto her back.

She wondered if she should drain her own brake fluid and go drive around for a while. But it occurred to her that that could result in a less-than-perfect death. Being mangled and disfigured or brain dead due to head trauma were not odds she was willing to take. "Damn men," she screeched at the plaster ceiling. "Damn them all." She looked over at Elvis. "Except for you, of course, darlin'." *I should have camped out at Graceland and never left*, she thought. Elvis would have loved her tender, loved her true. She hugged herself.

I wondered if she might consider giving up on this plan for death. If there was the slightest possibility that she might think, *Since this seems to be so much trouble, maybe I'll just hang around for a while longer and try to deal with it all and muddle through*. But, no, when Jack Bland had stepped onto Louisa's porch Genevieve knew she had no other recourse but to die. She had lied her whole life, to everyone she loved and to everyone who ever crossed her path, but she couldn't lie to herself about this. She couldn't live with the horror and knowledge of her own daughter in love with the man she had always loved. She had given up everything for the fantasy of this man, this man who never wanted her, but who now wanted only Louisa.

She also knew she couldn't sustain the rigors of what she would have to do, the lies she would have to unearth, the pain she would have to cause Louisa and Anna Beth to explain it all—not to mention herself. She had sold her soul for Jack Bland, a man she could never have. She would rather kill *him* now, but she couldn't do that. As low and scum-sucking as he was, Genevieve loved him more than life— although the perversion of Grandpa Clancy's abuse had warped her idea of how to show love and accept love in return. With only that pitiful foundation to go on, Jack Bland's caring had looked like the real thing to her clueless heart. Her doom was commenced and sealed.

When she clomped up the stairs to the attic, dripping blood from her ragged wrist all along the way, I really started getting worried. This was no joke anymore. She was serious. I was scared. I glanced over at my door and wondered if it wasn't about time I pushed on through it. *Aren't you going to do something, God*, I shouted? *You know, I could use a little help here.*

I hadn't asked too many questions, hadn't bothered Him with trivial things. So, why wouldn't He ever answer? Did my prayers have broken wings? Oh, sure, He nudged me this way and that at His leisure, or infused me with that warm and fuzzy feeling that everything was going to all right. But I could have used more directives. I needed specifics. I wanted facts.

I wanted abilities to change things, especially to keep Genevieve from killing herself. But no *boom* of authority gave me answers. God didn't call me in for a meeting and lay out the plan. He just kissed my forehead with awareness, and I knew there was nothing to fear. In spite of all her failings, Genevieve was in God's loving hands.

She stood hunched over in the attic and knew it had to be up there somewhere—Ned's handgun, the one he had kept hidden under the mattress of their bed. She had found it one day on a rare occasion when she changed the sheets a few years back. She had been disgusted then with the realization that she'd been sleeping on top of an object of death. In the attic, she rifled through box after dusty box, now craving that pistol in the worst way.

It was a real struggle but she managed to scoot back down the stairs on her rump, her limbs sodden and heavy, her mind frazzled and dazed. She was so tired. Dying took too much effort. She thought about leaving a suicide note, a confession, but that would take energy and thought—two things with which she was running short. She'd leave that to Elvis. She had confessed everything to him so many times. Plus, she couldn't hold a pen if she tried. Besides, she'd worked so hard to cover up her blunders, her sins, her infidelities, she decided that everyone would be better off if she just buried them with her. Let the lies die. Let the pain end.

I did everything I could do to stop her, ruffled the curtains, threw perfume bottles and hairbrushes across the room. I slammed doors, and turned over furniture, heck, I even slapped her around a bit, stomped her foot, held her wrist to slow the bleeding, but it was as if she expected a tornado to accompany her exit. My feeble attempts to save her or scare her out of it gave credence to her choice instead. She lay down on the bed and held a pillow against the opposite side of her head, thinking it might absorb some of the mess. She didn't

was no telling where she'd be on the weekend.

Out with Jack Bland or up at the lake, she supposed. But now, with so many unanswered questions, she guessed it was better not to catch up with her just yet. "How will I tell her, Olivia? How will I tell Louisa what Moody has done?" I kissed her cheek softly and whispered, *You'll know when it's time.*

The fingerprint ink and gunpowder-test solvent wouldn't budge off her hands. She rubbed them compulsively on her jeans. Even though she could no longer see the residue on her skin, it was there; it was a part of her now. It had shocked me at first, the police considering her a suspect. How could anyone think that she, of all people, could hurt someone, anyone, even Genevieve, especially Genevieve?

She didn't wonder this, though. The memory of finding Genevieve gushed forward again—the ragged emotion that had surged though her when she had stumbled upon her, when she had pushed the bedroom door open and saw her there, sprawled out on the bed. She had wanted to kill her herself at that moment, kill her for doing this. But I knew that kind of fury wasn't in her. Even now, though, after hours to calm down, she still believed she could have pulled a trigger; that she could have blown the brains out of a mother she never really had. She hated her for what she had done, to herself and to our family. But it was too late now. As usual, Genevieve had acted as *she* thought was best, leaving everyone else to either go along with it or clean up the mess.

Willard and Madson burst through the door, breathless. I'd never been so happy to see two people. They could offer Anna Beth a support I could never give. They swept in, hugging, holding, patting, kissing any part of her within reach. I moved out of their way. She just stood there, limp and unmoving. She couldn't cry, couldn't hug back. They ushered her to the sofa and sat her down. And at my urging, the vigilant police officer disappeared from the room.

"Oh, sweetheart, we're so sorry," Willard said. "How awful. Are you okay?"

"What happened, sugar. Take it slow, but tell us what you know," Madson said.

I wished I could do this for her. I didn't want her to suffer through it again. She breathed in soured air, and let it out again, in and out, in and out, her throat raw and parched. It burned like she'd swallowed Listerine and seared as she fought to form the words she knew she had to somehow get out.

"Mildred Minniver called," she began, almost panting. "She got worried when, when Moo . . ."—*breath, breath*— "when she didn't come to pick up her check." It was hard in coming, but Anna Beth recounted, bit by heartbreaking bit, how we'd arrived at the house. Disjointed thoughts became fractured words that jumped off a tongue belonging to someone else, thick and dazed.

She stared at the coffee table through most of it, her mind regurgitating the information in quick bursts, long pauses, dry sobs. She tarried over the simple details about sitting in the kitchen and wondering about the unplugged refrigerator and if they had left anything when they moved to Iuka, as if her brain refused to allow her to revisit our journey up the stairs and the grisly sight we found there. Finally, when the words failed to form, she glanced over at the stairway, and only her eyes followed our assent of a few hours ago. Tears brimmed as her gaze reached the top, and then she stared straight up, through the ceiling, hoping that *up* was the direction Genevieve's spirit had gone.

Madson and Willard's eyes trailed along the same path to the stairway, then to the ceiling just above their heads. "Good God, is she . . .?" Madson asked, assuming that her body was still spread out up there, blood dripping from her veins.

"No, no, she's gone. The police . . ." Anna Beth composed herself, and she motioned toward the policeman who was nowhere in sight. "They took her. She's in, in, in the morgue, now." The howl that had been pent up inside her for ages finally escaped in a rush, and she went along with it, letting it all go. Through hiccups, coughs, and squalls, she cried harder and with more gusto than she had ever cried in her life. It hurt me to listen, but I was so glad for its release. Madson and Willard cradled her, scooped up her tears into competent hands, and shooshed and patted until the tempest played itself out. It was a marvelous sight, so tender, so loving. I stood in prayerful vigil, thankful that healing had already started to take shape.

"Now, now, it'll be all right. Oh Lord, how did you handle this alone? My poor, poor, sweet child." Willard's eyes blinked and danced about the room nervously, wanting to focus on something, anything, but of their own accord, they gravitated toward the ceiling again. I knew it was coming, knew that she would have to see for herself. She stood up as if manipulated by a puppeteer's strings, and moved toward the stairs.

Anna Beth gulped, sniffed, wiped her nose on her shirttail, and shook her head, pleading with outstretched her arms. "No, Aunt Willard, don't. You can't."

"She was my sister. I've got to. I've got to see . . . "

Madson and Anna Beth followed her. At the top of the stairs, their stricken faces gawked through the doorway, no discernible expression registering, only disbelief. The left half of the room remained spotless, unfazed by the devastation of its other half. The cardboard Elvis lay face up, upended, dangling off the edge of the bed, its pouty mouth degrading, its squinting suggestive wink adding tawdriness to the scene.

I wished they wouldn't look elsewhere, that their eyes would travel no further and remain still. This side of the room seemed unaffected by the discourse and destruction that lay so close within itself. But there was no way to prevent it. Eyelids widened as they panned the room, and I was sorry that all my efforts to stop Genevieve had only added to the devastation.

The right side knew no sanity, every inch screamed of pain. Propelled by my angry wind, knick-knacks were scattered about like broken playthings, curtains were ripped from their rods. From the gun blast, pink feathers lay strewn as if fallen from angels' wings in hurried flight, and they stuck like colored snowflakes to crimson-splattered walls and floor.

Madson uttered, "Lord have mercy," and he crossed himself a few times. The shiny toes of his shoes stood one inch outside the doorway, refusing to cross the threshold, the invisible boundary between life and the foreboding realm suicide conjured up. Willard crossed herself spontaneously, folding and refolding her hands, tears streaming from tightly squeezed lids. Her lips moved without sound in inaudible prayers that were too late.

Anna Beth pushed past the human wall that failed to protect her. We all reached to stop her, but she shoved through us and went to stand by the bed again. It looked so different now, so empty. A red speckled outline of Genevieve's left side proved that she had been there, forever imprinted on the cream spread. This half-perfect silhouette suggested lifting, implied ascension; I was glad of that. A subtle stillness settled over us as we stood there, a gift from above, I'm sure. Finally, Willard and Madson reached out and pulled Anna Beth to them, and we descended the stairs.

Back downstairs we huddled on the couch and stared at the floor. "I wish she had loved Daddy the way the two of you love each other," Anna Beth said, squeezing their hands. "Maybe he wouldn't have left us, and this wouldn't have happened." Such simple statements. She had no way of knowing what freedom they held.

I snuggled in close to my mother. I knew she'd need all the support I could give. "Lord, honey, we do love each other dearly, but not in the tawdry way your mother dreamed up," she said. "Genevieve thought she knew everything about me, but I couldn't let her know the truth. Her prejudices wouldn't have allowed her to handle it. Society wouldn't allow it either."

She laughed to herself for a moment, shaking her head at how silly it had been to keep quiet about her life for so long. And realizing, too, that it was time to speak up. Then, as if Genevieve's death had unlocked a jeweled case, hidden in a cave far away, my mother spilled her heartache out onto the coffee table for us all to see. She spoke simply and clearly, as if she had rehearsed the speech in the mirror or had prepared to tell it at the woman's luncheon. Her hands were her audience.

She told the sad tale of Grandpa Clancy, a man with no conscience who had flown into a rage and beaten her mercilessly when he discovered she was in love with Madson and pregnant with his child. She explained how she thought she'd lost the baby because of that beating and had fled to the convent for protection, and how the nuns had taken her in. "My babies were born right there at the convent. Yes, that's right, babies. I had twins. They survived. It would have been such a scandal, if word had gotten out. So, Reverend Mother prayed over it long and hard and decided to give my babies away to a good, loving home. She promised me that they'd be well taken care of. I knew it was for the best. Later, when I was able to talk to Madson, he understood. What else could we do? What else? I've asked myself a thousand times." She reached for his hand. "But I never even got to hold them. I didn't get to say good-bye."

She paused for a moment, remembering, and it was as if the room held its breath in respect. I wondered if her thinking I'd survived had kept me here, if the hope she had for me had tethered me to this realm. I exhaled for the first time, knowing she'd be all right now that she could talk about it, now that she had scattered her grief.

Her sorrow was arresting. It tugged at my essence and I struggled again to understand why it had to be this way. I knew it was for the best, but I didn't understand why any more than she did. No one spoke for several long moments, as if the three of them prayed in unison for the babies they were sure they would never get the chance to know and love.

Finally, Willard shooed her mourning back into its place in her memory and tucked her handkerchief back into its place in her pocket. "But there is more, my dear. So much more. Our dear Madson . . ." she said, looking up into his eyes, "is also my uncle. He is Grandpa Clancy's son. Of course, we didn't know this at the time, either of us, and our relationship changed completely after we found out. Grandpa Clancy made sure I knew, though. Yes, he made sure we both knew."

A lifetime of sorrow passed between them. He would have never divulged this secret heritage; she knew that. But he seemed relieved that the time had finally come for the truth to be told. "Grandpa was a horrible person, Anna Beth. He abused your mother and me often, repeatedly. We suffered horribly because of that man. He was the product of philandering men that go way back to slave times. He raped a woman who worked at the flower shop—one of many, I'm sure—and Madson was born right there in the basement where he has always lived."

"Oh, Madson," Anna Beth began, "I'm so . . . "

"It's all right, child," he said, his head held high. "My mother was a good woman, I know that. I just wish I'd had the chance to know her. She died giving birth to me."

Willard explained that when Grandma Olivia, God rest her loving soul, found out what Grandpa had done, she kept the secret and helped Madson's mother through her pregnancy.

"When my mother passed, Miss Livvie wouldn't let the old buzzard kill me or throw me out," Madson said. "She took me in, raised me up and gave me a home, in spite of him. She was one tough woman, Miss Livvie was."

"So, you see how complicated life can be? How complicated love can be? But, of course, you know that, don't you? We've all learned about love the hard way."

It took Anna Beth a few minutes to absorb it all, but in the end, it all made sense. She ached for Willard and her tragic life and loss, as I knew she would. She realized, too, that Genevieve would have never accepted Willard and Madson's love for each other, not to mention the fact that he was her uncle. Even with all he had done for the family, it was hard enough for Genevieve to accept him as a friend. "But Aunt Willard, hasn't Reverend Mother ever told you about your children?" she asked. "Why couldn't you see them or know where they are?"

"It has been hard, yes, but I trust her, sugar. She's my dearest friend. If God wanted me to know, she'd tell me. I know she's prayed over it and over it. Just one of those things I have to accept and trust."

Madson nodded as her story played itself out. He had experienced it with her and stood by her still. Anna Beth sat, thoughtful for a moment. The details trailed through all the questions she'd had and wiped them clean, one by one. Of course, she realized that the convent was *her* convent, *Beaver's Auto Parts and Shop*. She would see it with even more compassionate eyes from now on. But she didn't tell Willard she'd been there. It wasn't the time. Not yet. Then, nodding, she accepted Willard's confession as a gift, and a silent emotional bond ran through them like a shaft of gold. "I always wondered about you two," she said, embracing them both. "I knew you belonged at the home place, Madson; I just couldn't figure out how."

"Yeah, this family is one convoluted mess, huh? Some things are hard to explain."

My spirit lightened a bit. At least that much of it was out. I wondered when the rest would come. I was proud of my mother and how she seemed at peace with it all. I wished I could read her the way I read the girls or Genevieve. I wanted to feel her pain. I wanted to know if it resembled my own. And I worried that maybe my time with her was over now. Wondered if her telling would be what needed to happen before I could go through my door. I moved over to it. It hadn't opened. I pushed against it. It didn't give. *Guess not*, I figured. And speculated about when it would.

The policeman reappeared, drying his hands on a kitchen towel. He cleared his throat to get our attention. "I thought I'd make myself useful," the officer said. He stepped reverently into the living room, holding something in his hands. He studied his feet. "The Frigidaire caused quite a mess. I thought I'd help you out and clean up a bit."

Anna Beth shifted toward him, frowning with curiosity as she studied the object in his hands.

"I tossed out most of what was in there. Mostly spoilt meat that looked kind of ancient, and a bag or two of Veg-All. I put all the vodka in the cupboard with the canned goods and mopped up the floor best I could."

"Thank you, Officer," Anna Beth started. "But . . ."

"Awh, it weren't no problem. It was the least I could do for you and Miss Genevieve. We're gonna miss her down at the precinct, I have to say. I'm just real, real sorry that you good people are getting put through all this. It's a shame, a sad, sad shame."

"We appreciate your kind words, " Willard said, with a sad smile.

"I found something in the freezer, though, that you'll probably wanna take a look at." He handed Anna Beth the plastic bundle with a small stack of papers inside. "People are kind of funny, you know. They hide important stuff in the oddest of places.

"Heck, one man I know of buried all his money in the flowerbed under his begonias. He was some kind of upset when he realized that shoe boxes leak." He chuckled to himself and wiped his hands off again. "That there is a death certificate, looks like to me. I took a look at it. Might be for someone you know. A relative, I'd s'pect. Now, why she put the ol' guy's blood donor card in there with it is a mystery beyond me. But like I said, people do some pretty peculiar things with important papers and such." The man toed the carpet, then told them, "I'll leave you then," and turned and walked out the front door.

Anna Beth's eyes were riveted on the papers. She had hardly heard anything the man said past, "You might wanna take a look at these." She unwrapped the wrinkled plastic with all the care one might give the original manuscript of Jesus' *Sermon on the Mount*. She let the plastic drift to the floor, and fingered the yellowed parchment it contained. *Death Certificate* was written in bold script on the top of the page. She traced Ned's name with unsteady fingers.

Name: Nevens Poindexter Baxter
Cause of Death: Severe bodily trauma caused by automobile accident.
Date of Death: July 12th, 1966

Nineteen sixty-six. The same year Ned disappeared, July twelfth, the very day. We'd just moved to Memphis, and he was so excited to have the family together again. We'd spent one night in the house together, then he had left early the next morning to go back to Iuka to get the rest of their stuff. He had never returned.

Anna Beth had never understood why he would abandon them. What would make a man leave his family, especially when he had finally gotten his wish to have them live together in the same city, in the same house? Her mind paged through memories she had tried to dispose of long ago but that kept recycling themselves into scenarios that never made sense. Why? Why would Moody not tell her own children that their father was dead?

Her eyes moved from the death certificate and focused on the red-and-white card she'd been turning over and over with her fingers while she reminisced. Now she looked hard at it. What was it? Why was it here? What did it mean?

American Red Cross Donor Card:
Nevens Baxter. Blood type—blood type—blood type. This didn't make sense.

"What, what is it, darlin'?" Willard asked, coming to her feet.

Anna Beth shook her head. She didn't respond for a few seconds, so struck with betrayal she couldn't make her thoughts follow the lines on the page. She stared at the yellowed paper, and murmured, "Aunt Willard, something is wrong here. Moody's blood type was A, A positive. Right? She bragged that she'd flunked out on many things in her life, but somehow she'd managed to score a "perfect blood, A+ blood, the blood of kings and queens." Elvis' blood type, too, she was sure.

"Yes, sugar, but what does that matter now?"

"And Daddy, Daddy had type O blood, Aunt Willard. Type O. Don't you see? O and A+ don't add up to B. We just studied this in science class."

"Well I suppose, but why?"

Anna Beth slumped into the nearest chair. "If she was still alive, I'd kill her. I don't understand why she would do this. Daddy isn't mine, Aunt Willard. O and A+ don't add up to B. They don't add up to *me*!"

I Got Stung
Top 20 *Billboard* Single

Two years later, the mid-August heat wafted through the loading dock door of *Flowers by Ned* as the Bland-Hersh deliveryman unloaded the shop's weekly order. Inside, paddle fans churned the steamy soup, wilting designers and flowers alike with a blast of natural sauna. After much begging from a whiny Louisa, Anna Beth had just arrived back in Memphis from Iuka, and we had moved into Genevieve's house with Louisa—who had given up her swanky apartment for the decrepit old place in an effort to 'take control of her life.'

Since when? Anna Beth and I still wanted to know. The fact was that Louisa didn't like living *alone* any more than Genevieve had. Also, with a baby that we all thought actually had a chance of making-it-into-the-world-alive on the way, she'd need help taking care of the little tike.

I had made tracks back and forth between them since right after Genevieve died and Anna Beth moved to Iuka, choosing to take a break from school to rethink her life. She had lived at the home place for a while, but shocked everyone, except me, when she moved to the old auto parts convent. We had spent so much time there it seemed silly to be anywhere else.

Willard struggled with Anna Beth's explanation of how she'd found the place—she was honest and gave me the credit for leading her there—but tears came to Reverend Mother's eyes as she listened to the tale. Her face grayed to a shade just this side of pallor, when Anna Beth called me by name. She got so choked up and upset she couldn't talk and had to leave the room. I'm sure she did some big time praying to make sure she was doing the right thing by keeping her mouth shut. But, as always, she acted on God's direction. She had faith that He knew what He was doing. She stayed out of his way, unlike me, and birth this child. A baby's squalling will be music compared to your whining. Maybe then you'll stop your moaning, and we can have a little peace and quiet around here."

Whoa, girl! At one time she would have just cursed under her breath and stifled those sentiments, but no longer. Genevieve's death and the revelations it delivered instilled Anna Beth with a determination for truth in all things. She didn't care what the situation dictated; she now voiced her opinion and stuck to her guns.

"No chance of that, either," Mildred moaned.

Anna Beth glanced at the clock over the phones. "Good Lord, I've got to get outta here. Who's eating, and what do you want?" She slipped her backpack over her shoulders and grabbed her keys.

"Where're you going? Some place good, I hope," Louisa said, taking the opportunity to stop working and sit down again.

"Got a delivery near the Half Shell. Plus, I've got an important stop to make."

Louisa slammed her clippers down on the table, and her mouth screwed up into a knot. "For Christ's sake, Anna Beth, when are you gonna give it up? You will *never* find out who our father is no matter how much research you do."

She was almost as good at reading people's motives as I was, but then again, Anna Beth had never owned a decent poker face. "Moody left us nothing to go on, and you're just wasting time fiddling with it."

She had decided that she didn't care who deposited the seed that created them. She knew Genevieve was their mother; that was bad enough. This litany between them had been going on for over two years now. I did my best to butt in when I could. I took the opportunity and knocked a box of floral pins off the shelf. It hit Louisa's table hard, but sadly, didn't fall open and spill a zillion little spikes onto the floor. Much to my chagrin, everyone around there had gotten so used to me disturbing the peace no one even flinched.

Anna Beth ignored Louisa's remarks and my antics—again. She was on a mission and she wouldn't let it go. "Don't you want to have at least one grandparent for your baby? Lord knows, it won't be seeing much of its daddy. Stolen weekends are no way to raise a child, Weesa."

Louisa grimaced and snapped the stem off a Tropicana rose.

"You're a fine one to talk. What do you do at that old *convent* of yours?"

Anna Beth hadn't let anyone visit us yet. Wouldn't even give Louisa directions. I couldn't understand her apprehension, but she just wasn't ready, feared they'd make fun of her when they discovered how she spent all her time. "None of your business. You'll find out when I'm good and ready for you to."

Mildred shook her head and hummed a little louder. The deliverymen didn't break stride. They'd heard this kind of fussing before. The girls took out their frustrations on each other now that Genevieve wasn't around as the perfect target, and since she'd left them with so many unanswered questions. Anna Beth puffed up with un-righteous indignation.

"Do you believe her?" she asked, in Mildred's direction, but pointing her keys at Louisa. "My private life is none of your concern I'm trying hard now to let you live your life, whether I agree with your choices or not. I deserve the same consideration. Let me have just this one thing to myself. " She strode to the back door and threw it open, but did not step out. A hot hand of humidity slapped her. "If— no, no, make that *when*—I find *our* father, I'll just keep him for myself, too, if you don't want to know. But I am going to find him, Louisa. You mark my words."

Just then the radio station broadcast the high-pitched '*beep-beep*' warning of an important announcement. Anna Beth glanced outside, looking for angry clouds, then, not seeing any, closed the door and stepped back inside. Everyone held their breath and listened to dead air, until WHBQ's legendary disc jockey, George Kline, cleared his throat, and said, "*We interrupt this broadcast, faithful listeners, with some tragic news today. The King of Rock and Roll, Elvis Presley, is dead.*"

The whole flower shop, all of Memphis, heck, the whole country gasped in shock. The girls shot looks at each other.

"What?" Louisa mouthed. Mildred turned up the volume. Anna Beth dropped her backpack on the floor at her feet.

"*Memphis' beloved resident, Tupelo's native son, and my dear friend, Elvis Aaron Presley, was transported from his home at Graceland to Baptist Memorial Hospital where he was pronounced dead of apparent heart failure. He was forty-two years old."*

Louisa sprang to her feet. "Oh, my God, Anna Beth!"

Anna Beth nodded, too stricken to speak. Her mind suddenly reeled with the same illogical possibilities she knew Louisa was also thinking, things they had thought, but quickly dismissed as ludicrous right after Genevieve's death. Now, she couldn't get her mouth to cooperate and say the words. She wished someone else would put them together for her.

Louisa obliged. "But what if he? . . . Could he be? . . ."

Finally, the ramifications slammed hard. Shaking her curls violently, her hands covering her ears, Anna Beth said, "What? What if what, Louisa? What if he what?" But she knew exactly what Louisa meant. Maybe it was because they'd just been discussing their parentage, maybe it was because it all seemed just crazy enough, but Genevieve's truest love became clear.

The object of her devotion. The subject of her hopes and desires. Genevieve had spent her whole life mooning over Elvis. They wondered why they hadn't seen the wisdom in it before. What if she'd slept with him? She certainly had plenty of opportunities. And what if they were Elvis's love children, they wondered, the products of some groupie affair when the rocker was just starting out?

My memory took me back a few years to the night Genevieve reamed out Jack Bland at the wholesale house. She'd suggested that he was the father of her child. At the time, I thought I knew better, but she—and God—had a knack for keeping secrets, even from me. I couldn't believe my own longing, but I wished she were around so I could pick that convoluted mind of hers again. Had I read her wrong? I had to wonder. What was the whole truth?

"Naw, couldn't be. She would have told us," Louisa said, trying to convince herself and everyone else in the shop. "She couldn't have kept *that* a secret. It would have killed her, keeping something that juicy to herself." Yes, that sounded logical, even coming from Louisa, the Queen of Illogicality.

Anna Beth and Mildred nodded, but were unconvinced. Even the deliverymen and designers paused as if considering the possibility for a moment, but they shook their heads. They all knew Genevieve was capable of it. She could keep a secret better than anyone. And she could lie through her teeth while she kissed you on the cheek. She might have been irresponsible, but she was as loyal as a yard dog. She'd do anything to protect Elvis, even hide the fact that he had fathered her only kids. They all believed it to be true, and they were convincing me. I knew that Madson had fathered one of the girls, my sister, of course, but it just might be possible that Elvis, not Jack Bland, had fathered the other.

The radio station began an Elvis marathon, playing nothing but Elvis songs from that moment until his funeral, which wasn't even scheduled yet. Anna Beth still stood in the middle of the workroom, keys in her hand, ready to get dinner—if she hadn't lost her appetite—but it was Louisa who left. She had already snatched up her purse and was headed toward the door when Anna Beth looked up.

"Where do you think you're going?" Anna Beth hollered after her.

"Home," Louisa said, pausing only briefly. "That house is full of Elvis crap. It's a gold mine, Anna Beth. A gold mine in more ways than one."

Every light on the phone bank lit up all at once. Incessant buzzing ensued. Anna Beth glanced over at Mildred. As stupefied as they were by the possibilities, they first had work to do. Louisa, however, disappeared out the front door

"Help me with the phones, Mildred," she said, in a panic.

"This'll be worse than twenty Christmases," Mildred said, grabbing the first line.

"Good Lord, has word gotten out already? This is crazy. Call Aunt Willard and Madson. We're gonna need them to come up here and help."

*

We left the shop in the wee hours of the morning. Anna Beth drove home in a dog-tired stupor. She stumbled through the front door of Genevieve's house and collapsed onto the couch, too exhausted to still be angry with Louisa for leaving the shop in the middle of Elvis' tidal wave of grief-stricken fans.

I have to admit; I had never seen anything like it. The shop's phones were still buzzing when we left at 2 a.m. The FTD machine

impeding her determination. Once again, my best effort wasn't
sufficient to prevent her pain. That damn free will got me every time.
Why had God left me here to look after them if, when they needed me
the most, I could do so little to help? I had yet to figure that one out.
She shoved her weight against the open doorway as if the door were
there to push against. "Let me through, Olivia," she demanded. "I
know more pain is in there, but I have to know. You have to let me
know."

Of course, she was right, but I loved her. It was hard to sit back
and watch her jump right into a pile of razor blades. She had pieced
together their lives the best way she could, now she had to find the
truth of it, feel the pain of it, and deal with it so she could move on.
The missing pieces were all in there; she was sure of it, right there in
that house, in that room—or at least they had been before Louisa had
gotten a-hold of the place.

I knew Genevieve had left every good clue, and probably a few
bad ones, but all this time Anna Beth had been looking in all the wrong
places. I guessed that I should have sent her there sooner. Hindsight is
the pits. But I acted at the pleasure of my Lord. We both knew that it
would take His help to figure it all out. But now, the fight was over.
She stood erect, took my hand, and we stepped into Genevieve's
room again.

Elvis lay face up in the middle of the bed, his white sequined
cardboard jumpsuit torn open at the waist. Magazines and empty
album covers lay with him. Elvis scarves, blue suede key chains,
Graceland postcards, fan club buttons, concert ticket stubs cluttered
the floor. A hank of broken guitar strings dangled from the ceiling with
a blue suede guitar strap, twisted like a snake and ragged on the edge.
Its wiry strands spiraled in all directions, held together with one of
Louisa's old ponytail hair bobs. Louisa had torn through everything.

Scraps of paper, some rumpled, some folded into tiny squares
and triangles, lay like cheap confetti on the floor and across the bed.
She leaned over one that lay face up on the bed, unwilling to touch it.
I stole a handbag and three pairs of hose from Goldsmith's today,
it read in Genevieve's flowery cursive.

Another note stuck out of an old Music Beat magazine. Anna
Beth flipped open the page with her fingernail, revealing the inscription

and a full-page picture of a young, skinny Elvis smiled up at her. The message read: *Grandpa Clancy beat the tar out of me when I was ten. I killed him for it when I was twenty. Right there in the parlor. My dear, sweet Madson keeps telling me it was not my fault, but I wanted him to die. I wished death upon him.*

Anna Beth's hand went to her throat. She swallowed hard, but bile rose and its bitter twinge burned in the back of her throat. "Oh, Moody, why did you write all this down and leave it for us to find?"

Another lay on the floor at her feet: *Oh, Elvis, I am so bad. I poured piss in Ned's beer can and he drank it.*

And another on the dresser: *Sweet, Elvis, I miss your arms around me. Kiss me, please kiss me again soon.*

She eased around to the side of the bed where the innards of Genevieve's *Kissin' Cousins* alarm clock littered the bedside table; a long strip of pink paper lay among the springs, coils and bell. With only the tips of her index finger and thumb, she picked it up. *Willard had a baby in the convent. And I know who the daddy is!* We could almost hear Genevieve's voice in a childlike chant, "Nannie nannie boo-boo, I know something that you don't know."

So many confessions lay scattered around us. Anna Beth wondered how she would ever survive reading them all. *I'll help you get through it*, I told her. *I'll lead the way.* And the formation of those words held more certainty for me than any other words I had ever said.

I knew that God would help me. I knew He had never abandoned me, and that He'd show me the way. He had led us all to these very moments of illumination just as surely as He'd given us the bond of belonging we shared. I felt buoyed by this assurance. Finally, my objective was coming to fruition, I would be able to help "my girls" unravel the knotted mess of their lives. But also the first fear I'd ever experienced crept upon me with the knowing that my time was nearing its end.

*

Sweat trickled down Anna Beth's stomach from the little pools that had formed under her breasts. I couldn't believe she was out here after all we'd been through the night before when she had stood in one spot in Genevieve's bedroom, never sitting down, and read aloud every scrap of paper Louisa had unearthed and left scattered about. Then she had stacked them up neatly, smoothed their creases, placed them in a box, and offered them up in prayer as a testament that Genevieve had at least tried to expunge the evil from her life.

And now, spent and listless, she perspired from the physical labor at hand at the base of the place Elvis would be laid to rest. She and a host of others from the Memphis flower industry were responsible for managing all the bereavement deliveries. It was ninety-eight degrees in the shade, and shade was in short supply anywhere close to the mausoleum at Forest Hills Cemetery. We'd been there all day.

Louisa had never shown up at the house—we'd waited up all night—or at the shop that morning, but Willard and Madson had arrived before dawn. I was glad for that. We had put them to work helping Mildred, but before we left for our shift at the cemetery, they kept asking where Louisa was and if she was okay. Anna Beth didn't know how to respond.

Now, surveying the madness before us, all she could think about was Louisa. "Where is she, Olivia? Can't you find her?" But an unspoken question lingered unasked: "Oh, Olivia, what did she find? Which of the notes did she take with her? Does she know something I don't know?"

She paused for a moment and looked up from the mounds of floral arrangements at her feet, dabbing at the sweat dripping from her brow with her T-shirt sleeve. Genevieve's grave was just across the driveway from where she worked. Twenty yards, at the most. *Too convenient*, she thought, *for Genevieve to be buried so close to this spot*.

Had she and Elvis planned ahead of time to rest side by side in death? We had come to visit Genevieve's grave a few times since the funeral, but now Anna Beth's eyes were drawn to the marker. She wanted to scream across the way, "Who's my father? Why did you lie?" but she remained silent and gnawed on the inside of her cheek instead as she helped unload another flower shop van laden with sprays.

I had never been to a public cemetery before. I was taken aback. It was so empty of spirits, so lifeless. None lingered here. Why would they? I wondered why people visited their dead in this way, when all they have to do is expect them, be open. We're here. People talk to God. Why not to their dearly departed? Those they loved in life can still be loved in death.

The cemetery looked like Saturday afternoon at the State Fair. Television trucks blocked traffic, their antennae raised; reporters were poised with cameras, trying to get a shot of *the spot*. Florists rushed around like carnival freaks, huge plumes of flowers streaming from beside them and over their heads.

The site was overcome by the flood of arrangements as more vans pulled up in a steady caravan; doors flew open, and drivers tossed their wilting cargo to a line of people who passed each 'bereavement arrangement' to the next person up the hill. Anna Beth stood at the pentacle of the folly, just in front of the mausoleum, giving orders like she'd choreographed Elvis' funeral on Broadway for years. How she had managed to draw the short stick as graveside foreman, I wasn't sure, but she was good at it, and was getting the job done.

Massive sprays lay in heaps of aromatic chaos all around us. No grass could be seen. She ushered deliverymen this way and that, showing them where to place each offering, and every so often, one spray would lose its footing and fifty would fall like dominos crashing in a mass of lost petals and broken flower heads.

"The customer wants this one placed on the grave for a minute, then picked up and delivered to their home," a Sandy's Florist deliveryman said, holding up the order as proof.

"Must be his first trip, huh?" Anna Beth said, glancing over to where I watched. We'd heard that request too many times already this sweltering day. "Yeah, yeah, just put it over there for a second, then take it away," she barked, and kicked the metal legs out from under a spray easel. "They've all lost their marbles, Olivia. They spend a fortune so their 'condolences' can stand next to an empty crypt for a split second. This is nuts."

One of the cemetery employees asked her, "What are they gonna do with dead flowers?"

"Who knows?" she replied, but we knew they'd probably sleep with them, or dry them and make a St. Elvis shrine for their living rooms so they could pray to it and wish him back to life. Yep, that's what Genevieve would have done. We knew better than anyone the

Louisa followed her back down the hill and leaned against the side of the van to catch her breath as Anna Beth climbed into the back of it to help the driver.

"Let's go home and talk there," Louisa said. "We've got to cool off. But you're not gonna believe it, Anna Beth. You just won't believe . . . "

Then, as I watched in a kind of shocked pause, bees swarmed up around Louisa, attracted to her distress and the perfume Jack Bland insisted that she wear. At first, she waved them away calmly, a minor annoyance in light of her exhaustion and the heat. But their persistence became more aggressive, buzzing, buzzing. She swatted a couple on her arm, and their stingers dug in. Before I could react, her pain transformed into panic and she flailed her arms, turning in circles, trying to get away.

"Stand still, Weesa. You'll make them mad." Anna Beth jumped from the van.

I exhaled, just a puff did it, waved my arms and they dispersed as quickly as they'd appeared, but Louisa's foot caught on the wire stand of a funeral spray and she stumbled. She fell face first against the van, her feet tangled up. Then, pushing off to right herself, she arced backwards as gracefully as if she were showing off a new back flip maneuver off Jack Bland's dock at the lake.

The ground came up to meet her and I reached out, knowing I had the power to break her fall if God would only give me the chance. White roses and calla lilies caught her, instead. Petals exploded into the air when she landed, as light and delicate as angel feathers blown to the wind. When they settled, I looked down at her, lying there, so peaceful, so still. *Get up*, I said. *It's okay; they're gone, but she didn't move.* Anna Beth knelt beside her, and we both wept when blood oozed from Louisa's scalp. Men rushed over to help us, and when they pushed the flowers aside, the headstone that Louisa struck appeared—*Beloved Wife and Mother, Gladys Presley, Rest in Peace.*

Live A Little, Love A Little
Film, Metro-Goldwyn-Mayer, including
the songs, *Almost In Love,*
A Little Less Conversation,
Wonderful World, and *Edge Of Reality*

The painful heat of August gave way to the cool rush of autumn's colors, and then a mild winter, warm as bathwater and just as soothing, surprised us all. No brittle limbs or frozen earth to chill our heartache. Even the spirits seemed to languish and rest.

The early rains of March washed over the ground like a mother's splash, and sank deep, feeding perennial wonder and promising a rich germination within. And then, spring announced itself with great swathes of color. Hyacinth and jonquils dotted the grassy slopes on either side of the long driveway leading from the big house as we bumped along. Their purples, yellows, pinks and greens dressed up that old pockmarked fence in fine style.

We pulled out onto the highway, headed west. Just a few miles. Gazing out through the passenger side window, I watched cottony clouds make their eastward trek across the colorless sky. I'd never paid much attention to clouds before, but oh, what magical pillows of continuous change they are, kneading themselves into shapes of dragons and frogs, flowers, and if you look closely enough, the recognizable face of God.

It was moving day. The truck held only our last, few, lightweight belongings. Anna Beth had taken her time moving things over the last few months , an old dresser here, a chair there. Today was not a day for work. It was a day of renewal and bittersweet celebration.

Anna Beth was excited, in spite of her ongoing melancholy. It was as if she had waited her whole life for this day. We turned off the main highway as we had done so many times before, but this time onto a fresh asphalt drive. No more deep rutted dirt, no hitting her head on the headliner, on this trip or any other after this. She hadn't forked out the big bucks to redo the parking lot. Instead, she'd pulled every blade of Johnson grass by hand, plucked out each chickweed by its root. Then, she had filled all the cracks with concrete, and painted geometric figures, circles, spirals, and teardrops here and there; flowers, a checkerboard and bees, of course, flitted about across its surface, too.

Willard and Madson pulled in next to us when we parked. Reverend Mother was not far behind them. They'd all been there a few times over the past few months, but today was a kind of unveiling. They hadn't seen it all finished, polished so its brightly colored jewels shone in the clean morning sun. Anna Beth had saved one room as a secret, and was a little nervous about showing it off. She hadn't scraped *Beaver's Auto Parts and Shop* off the front window. Since the nuns never got around to it when they lived there, why should she? 'It adds character,' she said. 'Gives the place originality, in a campy sort of way.' I loved the tinkling sound the little bell made when we pushed through the front door.

"Welcome to our home," she announced, sweeping her arm, and moving to the side so our first visitors could come in. Her face beamed with the pride of the artist she'd become. I loved hearing everyone's *ooos* and *ahhs*.

"I don't know how you did it," Willard said, looking about. "Oh, Madson, you should have seen this place when I first joined the Order. It was such a filthy old dump. And then, after the nuns moved to the home place, it deteriorated even further being vacant all those years."

"I've been working on it for almost five years, remember. It didn't get this way overnight," Anna Beth said. Just like her to be modest about her masterpiece. She had saved up a down payment, and taken some money out of *Flowers by Ned* to purchase the place from the Sisters of Mercy—turns out Mildred had amassed a nice nest egg over the years.

Reverend Mother wandered from room to room with her hand over her mouth. Tears pooled on her lashes. We all moved through each room , and into the kitchen with its new black and white checkered floor. Salvaged cabinets, mismatched by style and Anna Beth's quirky choice of colors, lined the far wall. Everyone stopped, when we entered the living room/chapel, looking up. In its first life it had housed hydraulic lifts for working under cars. Then the nuns had used it as their crude chapel. Now, murals adorned the walls, reaching high up to a ceiling matching exactly the clouds I'd just admired in the real sky. Angels were everywhere. Painted into the murals, sitting on shelves, standing guard on the floor, perched in the pews. They were made of every material imaginable and had individual personalities all their own.

"Madson tells me I could make a fortune selling them," she admitted, "but I haven't been able to let go of any. I can't imagine my angels not being here. I'll sell the other artwork, but my angels won't get price tags."

A portrait of Louisa caught everyone's attention. Anna Beth had hung it that morning. No one had seen it yet. It could have been a photograph. She'd captured every detail of her likeness. We all stared at it, remembering. What a sad and wondrous day that had been.

They had wheeled Louisa into emergency surgery to do a cesarean section. White coats had fluttered like wings. Lights blared. Anna Beth wept. They had already told us that Louisa was brain dead. The blow against Gladys Presley's headstone had ruptured her skull and too much internal bleeding had occurred, because the ambulance couldn't get to us with all the Elvis fans crowding the cemetery, cars blocking the roads, flower shop vans filing in. All anyone could do was apply pressure to help the bleeding and pray until the ambulance made its way through.

As Louisa lay there on the operating table, I realized what my purpose had always been. I had never taken a breath, never entered her world, but I couldn't cross the threshold into heaven without my sister. I was to watch after her, be her Guardian Angel. What a special mission I'd had and we were meant to meet God standing side-by-side. I watched as my door opened, inch-by-inch, with Louisa's diminishing breaths. It was as if I were dreaming. My light now extended down to Louisa. It encompassed us both, a cocoon of warmth and breath. Then, my attention was drawn away for a moment. I watched as the doctors lifted the child from her womb. It was blue. It wasn't breathing. I prayed they could save it. With both of us gone now, I wanted our mother to finally have a baby to love.

While the doctors worked on the baby, Louisa slipped so

effortlessly into my realm. I took her hand and we embraced. Oh, how I had waited for that day. She finally accepted me completely. No more fear. No doubts. And God's palm moved in around us, all fog and stars, memory and thought and calm. We moved together toward our doorway. It had been waiting there behind me, but would open only when we both approached. The light was more intense than life. I glanced over at Louisa. She smiled and whispered, "I love you," and waved her hand. I looked back toward the light, and it blinded me for a moment, confusing me. Then, when I looked again, *poof*, Louisa was gone.

I tumbled, falling, falling, deeper, deeper. I couldn't stop myself. I couldn't scream. I couldn't see anything, and couldn't move. I thought, *Oh, God, don't send me south now. What did I do wrong? Why can't I come into Paradise with Louisa? Don't leave. Don't leave me alone.* I remembered the other spirits, the ghosts with no purpose that haunted the home place. I didn't want to be one of them. I was so confused and so frightened, and then, it all ended. I landed softly and I opened my eyes. The bright light was back. It felt peaceful. *Phew*, I thought. I blinked and wiggled, and then I screamed!

Anna Beth cornered Reverend Mother in the waiting room for a little pow-wow. God's plan had come full circle. Reverend Mother explained everything to Willard, Madson and Anna Beth. Then Anna Beth left the hospital armed with Louisa's lab results, blood tests done on Willard, and a few more questions that could only be answered by one man. She pieced things together, thanks to Genevieve's confessions, the seeds of suspicion I'd planted, and a little direction from God. But she still didn't want to believe it all. She drove straight to the Bland-Hersh wholesale house. Jack Bland collapsed from grief when she told him Louisa was dead, and from relief when she assured him that Louisa was not his child. Even after Genevieve had told him that "one of my girls is yours," he had done nothing to stop his affair with Louisa.

"You are scum, just like I always thought," Anna Beth told him. "You will pay for what you did to my sister. I will see it, somehow." It was harder for her to get the next words out, "It makes me sick to tell you this, but I'm your daughter, Mr. Bland. I have proof of it now." And she handed him the confession note of Moody's, which she'd found in Louisa's handbag.

*Elvis, love, I've done a bad thing again. I killed my husband,
Ned. Just as sure as anything, I wished him dead and it happened.
I didn't kill my kids' father, at least. No, Ned wasn't their daddy.
I've always sworn Madson is Louisa's father, him loving Willard,
you know, but I may be wrong about that. At any rate, Louisa is
the baby Willard gave up for adoption. And I know this much for
sure: Jack Bland is Anna Beth's daddy. My girls'll get over losing
Ned. See? He wasn't their daddy, either of them, and he wasn't
much fun anyway.*

It was written on a scrap of blue paper no bigger than a thank-
you note. She wasn't sure where it had been hidden. It could have
been anywhere. It didn't seem more special than any of the others.
Just a weekly confession to Genevieve's god. Anna Beth wondered if
Genevieve had said an *Our Father* or any *Hail Marys* when she
wrote it. No, probably not.

Now, more people were starting to gather at my new home with
Anna Beth. The nuns were gawking at the living room/chapel. They'd
never seen anything like it. Nobody had. Their own supportive spirits
stood with them. And Reverend Mother was chatting in the corner
with Willard and some others, retelling the tale of the day Willard gave
birth. "No, I didn't understand it at the time, but the little baby that
died was dark-skinned. And little Louisa was just as light as she could
be." She smiled over at Madson, who join them.

No one knew about my mother's biological relationship to
Madson. There was an unspoken understanding between close friends
that Willard and Madson had been lovers, but some secrets are best
left alone, when no one is hurt by them being kept.

"There is a great deal of healing ahead of us," Willard said,
thoughtful, gazing up at the angels surrounding us. "But I'm sure God
will be patient with us and grant us the faith we'll need to see it through."

Anna Beth ran her finger along the smooth edge of the frame
she'd carved for Louisa's portrait. "Yes, and maybe He'll send us
some spiritual guidance, too. What do you think?" Everyone agreed.
"There is one more room you've got to see. Come this way, please."

Several people followed us upstairs and down the long hall to the
room where Willard gave birth. Anna Beth swung open the door and
applause rang out. It was a magical place, all pink chiffon and antique

lace, happy insects, bees and birds painted on the walls.

It is fascinating, watching all these people. And a little strange at the same time. I'm not used to this perspective. Kind of like those first few years as a spirit. Guess it will take me a while to learn the ropes. Like then, I have this knowledge, this knowing and consciousness left over from my previous realm that bursts out of my cranium like a rainbow. But I will lose this understanding before my third birthday.

Least that's what I hear from the Big Guy upstairs. My insight will dissolve into wisps that will rise to heaven and wait for me until I return to claim it again. My new experiences will meld with it and my education will continue until God calls it quits. Spirits have transcendence, but this little body will take some getting used to. Maybe that's why God starts us off as babies. He has to pack our spirit into a tiny spot with give, so we can continue to grow, and grow, and grow. It is all about learning, this existence we share, and trusting that everything has its purpose, whether we understand at the time or not. So I'll be patient, let my knowing go, and then accept it as it comes back to me again.

Anna Beth is leaning over me now. Her face is my most favorite to gaze upon. I love it when she touches me. I had always dreamed about what it would feel like, skin meeting skin, warmth joining warmth, and now I know. It's like heaven itself, I think. I'll know for sure someday. Everyone makes funny noises at me, though. *Goo, goo. Gaa, gaa.* They call it baby talk. Not Anna Beth. She talks to me just like she always did. I'm glad of that.

Now, we're going back downstairs. She's dressed me up for this party. What a dress. I've never seen the like. She would have never worn something this fussy. It hangs down, way past my feet, and has white ruffles and ribbons all over it. What a sight I must be. We're headed out the back door now.

There's the oak tree where my old body is buried, and my mother's, Louisa's, is next to it there. The priest is getting ready. Everyone is gathering around. Again, so many prayers and fancy rituals, all this to welcome me into the faith. He is dipping a gold cup in Holy Water and dribbling it over my head. "And I baptize you, Olivia Abigail Clancy Baxter. In the name of the Father, and the Son and the Holy Spirit. Amen."

Author's Note
&
Acknowledgements

I began writing *Flowers for Elvis* over six years ago after having lunch in a small restaurant in Charlotte, North Carolina where I overheard a conversation between two women sitting at the booth behind me. One of the women had recently been pregnant and delivered twins, but sadly, one of her children was stillborn. The agony in her voice was palpable as she lamented the loss of this child and wondered aloud to her friend about what had happened to her child's spirit. She wanted to know why God had taken one twin away, and what purpose there could be for this tragedy. She also wondered if God was punishing her for the sins of her past.

I felt guilty for eavesdropping on her misery, but was drawn in by the woman's questions and her desperation for answers. I wanted to tell her, "No, God forgives. He doesn't punish one for the sins of another. He has a plan for every soul." Instead, in my silence, the idea for this book bloomed in my imagination as if God had watered a dormant seed that had been buried deep within me for many years and had somehow been unearthed. The basic plot emerged from a cloud of imagination, and I recognized the shadows of the characters that were already taking shape in the recesses of my mind. The fragments of story began there, but it would take me years, and too many plot twists and revisions to count, to extrude the true meaning to my characters, and to myself.

Flowers for Elvis is a work of fiction. None of the characters are real—except Elvis, of course. But, like my characters, I have known heartache and tragedy. I have lost loved ones to death, through my own abandonment of them and, yes, even to suicide. As I wrote this story, I worked through past experiences that still tugged at my heart and worried the frayed edges of my confidence. Those nights at the keyboard, when I allowed myself to explore those places of hurt, I was startled by a voice and an understanding I didn't recognize as my own. I accepted this visit into my soul as Grace that revealed *me* to myself through my characters' convoluted lives. And I prayed that the lady in the restaurant would also, somehow, receive peace.

So, I guess you could say that *Flowers for Elvis* was born of a desire to prove to myself that God's benevolence is boundless, and that He has a plan for everything, even those things we cannot comprehend.

Many people have helped me along this journey. My editors, Deborah Smith and Debra Dixon, the opinionated "belles" at BelleBooks, deserve polished tiaras, tall glasses of sweet tea and a hoop-skirted ball thrown in their honor. I appreciate your gentile guidance and encouragement. Thank you, Debs.

I was privileged with the opportunity to work on later drafts with the literary mentors at Spalding University's Master of Fine Arts in Writing program in Louisville, Kentucky. Acclaimed authors, Silas House, Kenny Cook, Connie May Fowler, Kirby Gann, Neela Vaswani, Julie Brickman, Mary Clyde, Robin Lippincott and Jodie Lisberger urged me to go deeper and to stretch my imagination with thoughtful "What ifs?" I cannot thank you all enough for your generous tutelage and support.

Amy Garrett and my Charlotte, North Carolina book club friends read the first draft and offered me hope, a virtue no writer can live without. Judith H. Simpson of the Queens Writer's Group in Charlotte told me, "It's good, but take out 98% of the adjectives." Her encouragement gave me the confidence to revise. The members of Emerald Coast Writers in Destin, Florida, especially Sue Lutz Hamilton, Ellen Martin, Darlene Dean, Joyce Holland and Vicki Hinze, taught me the art of networking and that writers are the most charitable members of the human race. And this upteen-millionth draft would not have been possible without my fellow students at Spalding University, especially Lisa Marzano, Loreen Niewenhuis, Vickie Weaver, Terry Price, Bonnie Johnson, Maija Stromberg, and Matt Ryan, who mentored me, read draft after draft, and examined it through the eyes of literary criticism. I thank you all.

No, I'm not quite finished. I have a long list of gratitude. To my friends, the faculty, staff, students and parents at the best Catholic school in world, who whooped and hollered their congratulations and honored me with the blessing of "extended family," I love you all and thanks. And a special thanks to my friend, Larry Inman of Inman Images, for the beautiful book cover photography.

My family deserves much more than a simple paragraph of thanks. The words I need, however, are lodged somewhere in the back of my throat and threaten to overtake me with perpetual sniffles that will require mounds of tissue to quell. You will never know the depth of my appreciation. To my dear Peter, you have taught me patience and perseverance. (Lord knows, you own those virtues.) I love you—always. To my daughter, (even though you can't read this book until you're *forty)*, you taught me to expect miracles, to grab my dreams and never give up, and to do what I love. You are the air that grants me the ability to breathe. My greatest honor is being your mom. And Sissie, oh, dear Sissie, my best friend. We are joined, hearts and hands, hopes and dreams in the miracle of sisterhood. Love and thanks.

God Bless!
Julia H. Schuster

Flowers for Elvis
Book Club Discussion Questions

Titles are always important. Why do you think the author chose *Flowers for Elvis* for this book? What symbolism do flowers play in the novel? How do the various settings, including Elvis's funeral and the backdrop of the floral industry, support this theme? Likewise, discuss the symbolism of bees in the novel.

Discuss the interconnectedness of the spiritual with the physical in the story. What bonds do you think exist between the dearly departed and those living on this physical plane? Do individual souls have purpose beyond the here and now?

What connections did you discover in *Flowers for Elvis* that mirror events and situations in Elvis' life?

Faith and trust in God are recurring themes in *Flowers for Elvis.* Faith that God has a plan for each person (or soul) and trust that He knows what He's doing. The characters' free will, however, often runs counter to God's plan. Discuss how each characters' faith evolves through the story.

Recount the evolution of Olivia Abigail through death to life. How is this narrator relevant to the novel as a whole? Could the story have been told from another character's perspective? How would this shift in perspective change the tone and/or outcome of the narrative?

What is your interpretation of the precise nature of the love between Olivia and her sister, and her love for the other members of her extended family? Discuss the relationships of other characters? Family, sisters, twins, mother/daughter. What are your thoughts about the transcendent nature of love?

Examine the concepts of forgiveness and redemption in *Flowers for Elvis?* Olivia states, "No one needs love more than a person who does not deserve it." Do you agree with this philosophy? What questions are posed about forgiveness, both human and spiritual? Does Genevieve deserve forgiveness? What about Grandpa Clancy? Willard? The Reverend Mother? What effect does Genevieve's unwillingness or inability to forgive Grandpa Clancy have on her life? What about her unwillingness and/or inability to forgive herself? How does Anna Beth's (posthumous) forgiveness of Genevieve shape her thereafter? How are each of the characters redeemed?

Does Genevieve achieve the stature of a tragic antagonist? Discuss the choices Genevieve makes throughout the novel. What is her tragic flaw? What are her admirable qualities?

A myriad of secrets litter the plot of *Flowers for Elvis*. What effect do the secrets of generations past and present have on the characters and their understanding of life? What overshadowing fear makes them perpetuate secrets that are so obviously ruining their lives?